THE PEOPLE'S LIBRARY

ALSO BY VERONICA G. HENRY

Stand-Alone Novel

Bacchanal

The Mambo Reina Series

The Quarter Storm

The Foreign Exchange

The Scorched Earth Series

The Canopy Keepers

A Breathless Sky

PRAISE FOR VERONICA G. HENRY

The Canopy Keepers

"A fascinating tale . . . Henry digs in to themes of family, environmentalism, and the connection between humans and the natural world."

—*Publishers Weekly*

"Henry's near-future fantasy world is interesting and beautiful, with lush descriptions of the forest and the fantastical world hidden within."

—*Library Journal*

"Henry adeptly navigates the communication struggles among families and the destructive forces of climate change in this thrilling fantasy."

—*Booklist*

"Perfectly balanced between the fantastical and sharp reality, *The Canopy Keepers* is a genre-defying work as prescient as it is brilliant. Henry has written yet another extraordinary novel everyone should be reading."

—Cadwell Turnbull, award-winning author of *No Gods, No Monsters*

"A gripping, compelling story with themes of great significance to us all."

—Shiv Ramdas, author of *Domechild*

"*The Canopy Keepers* is a gorgeous love story for national parks, trees, and the people who protect them. Veronica Henry's characters are strong, complicated heroes, and her world is delicately, lovingly drawn—and an anguished reminder of everything we are losing day by day."

—Yume Kitasei, author of *The Stardust Grail*

Bacchanal

"Henry skillfully layers historical realism with fantastic elements to explore the way times of desperation test the ethics of oppressed communities. Henry is a writer to watch."

—*Publishers Weekly*

"Henry's debut draws on a rich history of folklore from various African traditions, as well as African history and Black American history, and almost the entire main cast is Black. The carnival setting works perfectly for bringing together various strange and magical people who aren't at home anywhere else . . . Come one, come all, this magical carnival has all the delightful dangers a reader could wish for."

—*Kirkus Reviews*

"[*Bacchanal* is] gorgeous while somehow never losing sight of the need to unsettle. It captures a sense of wonder and reminds you that too much curiosity can lead to danger. And most importantly, it's Black and never lets you forget it. If you want endearing characters, a charming setting, and characters that refuse to bend to the world's injustices, then *Bacchanal* is the book for you."

—*FIYAH*

"Set in the Depression-era South and featuring a mysterious traveling carnival, [*Bacchanal* is] a novel of Black history and magic that makes for a terrific read."

—*The Washington Post*

"Beautifully descriptive prose that fully captures the places, people, and time period."

—*Booklist*

"Think of a Southern Gothic version of [Jane Yolen's] *The Midnight Circus* with a touch of *Lovecraft Country* . . . nail-biting scenes of tension."

—*Lightspeed*

"Filled with magic, danger, and dynamic characters."

—*Woman's World*

"With a powerful voice that grips you from its very first pages, *Bacchanal* casts a spell on readers . . . Eliza is a wonderful character . . . Not a traditional superhero, Eliza's special power is a highlight of this work, and readers will root for the young conjurer and for Henry as she explores the limits of her gifts."

—Sheree Renée Thomas, editor of *The Magazine of Fantasy & Science Fiction*, award-winning author of *Nine Bar Blues*, and featured author in *Black Panther: Tales of Wakanda*

"Veronica Henry pulls on a mix of African folklore, Black histories, and carnival culture to weave a story of mesmerizing, bizarre, and dangerous magic. With a heroine of unique powers and a cast as colorful as any sideshow, this story offers up its share of delights, adventure, and frights! Welcome to *Bacchanal*. Enjoy the sights. Hope you make it out alive!"

—P. Djèlí Clark, author of *Ring Shout*, *The Haunting of Tram Car 015*, and *The Black God's Drums*

"Readers won't want their travels with the seductive and dangerous Bacchanal Carnival to end. If you took [Erin Morgenstern's] *The Night Circus* and viewed it through the gaze of a young Black woman in the Great Depression, you might get Veronica Henry's *Bacchanal*. Demons, lies, and secrets [await]."

—Mary Robinette Kowal, Hugo Award–winning author of *The Calculating Stars*

THE PEOPLE'S LIBRARY

VERONICA G. HENRY

47NORTH

This is a work of fiction. Names, characters, organizations, places, events, and incidents are either products of the author's imagination or are used fictitiously. Otherwise, any resemblance to actual persons, living or dead, is purely coincidental.

Published by 47North, Seattle
www.apub.com

EU product safety contact:
Amazon Media EU S. à r.l.
38, avenue John F. Kennedy, L-1855 Luxembourg
amazonpublishing-gpsr@amazon.com

ISBN-13: 9781662520297 (paperback)
ISBN-13: 9781662520303 (digital)

Cover design by Jarrod Taylor and Logan Matthews
Cover image: © Mark Fearon / ArcAngel Images; © metamorworks, © SkillUp, © StarLine / Shutterstock

Printed in the United States of America

For librarians everywhere

Prologue

Welcome to a place called Promise. Vast and open as a rose in full bloom. Formless and adrift. Absent smell and taste and touch and sight. Promise is as unknowable as it is inaccessible. A place of pure potentiality. Guided by cosmic hands of infinite wisdom, substance and reality are birthed.

It is not a place for corporeal beings, not in the sense one would understand. Neither warm nor cold. Brilliant darkness swirling with limitless possibility. A mosaic of consciousness. Biding time. Content to wait.

From this fertile wellspring, it all begins.

Years from now, as Echo London sucks in her last breath, she will recall with a certain detached horror the events surrounding her last week at the People's Library and wonder if Time's Eye judged her harshly.

Part I

When it all began, in that time before time, existence did not exist.

—*Unknown*

Chapter One

If Echo London had been born in a different time, a remote setting where the velvet curtains of night parted around a fire where villagers gathered to feast on a story, she wouldn't have been the griot, but she would surely have been the one to point out the right person for the job. She loved all the elements that make up a good narrative as a five-star chef loves farm-fresh ingredients. Becoming a librarian was a foregone conclusion.

Echo rested a rounded hip against the moving walkway's glass balustrade as she watched her Ohio City neighborhood emerge from its glittering slumber. From the clear-paned scroll beneath her feet to the digital markers blinking like eager salespeople along the storefronts, an unbroken stream of dazzling advertisements appeared, each one extolling another of Cleveland's proud achievements—environmental-rebound awards, a rich history of artistic geniuses, its globally recognized leadership in ethical AI research. She tried to ignore the way the words flickered, recalibrating themselves when she blinked, as if sensing which slogans worked best.

This, the country's proclaimed "comeback city," had turned into an urban peacock, boasting about its past, present, and indisputable future, a thumbing of the nose to anybody who'd ever doubted it.

Echo turned away, only to find her gaze drawn upward to the mammoth billboard sitting atop a building that had hosted a variety of tenants over the years. The former bank, once and now again a space for green-themed small businesses. The ad shone with the city's young mayor and a crew of hangers-on posing in front of the People's Library, dubbed TPL. Toothy grins wider than the chasm between what they thought the public wanted and reality, had they bothered to ask.

The text scrolling along the bottom of the display announced the imminent opening. She sensed a date at the end of that sentence and turned away, even though she'd been practicing how to allow her gaze to gloss over numbers. Because there was a cost if she didn't.

Less than 5 percent of the population had synesthesia, and Echo was one of them. Each case manifested differently. For her, the grapheme-color strain meant that numbers weren't just figures; they had an associated color and emotion. Zeros were mostly neutral, leaning toward either gray, evoking a kind of melancholy, or an ambivalent, impartial black. Ones were another thing altogether. And don't even mention combinations. Those frenetic emotions had cost her so much.

TPL would be the first library whose offerings comprised the world's only digital human collection. Copies of history's most fascinating people, reduced to pixelated knockoffs so that patrons could interact with them for a supposedly richer experience than text or audio alone could offer.

It was hard to even picture it, but people would be able to "check out" a member of the collection with the help of an AI librarian named Ada, after the famous programmer. Then all you'd have to do was close yourself off in a kind of cubby or booth and chat it up with this facsimile of the real person. Not just rote, preprogrammed responses either . . . real conversations. Rumor had it they were working on a feature that would let you do walk and talks throughout the library too. Sounded to Echo like all the denials about curtailing artificial general intelligence advancement were just political sound bites. Some marketing genius had coined the term "virtual personages" for them, but a kid from Garfield Heights had trimmed the name to "virtus," and it had stuck. "Dupefakes" was another, more uncharitable alternative.

What an ostentatious absurdity. At least she'd never have to set foot in the place.

With one last eye roll, Echo turned away from the billboard. The Lorain Ave exit was next. The city's new solar-powered walkways, "solarways" for short, were another, speedier attempt to reduce car traffic, replacing some of the sidewalks on all major thoroughfares. They weren't all that different from the ones found in airports. You'd think she would have gotten the hang of them by now. Barely two feet separated one lane from the other, and if you wanted to cross over—well, especially after being shot off the thing like a missile—you'd need the dexterity of a star running back to twist your way out of an oncomer's path. A design flaw if she'd ever seen one. She braced herself for the somewhat jerky dismount and hopped off, only to be pitched into a man who smelled like he'd dragged himself out from the Flats, with last night's booze still clinging to his unbuttoned shirt.

"Excuse me," Echo said, putting some distance between them.

"Wha . . . ?" the bleary-eyed man grunted and kept walking a crooked line.

The subsurface smart panels lit up; then an alert sounded. "The pattern of your steps suggests you may have consumed an excessive amount of alcohol. Would you like for me to call a transport for you?"

"Screw you, man," the drunkard said and tottered off, stumbling through a mountain of neatly collected fall leaves.

"That's unfortunate," the alert responded. "Authorities have been notified. Please proceed to your place of residence without delay."

Shaking her head, Echo made her way to the intersection of Lorain Avenue and Fulton Road, where she hung a right. The neighborhood was a mix of low apartment buildings and restored Victorian-era houses in a variety of styles. Aside from the homes, two standouts shared these narrow streets: a Gothic church whose bell still rang every Sunday before service and the neighborhood park that housed the F. M. Lewis Library.

As soon as the building's familiar silhouette appeared, framed in the soft hush and rustle of a copse of northern red oaks, a calm settled around her too. It loosened the tightness in her shoulders, the constriction in her chest. It was almost as if the library saw her coming and reached out with a grandmother's welcoming arms, saying, *Come, come inside. You're safe here.*

A renaissance masterpiece of terra-cotta bricks and fluted columns, with the branch name proudly etched into the stone above the entrance. Now this . . . this was a fitting home for books.

A couple of police cars and an unmarked van sat parked at the curb down the street. She saw a few folks casually strolling down the sidewalk and another couple pushing a double-wide baby carriage, but no officers or security sentries. *Strange,* Echo thought.

She turned away and trotted up the stairs and let herself in with a quick scan of her fingerprint. As she closed the door behind her, a few patrons were already gathering in the grassy area out front waiting for opening, always at nine sharp. After a quick wave, she turned to get ready for the busy day.

It was the lights that threw her off. Coming into the entrance hallway, she noticed the glow against the wooden floor, to the left of the circulation desk. It had to be coming from the staff room. But nobody ever beat her here.

She rounded the corner and found the door slightly ajar. She pushed it open to find her boss, Percy, sitting at the table with his hands folded in front of him, as if in deep contemplation, or prayer. He had hired her to lead this library twelve years ago. In all that time, all but two of their frequent conversations had taken place on-screen, since he lived in Atlanta.

He looked up at her wearing an expression reserved for delivering only the worst news. Echo's heart sank, even if she had no idea why yet. He stood. "You may as well sit down for this one."

Percy Grafton was older than Echo by at least twenty years, though still young by today's standards, with the average lifespan pushing ninety. He seemed to have aged considerably from when she'd seen him last, his skin now as ashen as rocks on the shore.

"Sitting down never made hearing bad news any easier for me," Echo said, still hovering in the doorway.

"Up to you, then," Percy replied. He'd emigrated from the UK as a teen, but the accent came out of hiding when he was stressed. He trudged over to the window and shoved his hands into his pants pockets. He slumped against the wooden frame and exhaled softly. "Caught me completely off guard, this did. You must understand. I would have warned you otherwise."

Now Echo's hands were trembling. "Warned me about what?"

"The vote was unanimous." He rapped his knuckles against the wall. "Leadership at the National Literary Commission, in their infinite lack of wisdom, have decided to close this old place." He turned to face her then, with a look akin to pleading in his eyes.

Echo pulled out a chair, sank into the worn vegan leather, and buried her face in her hands. After a few moments of fighting back the flood of emotion, she asked, "Closing? The library? What on earth for? You—" With a look from Percy, she corrected herself. "*They* can't be serious. We'll change their minds. Both of us. We'll go talk some sense into them."

"Requested and already denied," Percy stated.

Other branches had closed, that was the reality of their time, but the ones that remained were strong. The communities they served loved them. She'd somehow thought that what she and her staff had done here would make them immune.

"They can't do this," Echo said.

"Oh, but they can and they did," Percy countered.

"The Christmas program," Echo said, sighing heavily. "It'll be the end of the year. They're going to close us after that, aren't they?"

His chuckle had not one ounce of mirth. "We have about an hour."

"Percy, do not play with me! What about the staff? The books? I mean . . ." Echo got up and joined him at the window, pointing. "Look. We've got patrons outside right now waiting for me to open those doors."

He cupped the back of his neck. "I won't say I'm sorry, because what I am is angry that I wasn't able to save you or this old building. I know what this place means to you." He paused then, and they exchanged a knowing glance. Percy was aware of her condition, but like a true friend, her only friend aside from Gina, he never mentioned it. "You turning this into the most popular branch is the thing that did us in."

"What do you mean?"

Percy made an exasperated sound.

Echo watched him for a moment. His head was down, tilted ever so slightly away from her. "Why do I have the feeling you're not telling me everything?"

Percy moved over and hiked himself up on the edge of the table. "You've seen the ads, right? For the People's Library?"

Echo nodded, feeling even more dread, if that was possible. This library full of books and quiet corners . . . she sometimes spent more time here than her apartment. "You're not saying they're going to close all the libraries with physical books?"

"Thank heaven for small miracles, no," Percy said.

"So why this branch—what makes us so damn special?"

Percy fidgeted and pulled his lips back into a nervous smile. "Not 'what,' but 'who.'"

At first, Echo had no idea what he was skirting around, but then her mouth formed the small o of an unwelcome realization. "Me?" She barked a sound of outrage. Then, once more, louder this time: "Me? You think I'm going to go work at that place?"

"There aren't any other director openings in the district."

"Then I'll quit. The staff can make their own decisions."

"Don't shoot the messenger on this. *I'm* going to have to oversee the place. I'll be there with you. Because, if you don't, if we don't, then . . ."

Echo filled in the blanks. "There aren't any other openings for you or my staff either."

She got up and peered through the window. Those patrons who had expected to visit the library had gathered near the entrance. But they weren't alone. The commotion was enough that the police had started herding people away from the doors. Some weren't going willingly. When she turned to rush outside, Percy fell in behind her. By the time they got to the door, they were greeted by an officer and some bureaucrat pasting a sign on the door, announcing the closing of the F. M. Lewis Library.

Echo shouldn't have been surprised. News traveled faster than ever these days. She stood at the top of the stone steps leading down into the courtyard and struggled to make sense of what she was seeing. One snarling woman had turned a book bag bearing the library's name into a formidable weapon. She swung it overhead and connected with the cop trying to tackle her. A few paces away, a short, thickly muscled man grabbed a baton off the ground and pulled another officer into a chokehold.

The activists had also arrived. A swarm of them, brandishing signs that read **Humans for Humans, We Won't Be Replaced, Death to AI**. Echo knew that for them, this show was only the beginning. They'd never been afraid to get physical. One punch had already been thrown, and soon a flurry followed.

"We better get back inside." Percy tried to take her by the arm and marshal her through the double doors, but Echo yanked away. She turned her ire on the bureaucrat still standing there, gone pale as a glacier. He gripped another one of the closing notices in trembling hands. Echo snatched the paper from him and balled it up before tossing it on the ground. Then she found a seam beneath the one plastered on the door's glass pane and picked at it with her thumbnail.

"Have you lost your mind?" Percy screamed behind her, but Echo barely heard him. She didn't stop until she'd clawed off the notice. She turned to her friend, chest rising and falling in great waves.

"You go back inside. Call . . ." She trailed off. Who was there to call? The police were here already.

They were going to take away her library. They were launching an assault on books, *again*. Echo wanted to stop them. She wanted to make someone pay. If only she'd had the guts to join the resistance.

Shouts. Screams. Kicks. Chaos churned on all sides, an upheaval. And she wanted in. Echo eyed the staircase. Walking down the first step was easy, as was the next. But when she found herself just an arm's length away from a protester, crumpled beneath a storm of boots, she froze. For the briefest of moments, the man's eyes, wild with rage, locked onto hers. Still, she couldn't move. If only someone would flash a number one in her face, maybe she could find the courage.

Shame made her turn away. Self-loathing allowed her to be guided by Percy's strong hands. Guilt and contrition ushered her back into the staff lounge, where she sat, cold, numb, listening to the clamor that marked the end of her time at the job she loved.

Chapter Two

Nine months later

Thanks to robot-assisted construction crews, the transformation of the old F. M. Lewis Library branch into a shelter for the unhoused had been swift. She wasn't angry at the new residents, but a part of herself she wasn't proud of resented them for occupying the space.

Speckled sunlight broke through the clouds and shone on all the places on the structure's red-brick facade that in such a short time looked so much worse for wear. The octet of neoclassical white pillars was cracked and yellowed. The windows could've done with a good washing. The grass looked like a wilted salad of mixed greens and browns. And the air, the air was starkly absent of the scents of leather and old paper. Echo remembered when this place had been maintained like a national landmark, largely because of her pestering. She guessed the city didn't think its current inhabitants deserved the same attention.

One person braved the early hour. He sported a hoodie featuring the Human.exe logo. Two arms raised, parallel, fisted. A black dot between the subversive *H* representing the resistance group. No one in the new government wanted to admit it, but the group's opposition to artificial general intelligence was what had turned the tide, instigating the laws put in place to set clear parameters around how the AGI technology could be used.

He nodded at Echo. "You used to work here, back when it was a library, didn't you?"

"I did," she confirmed.

"And, what? You're mad now? You think we should have found someplace else to live?" His tone was calm, probing.

"The fact that I'm here and not where I'm supposed to be should tell you that I miss the place, but if *we* had to go, I can't think of a better use for it."

He smiled and gave her the resistance sign before retreating inside.

Those same doors she'd sometimes propped open in the fall were shuttered to her now and forever. She closed her eyes and pictured herself striding through the entrance hallway, stopping in the conference room for coffee, then making the rounds of the building. The smooth feel of a book's dust jacket beneath her fingertips. The soft flutter of turning pages. The sublime pastries the local bakery dropped off every Friday, the tastes of cinnamon and vanilla lingering on her tongue.

It was like the ghosts of all the books that were once housed here still clung to the place. A feeling more than anything substantial, of knowledge, unmoored and mourning.

The rapid slap, slap, slap of several pairs of fast-approaching footsteps yanked her back to the present. A trio of oncoming joggers performing their track shoe hustle breezed past.

For the second time this week, Echo had taken this detour to come and reminisce. It was time to go. In a little over an hour, she was supposed to start her shift as director and curator of the People's Library. She turned to head back down Fulton and stopped.

The pearly-gray July morning sat snug in that sizzling sweet spot between early and late summer, but she shivered anyway. The hooded man was gone, but a tingling at the nape of her neck told her she wasn't alone.

She did the thing where she relaxed her gaze, seeing but not focusing. The wide brick path was clear. Same for the steps and double doorway. Nothing but air weaving between gothic columns.

A catlike purr preceded a flicker of staticky movement. There, near the bush where Echo had found a soft landing when she'd tripped on a patch of ice during the handful of days that had masqueraded as winter a couple of years back. A pool of thin sunlight cut through the clouds at that moment. TPL's virtus were hard to spot in the sun, but there it was, hidden in plain sight.

The look of them was still difficult to fathom, and outside TPL no less. Drawn with the precision of the most skilled artist's hand, they were as close to human as she'd ever seen digitally. Ensconced in what she could only compare to a playing card, about the height of an average woman and a width less than that of a baby's first hair. It was like watching a giant piece of paper floating around.

Like Echo, were they drawn to places where real books used to live? More often than not, when they escaped, they ended up here, or at other nearby branches. It seemed that even lines of AI-mangled code weren't enough to confine a virtu with determination to explore.

But how?

The administration must have filed away all her inquiries about the matter behind one of the quantum shields that were supposed to lock down access, because she'd never received an answer.

Echo moved slowly, coming at the virtu from a different angle. You had to be fairly close to one to check it back in. Echo was almost there when her foot came down on a small branch. Too late, she shifted.

The virtu bolted. The 3D image sped off and charged around the corner of the library.

She didn't have time for this. Being late for work was not something she did. With a single tap to the subdermal chip behind her right ear, she accessed her AI companion, Gina. *What time is it?* With the latest upgrade, she didn't have to speak aloud, but she still found it difficult to break the habit.

Hey hey, Echo, it's 7:50 a.m. The forecast—

Stop, Echo said, and then adjusted the strap on her leather tote bag, which was biting into the soft flesh between her neck and left shoulder. On the move again, she wound her way around the right side of the building.

Abruptly, near the curved edge at the stairs leading to the basement door, the virtu appeared, back turned.

Echo advanced, ready to utter the words to return it to the collection. But in a move that fluttered the collar on her shirt, the thing flipped around to face her. What she saw curdled those words on her tongue. The figure enclosed in the plane was dressed in all black. The fringe along the bottom suggested it was a long shapeless dress. But the face . . . it was hidden behind a strange white mask. Polished to a high gloss. The cheekbones and forehead pronounced, almost exaggerated. Dim recesses for the eye sockets.

She opened her mouth to speak. All she had to do was say the word, but she could only gape stupidly at that mask.

The virtu spun again and raced off in the direction of Edgewater Park Drive.

"Stop!" Echo called and ran after it. She eyed the solarway, now clogged with commuters and baby carriages. She ran alongside the railing, ignoring everyone except the person dressed like a rainbow, who pointed down a side street and said, "If you're after the dupefake, it went that way."

Walking to and from work was Echo's exercise of choice, not running. With only enough air in her lungs to sprint off again, she gave the person a curt head nod as a thank-you. But she soon stopped. The virtu wasn't anywhere in sight. Hands on her waist, she gulped in air and tugged at her moisture-wicking shirt while catching her breath.

She felt the tepid warmth on her skin and wished that the bunch of clouds to the west would grace her with some shade. In a few more breaths, she'd recovered enough to continue the search. She turned right onto West Fifty-Eighth Street and before long approached a turn onto Detroit Avenue. It took her a moment to realize that the path she'd been following led straight to TPL. Was the virtu going back all on its own?

Echo slowed to a walk, scanning. With Fulton Road in sight, in the wide-open expanse of the area that now comprised Edgewater Park and the library, she spotted it.

Something was definitely off. Virtus had slipped out before—not often, but it had happened. This cat and mouse game and the weird mask, though? No, this was a new twist. One that made her stomach churn. She got closer, her steps tentative. The facade of the virtu came into view.

The developers had thought it would be good to give some kind of surface-level autonomy to the virtual personages, so they'd instituted a dual-check-in policy. A person who borrowed a virtu could signal that they were ready to end their time together, but the virtu had to agree. They'd been known to drag out these sessions when either party might be feeling needy.

When she got closer, she saw that the virtu had become more visible. Her dress was a long, black, high-collared, long-sleeved affair, bows at the wrists. A dainty, pale hand rose toward the masked face.

The virtu remained still for what Echo estimated to be the ten seconds she'd been holding her breath. Then the virtu stuck her fingers into her eye sockets and pulled. The mask dropped out of sight, somewhere in her virtual world.

Instead of a recalcitrant face, Echo saw darkness, interrupted by a celestial light show swirling with binary digits. Too late, she tried to look away. As the last of the ones faded, the color red, a siren, exploded in Echo's vision.

Chapter Three

Echo hadn't meant to scream. Hadn't even realized she was screaming until a group performing tai chi in the park crowded around her. By now her synesthesia-induced color storm had passed.

"You all right, dear?" An elderly woman's face was etched with concern. She wore the flowing two-piece ankle pants and long-sleeved shirt favored by her age group. The smart fabric was in the midst of shifting from seafoam green to a subtle red, a warning that the noxious air from the latest Canadian wildfires had finally reached them.

After a morning chase with a faceless virtu? No. Hell no, she wasn't okay. Sweat curled the fine tresses along her hairline and had colonized every crevice on her body. It took a moment, but then Echo recognized one pair of the eyes currently gaping at her. A regular patron of the library. Immediately, she swallowed hard and straightened. "I'm fine, really."

Those glances they shot back her way told her that she'd convinced only half of them. Someone else, arms and legs ensconced in exoskeleton supports, gave her a couple of gentle pats on the back. Even a child, happy-face emojis flashing on the headband holding back her long dark hair, made the kind of soothing sounds her parents probably murmured when she awoke from a bad dream. Once more, Echo mumbled assurances that she was okay and wormed her way out of their midst.

The delinquent virtu, of course, was nowhere in sight. And what was she supposed to make of what she'd seen? A bit of code gone wrong?

Some kind of bug? Or were hallucinations a side effect of chronic lack of sleep?

A quick glance around the perimeter of Edgewater Park confirmed that only the tai chi crew had witnessed her little breakdown. She asked her companion for the time and blew out a frustrated breath. This was not the way she was supposed to start the day. *Nobody to blame but myself,* she said to herself. If she'd come straight to work instead of detouring down memory lane, none of this would have happened.

The organic whisper of recycled algae fibers rustling with movement meant the tai chi group had gotten back to their practice, so Echo set off down the walkway. Unease swarmed every blank crevice of her mind. An escaped virtu was a rarity, for sure. But the mask and the whole vibe had every warning bell in her body firing. Her boss would be getting a call about these escalating glitches later.

If you were of a mind to appreciate such things, the People's Library was an architectural marvel. Layered like an upside-down wedding cake, it rose in widening rings, defying gravity. The smallest level was situated half on the Lake Erie shore, while the other half balanced atop supports erupting from its gunmetal-gray waters. Encircled by a sleek promenade, part of it cantilevered over the tide. The structure rose like a cathedral of knowledge, spun from glass and hempcrete and bamboo, housed with virtual people, their lives and stories eternally adrift.

At the front, grassy slopes stretched downward, dotted with now-empty six-seater tables. Small trees and seasonal flora added bursts of color. Windmills disguised to look like palm trees spun swiftly in the breeze, powering the library. A massive solar array on the roof took care of the rest of the structure's power demands.

Finally at the entrance, Echo sighed and raised her right palm. Invisible scan complete, the door slid open. Once inside, she repeated the process to close it behind her. A quick time check: forty minutes to spare before the library opened.

The quiet always soothed her, wrapping itself around her like a cashmere sweater. The hempcrete walls, chosen for their sustainability and carbon sequestration, also served another purpose. They absorbed sound, muffling the noise outside.

She glanced up at the large antique brass timepiece hovering about twenty feet above the information desk. Time's Eye, they'd named it. Ever watchful, the clock was visible from every vantage point, positioned to stand sentinel over all that took place within these walls. An arbiter. Maybe a judge.

The clock's brassy dials told her she had little time. The hour was a pumpkin-orange, high-energy eight, while the minute hand rested on a bluish-green four that usually calmed her. But together, the combination sent her adrenaline spiking. Her therapist had taught her deep-breathing exercises to help control the mood swings. Mostly the technique worked. Disaster ensued when it didn't. See the wrong number and freak out, and people didn't get it. Didn't want to. She hadn't wanted solitude, but it had chosen her all the same.

This time it took several minutes to calm down, time she didn't have to spare. The library opened at nine.

She turned her attention to the otherworldly faces of virtus that rotated in a semicircle behind the clock. They were like ads, a stream of suggestions for patrons to check out. Positioned as they were, floating behind the clock, you couldn't miss them when you walked inside. Echo grinned as her very first suggestion for inclusion in the collection scrolled past. Virginia Proctor Powell Florence, the first Black woman to earn a degree in library science.

As a lover of books, Echo had been miserable here during the early days. But that had begun to change.

Staff offices were on the rear of the first floor, so she quickly dropped her tote bag at her desk and made a mad dash for the nearest elevator. At the Lewis branch, Echo had known every book in her collection, could pluck an obscure text right off the shelf if asked. Suffice to say her reluctance to do the same at TPL had *not* gone unnoticed.

"It's not just you," Percy had told her. "We both have to know every single member of the virtual personage collection."

"Dupefakes, you mean," Echo had countered with a smirk.

Percy glanced over one shoulder, then the other, before he leaned in. "Fake as a three-dollar bank credit."

They laughed like a couple of schoolkids before Percy sighed. "We have to check out each and every one of 'em and spend at least half an hour in conversation."

"Until we cycle through the entire collection, plus the new ones we'll be adding soon," Echo said.

"The National Literary Commission commands—"

Echo had pursed her lips. "And we obey."

"Now, Ms. London." Walter Sprigg's familiar voice snared her back from the memory. "Where are you off to in such a hurry?"

Echo frowned. Walter wasn't usually here until fifteen minutes before his shift, and even then he usually had the good sense not to bother her right away. The elevator was right there. She could keep walking, hope he got the message about personal time and space. Instead, she plastered on a tepid smile and turned to greet her head custodian. "The question is, What are *you* doing here so early?"

Unlike the rest of her staff, Walter had been TPL's only new hire. Percy said that he'd been a renowned cameraman in the film industry before being booted out of his job by one of the androids that didn't need bathroom breaks or catered meals. He was a tinkerer by nature, able to fix a space rocket with a string of spider silk and a wish. That had landed him the custodian job at one small neighborhood branch. Soon they'd given him oversight of three.

"Whoever installed that HVAC unit may have slapped a 'smart device' label on the box, but that thing is as dumb as they come. You want smart, start here"—he tapped his forehead—"and add these." Walter held up both hands in a gesture that, for a moment, reminded her of something she couldn't place. "It'll void the warranty, but I'm tired of calling out that repair bot." He looked at her in that way of his that said he was once again going to make her a co-conspirator in something he'd already set his mind to. "I'm gonna fix the thing myself."

Walter watched her with that ridiculously open and honest look of his. If something went wrong, Echo would shoulder the blame. But Walter had told her ahead of time that he was going to do it, which meant he trusted her as much as he trusted himself. "I won't tell if you don't."

He gave her his odd little head tilt and nod, then smiled. She expected him to get on with it. How much time had passed since he'd stopped her? Another two minutes? Maybe three? Echo needed to log that time interviewing a new virtu before opening.

"Well . . ." she began, then paused, searching. "I need to look into an issue with an escaped virtu."

"Again?" Walter asked. His whole stance changed, suggesting he was settling in for a long story.

"Just like you said," Echo said, waving a hand. "Nothing around here is as automated and foolproof as they think."

"No doubt," Walter agreed. "You let me know if I can do anything."

Yes, please, just let me go. Echo nodded and dropped her gaze. More than a few seconds, less than a minute. Win. "You have a good day."

Echo didn't wait for a response but turned and kept walking. She didn't look up until the elevator was on its way to the fourth floor, the reading room. Through the glass rear, she gazed onto the lake and marveled at the morning light. When the elevator stopped, she maneuvered around the seating lounge and hurried into the left-rear private "reading" cubes.

The space was on the cozy side, the size of a walk-in closet or a safe room. Another layer of hempcrete behind the walls ensured privacy. She couldn't explain it, but she felt such a connection to something natural here, even at a library that was as far from it as possible.

The sound of the lake filled the space, piped in through a mechanism attached to one of the building's underwater steel supports. That sweet undersea melody carried away all worries of escaped virtus.

Echo nestled into the warm hug of the sole vegan-leather chair and leaned her head against the headrest for a moment to catch her breath.

If only she had a mirror. She smoothed her lips together, hoping some of the berry-hued color she'd applied this morning remained.

The entire front wall was a glass-like panel. It loomed in front of her like an accusation. A betrayal against every novel that ever was or would be written. She'd taken this job to save her staff and, to be honest, to soothe her ego. She wouldn't have been able to afford her small apartment without assistance if she didn't have a job.

And part of the deal was these tedious virtu interviews. Wasn't it Zeno who'd learned from an oracle that the secret to life was to have conversations with the dead? If he had, he should have clarified that they had to have something interesting to say. The first members of the digital collection had been chosen and installed by the administration before she arrived. A good number of them were outright bores. But she had to admit that wasn't the case with them all. She'd never tell anyone, but she'd actually enjoyed some of these conversations. *Really* enjoyed.

The same couldn't be said of her life outside these pods, however. Her challenges had all but ruined the possibility of ever having a social circle. She'd achieved everything she ever wanted, despite her challenges, yet chirpy, pet-like Gina was her closest friend.

In much the same way that staff inspected physical books for damage, Echo had to do the same for virtus, checking for any signs of human corruption. She scrolled through the list of options and stopped on one she'd skipped, hesitant to revisit this angering period in American history. This time, however, she opened her mouth and spoke the words: "Ada, I'd like to check out virtual personage Jesse Cooper."

Chapter Four

Selecting a book was one of the simple delights of Echo's life. Beautiful covers that hinted at the story within, fancy or block script on the spines—these things served to draw her in. Anticipation teetered as she read the jacket copy on the back. And only then, if her interest was sufficiently piqued, would she allow herself to read the first page or two.

Not so with this collection. A short biography was always available, but instead of artwork, there was only a face. Where was the creativity in that? The excitement just wasn't the same. All she had here was a moment where the glass display shimmered pleasantly before the virtu appeared. She expelled a breath and waited.

The man who regarded Echo on the other side of the display was Jesse Cooper, a member of the all-Black naval unit dubbed the Golden Thirteen. Wire-rimmed glasses covered thoughtful, curious eyes. He wore his uniform like an angel wears its wings. His double-breasted jacket featured those iconic gold stripes, marking his rank. A crisp white shirt and dark tie completed the look. His hat proudly displayed the US Navy officer's insignia, an eagle atop a shield with crossed golden anchors. He oozed a dignified aura so palpable she could almost see it.

"I'm Echo London, the director here at the library," she said. For some reason, Mr. Cooper's manner caused her to sit up straighter.

After the slightest arch of his right eyebrow, he said, "I would introduce myself, but you probably already read the biography."

He didn't smile like some of the other virtus. Or scowl. In fact, he didn't show much emotion at all. Even his voice was a bit deadpan, as if he had somewhere else to be and was only tolerating her out of some sense of duty. This was all the reminder she needed that artificial general intelligence was just that. Supporters were quick to point out how far they'd progressed with AGI, but to Echo, virtus were just expert mimics. Human? Far from it.

"I did," Echo confirmed. "But the way I see it, whatever summary the marketing AI drummed up only scratches the surface. First things first, though, you have any questions for me?" This information exchange was customary. The virtus supposedly wanted to "learn" as much as those who checked them out did.

The officer didn't speak immediately, so Echo busied herself trying to decide if the wall color in the cube leaned more toward sun-drenched buttercream or the soft tan of aged parchment paper. "Were you a part of the team that planned out how this kind of library would function?" Jesse asked.

An odd question. "I wasn't. I came on board after. I've worked at real . . . um, I mean . . . traditional libraries my entire career before this."

"Because you like being around people or because you like books?" Jesse asked.

Echo thought a moment before answering. "Being a reader led me to the line of work, so given the choice between an afternoon out with friends or a cup of coffee and a good book, well . . ." Mr. Cooper could draw his own conclusions from that.

A silence fell then that gave Echo time to take in Jesse's virtual milieu. Each virtu had a carefully crafted setting that was supposed to represent an important aspect of who they were. This was definitely a room on a ship. The light-gray back wall with the small open porthole told her as much. She could see the edge of what looked like a bunk, the rough woolen blanket neatly tucked beneath the mattress. A sailor's berthing quarters, then. Along with the light from the window, a shaft of yellow illuminated the right side of Jesse's face, perhaps from a lamp on a desk out of view.

She could dig into the obvious stuff. His time in the navy, going up against enemies domestic and abroad. It was a long time ago, but she always wondered what had led African-descended people to join the service back then. Echo chose another direction. "Tell me about where you grew up? DC, right?"

Jesse's neck drew back in the gesture of someone surprised by the question. But he went on to tell her about his childhood, full of good-natured boyhood mischief urged on by a crew of lifelong friends, lazy walks along the Potomac River, and scholarship. A father who was an engineering professor at Howard University and a mother who ran a hair salon from their home. Sundays were for church, even if Jesse's heart was never really in it.

"I was all set to go to Howard when the war broke out," he told her. "After that, I enlisted. Kinda felt like it was my duty."

To whom? Echo wanted to ask, but she found she understood. In the same way that she felt it necessary to do her job at a library she hadn't initially wanted to work at, Jesse and the rest felt a sense of responsibility to their ancestors to defend the land they'd helped build. "If you could share one lesson from your time with the navy, what would it be?" she asked.

Jesse removed his glasses, glanced up and then back at her. "Never let anyone define for you what it means to be a human being."

Echo wanted nothing more than to go deeper into that statement, and she would have if not for the virtual voice of the People's Library barging in. "Good morning, Curator London. The library is set to open in five minutes. The virtual personage is ready for a day of learning and exchange. Would you like me to unlock the doors?"

Ever since the day when she'd allowed the library to open itself and she'd come downstairs to find a flock of geese had entered, she'd never done that again. "No," she told the voice. Then, to Jesse, she said something she'd never said to another virtu before. "Mind if we continue this conversation another time?"

"Would it matter if I did?"

"I don't want to twist your arm, that's for sure," Echo said.

Jesse put his glasses back on and inclined his head, a tepid smile lifting the corners of his mouth. "Then another time it is."

Chapter Five

Echo headed for the staircase at the front of the lounge area. With each step and at each landing, she erected her private walls. One to fend off questions about her life outside, what she did, who she spent her time with. Another fortification against talk of the wildly swinging pendulum that was the weather and any other mindless chitchat that people so desperately used to fill up perfectly quiet space. And a final barrier to deal with the bureaucrats.

Before she'd been officially announced as curator, Echo had endured weeks of extensive coursework designed to prepare her for the role. Leadership classes, which she'd scoffed at, along with technical primers in artificial intelligence, ethics (*mm-hmm*), and library operations. Then there were the virtual personage interviews. Out of one hundred randomly selected candidates, from historical figures to entertainers and profound thinkers, Jesse Cooper was the one who'd intrigued her most.

The history of the Golden Thirteen was one of so many forgotten stories, but TPL was giving Jesse and his fellow officers a chance at redemption. Since when had learning more about her own history become a bad thing?

Normally, by the time her feet touched down in the lobby, she'd be the picture of calm, open, and engaging. Today her nerves were like brittle maple leaves, ready to be crushed beneath the sole of a sturdy boot.

Tomorrow she'd leave the past where it belonged, at least for a day, and forget about torturing herself by walking past the old F. M. Lewis Library branch.

As she passed the second level, which housed the People's Café and Coffee Shop, Echo inhaled the tantalizing aromas of their smorgasbord of breakfast treats. She smiled inwardly at one of the battles she'd fought and won. That clanging and banging of pots. The metallic scrape of spatulas on grills was because she'd insisted the administration hire real live human beings and not the admittedly capable robots that had taken over so many other restaurant jobs.

As she was prone to do, Echo took a moment to glance out the rear folding doors at Lake Erie.

"I don't get it," Carmen, Echo's library assistant, said behind her. "What everybody sees, ya know? It's not like that's the Mediterranean Sea out there."

Echo turned to Carmen and was greeted by a perfect smile that must have cost her parents a small fortune. She'd apparently thought better of the bright-fuchsia color she'd dyed her hair sometime back because she hadn't retouched several inches of glossy black new growth. A color that in Echo's opinion better complemented her café au lait skin.

"That's the thing," Echo said. "You don't have to get it. You can have your sea and I can have my lake, and somebody else may be perfectly happy with the puddle that forms in their front yard when it rains too much."

Carmen cocked the sparsely populated strip where her full eyebrows used to be. Gone after an ill-advised go at dyeing them to match her hair. "I was with you until you threw in that puddle business."

She handed Echo a tablet that outlined her entire day, right down to the breaks she always inserted to ensure Echo had time to get away and recharge. Capable Carmen, she jokingly called her. All that stood in the way of her library assistant running this place was Echo herself and the archaic MLS degree requirement.

Through triple-paned glass, Echo could see an eager congregation had already assembled. By midday, every floor would be crammed with people. Infants to centenarians, *everybody* was ready to worship at the altar that was the People's Library. It didn't hurt that the place was constructed like the old casinos. Food, lounging, tech, and development spaces designed so you didn't want or need to leave. Another draw was that the building boasted three-terahertz Wi-Fi, the best in the city. It was no surprise that everyone from Chagrin Falls to Westlake visited.

"Ada," she said to the library AI, "initiate opening."

A split second later, the front doors slid open, and the patrons streamed in. Without even wondering about it, Echo knew the back doors that let folks spill out onto the rear promenade had also been unlocked. Lights in certain areas came on, while others remained off until proximity sensors turned them on.

Echo corrected herself; it only *seemed* like everybody loved the library. There were certainly those who didn't. And they'd been all too open about how they felt.

Human.exe. She felt silly referring to them as a resistance group, like the administration was keen to do. It wasn't like she was the head of a military base here. What they were called didn't matter much anyway. Their mission had been clear: people first, technology a distant second. And they weren't afraid to enforce that message with force. TPL and all the tech that powered it had become a rallying cry, driving more people to their cause over recent months. They'd disrupted the opening and even swung a few punches at a member of her staff. So along with ramped-up security, Echo had begun scanning every face she saw for signs of ill intent.

Most were unremarkable, a hodgepodge ranging from the smartly dressed to those still wearing clothing her mother would have given her the side-eye for even thinking of leaving the house in. One woman caught her attention, not because of anything off, but because of her hair. A full, rounded, curly Afro that bounced right along with her as she waltzed past Echo with a nod. She glanced up at Time's Eye and gave it a little salute before trotting up the stairs.

A particularly cute toddler yanked on Echo's hand, drawing her attention away. Her father, an unnaturally tanned fellow with damp hair, scooped up the child, and the two settled onto one of the shape-shifting gel chairs in the lounge.

Echo was about to leave when she spotted someone who stopped her in her tracks. The woman might as well have stepped right out of one of the billboard ads. Smartly dressed in a navy-blue pantsuit. Matching pumps clunking along the bamboo flooring. She favored the touchscreen wrist cuffs that linked to her personal AI companion. She smiled when she saw Echo watching and marched over to one of the first-floor workstations.

Echo turned back to the entrance.

Shifty eyes were the easiest sign of potential trouble there was. The slender teen with a baseball cap pulled down and a gaze that refused to land on anything for more than a second—he could be a problem. She quickly approached him.

"This your first time in the library?" she said.

He shoved his hands in his pockets. "In this one, yeah. But before . . ."

He trailed off and didn't finish his sentence. And he didn't say anything more when Echo gestured for him to keep talking. "They can help show you around." She indicated the welcome desk behind them.

"Thanks," the teen muttered before shuffling over.

Echo watched for another few moments, then set off to do her rounds. *Gina,* she said to her virtual assistant. She'd gone back and forth about getting a wearable or an implant. Though new kinds of devices were being invented all the time, they could still be lost. In the end, she'd submitted to a procedure with all the sting of a mosquito bite and opted for earring wearables for the microphone. Single tap and you could have an hours-long conversation without having to utter one word audibly. *Ask security to keep an eye on the kid I was just talking to.* Echo described him as best she could.

You got it, boss! Gina chirped. Her voice and constant presence soothed Echo's nerves. Already behind on her tight schedule, Echo made a mental note to ask technical support about adjusting the voice again and surprised herself by jogging up the stairs to the second floor.

As she reached the second level, her hopes for coffee were dashed. The People's Café was a veritable zoo. Did anybody have breakfast at home anymore? If she didn't, why should anyone else?

Option one: Fire up the 3D cooker and wait impatiently while your meal, obnoxiously customized for your specific dietary and health needs, was prepared. Option two: Meet up with your friends or family at the most innovative building in the country and let someone else do it all for you, sans the finger-wagging about clogged arteries and calorie intake.

A serpentine line longer than an airport queue told her she'd have to wait for her morning cup and a pastry. The steps and the morning's virtu chase were also starting to take their toll—she was winded.

Still, she filed in with the group of patrons heading up to the Maker Space, where creatives and tinkerers like Walter came to take advantage of all the AI-supported development they could. Just after the grand opening, someone had created a gadget that had gone on to be submitted for a national innovators award. But Human.exe had put up such a fuss with protests that the award went to a product developed without artificial assistance. Echo wondered how realistic that was when nearly everything was powered by one sort of intelligence or another, whether you were aware of it or not.

This floor was reminiscent of a chemist's lab with a modern twist. Instead of Bunsen burners and vials, the tables had 3D printers and tablets. A trio of teens had set up shop, with a checked-out virtu overseeing their work.

"Take the film, place it anywhere on your forearm," the virtu said. Echo didn't know who she was, but she certainly commanded their attention.

One of the boys, a regular named Tommy, unzipped his jacket and tugged it off, letting it slip to the floor. Another applied the film, a replica of the signature *C* of the Cincinnati Bearcats. The virtu put a finger to her lips and said, "Apply pressure and rub it in."

Echo was drawn into their circle. One of the boys did as he was told, smoothing the film onto and then into the skin. It was one of those new tattoos.

"Go ahead, try it out," the virtu directed, beaming with pride.

Tommy double-tapped the design on his wrist, enabling the micro-directional speaker. "Ridleigh, what time is my first class today?" He cocked his head. The same gesture so many people used when talking to assistants.

"Good morning, Tommy. It is nine twenty," came the response.

The teen's eyes went wide. "It was my companion, no doubt about it. His voice was too low and kinda whiny, but it worked! We just made the first tattoo-wearable prototype." The virtu clapped, and the other boys whooped and hollered, a little loud for her taste, but this was a place where people made things. That meant the rules had to be a little more relaxed here.

She was ready to head back to her office just as the elevator doors slid open. The kid she'd alerted security to stepped out and froze when he saw her. His expression was unreadable. Again, his eyes met hers and slid away.

"Get over here, you're late!" one of the others shouted.

The kid sort of dipped his head and sidestepped past Echo on his way to join them. Echo shook her head. The administration had promised them security and then sent one person whom she feared a strong wind might topple.

There were people who hated the idea of this library. Echo had been one of them . . . for a time. The hate had softened into something less full. More permeable. Especially after the bomb. It had been rudimentary and technically wouldn't have done much more than scorch the floor beneath it, but the intent couldn't have been clearer.

But the National Literary Commission had responded swiftly. The culprit, likely a scapegoat, was apprehended before they'd completed repairs. Warnings flooded the digital ads and news streams. The clandestine group behind TPL, and she was sure there was one, was prepared to protect their investment. Echo wasn't so sure if that extended to the people working inside it. Zealots on both sides were warring it out, with Echo and her staff caught in the crosshairs.

Echo turned away, nonchalant as you please, and busied herself at one of the other tables. Ostensibly brushing away nonexistent crumbs and repositioning stools, she contacted Gina. *Get security up to the Maker Space and tell him I said "now."*

She heard the group of kids talking animatedly about what they were building. She had pretend-cleaned three more tables by the time security showed up and pulled the teen aside for questioning. He shot her a glance of disbelief but was ushered out with surprisingly little fanfare.

Echo thought there was no way she should be this tired, and it wasn't even ten a.m. This time, she stepped into the elevator and disembarked on the first level. From the moment she'd woken up, the day had been throwing obstacles in her way. She walked over and stood in front of the window facing Lake Erie, drawing little warmth from the sun. Lake Erie was a tempestuous mass today. One temerarious boat out there had decided to take on Mother Nature. If the sky were clear, and warm and cool air colluded to make an inversion, she could just make out the outline of Ontario, Canada.

Hey hey, boss lady, you have an incoming call, Gina announced. Echo stepped out back, out of earshot of a group of people near the guard railing just outside the back entrance. *Ready,* she said.

"Just got notification that you completed your next interview. I didn't get mine in yet, but I did begin recording my personal. What about you?" Percy was seated in his home office, the shelf behind him crammed with sports action figures. Each employee was supposed to go into the booth and record some aspect of their personal story or family history for addition to the communal collection. Echo had sidestepped that employment requirement for as long as she could before finally recording a comically pithy entry.

He continued, "From the look on your face and the lack of a coffee cup in your hand, I'm guessing you are in a mood this morning." Percy wore one of his vintage rock band T-shirts, this one featuring a group wearing all white called Earth, Wind & Fire.

"There was another escaped virtu. And I think the administration is lying about not knowing how. They have an answer for everything else. Their team built the place, didn't they?"

"Truth is fluid, a lie spoken with enough kick . . . well, you know the rest."

Echo gave him a side-eye. "Are you helping? 'Cause I'm not feeling like you're helping."

Percy snorted. "Look at it this way, we both work for this absurd hybrid government. Between the corporate overlords and the citizen councils, they spend so much time hiding shit from each other, it's possible the commission doesn't know any more than they tell me."

"I guess you could be right."

"Even if I'm not, drop it anyway. The next time you see a virtu sailing down Edgewater Drive, let 'em. See what happens if you don't jump in, trying to make everything right, for once."

You don't know me. Echo didn't say this aloud because she knew it was bull. Other people, *normal* people, gossiped and snacked at the tables outside or on the rooftop garden during breaks. Or they stared mindlessly at the ad streams. Read a book. But Echo sidled up to the library to pass her free time with virtus. What had she turned into?

Echo inclined her head. "Guess I better get to work."

Percy looked disappointed, then signed off, quoting from *Macbeth* as he always did. They would talk tomorrow.

Echo was on her way to her office when a woman appeared in her path. The woman in the navy pantsuit, walking straight toward her with the purpose of someone who knew these corridors well. Only Echo'd never seen her before today.

"You don't remember me, do you?" Her voice wasn't light, like it would be if she meant that question in a pleasant way; no, it was laced with something else. She smelled like the outdoors, kind of musty, a little earthy. Eyes the color of black jeans that had been run through the washer one time too many. A large tote bag hung from her shoulder.

"There are signs everywhere telling you as much, so you probably know this area is reserved for library staff."

"It was my first time at the Lewis branch," she went on as if she hadn't heard Echo. "You saw me wandering around, and when one of the other librarians was about to kick me out of the place, you waved her off. You asked me what kinds of things I liked, and then you recommended some books."

A librarian recommended a million books to a million different kids. How was she supposed to remember this one?

"It was what turned out to be the last novel published without artificial general assistance before the rebellion, the fracture. You know I kept it? Lost count of the overdue notices. Yeah, it all changed back to human only, but that book and what it stood for meant something to me. I've got more of them than food at my apartment. That's because of you."

Where was she going with this? Echo tried to read her expression, but she came up blank. "Is that why you're here? Are you looking for a recommendation for a virtu? If so, I can direct you to—"

The woman made like she was going to spit on the floor, then sneered. "You're a fucking hypocrite. You *know* this is only the first step. They won't stop until there isn't one real book left. And that's just the appetizer. Then they'll dive back into the main course. Spin those AGI programs back up and come after us again. But you go on fooling yourself if you want. There are people out here who ain't gonna let that happen. You with us or them?"

"You need to leave." Echo jabbed a finger toward the exit. "You can do it with or without the aid of my security team."

Navy Suit smirked, turned, as if to go quietly.

Echo saw it coming. Tried to backpedal. She double-tapped her earring. "Gina—"

It happened too fast.

The woman reached into the bag.

It fell to the floor.

Hands reared back, then something wet and dark landed with a sickly thwack, coating Echo's hair and body and oozing into her mouth.

Navy Suit flashed the Human.exe sign, then turned and ran.

Security was nowhere in sight.

The liquid dripped from Echo's chin and hair in thick ropes. It had no taste or smell. Nothing burned. She should have run after the woman or hidden. Done something. But she stood there, caving in on herself.

She blinked against the mess in her eyes. Through blurry vision, she saw that the hallway was empty.

Unless it wasn't.

Chapter Six

Echo's hands trembled as she groped around for a clean wedge of clothing to wipe her face and mouth. Blood, paint, something more toxic? The thoughts of what was coating her hair and eyes threatened to overwhelm her.

Capable Carmen, of course, got to her first.

"What the hell?" She rushed Echo off to the bathroom. First she made her rinse her mouth out at the sink. Then she snatched a wad of compostable napkins from a plant near the door and wiped Echo's face, ineffectually trying to pat her dry.

"Gina, call the police," Echo said, an inorganic taste still cloying on her tongue.

By then, the security guard, Peter, burst into the bathroom.

"I was distracted dealing with the kid you pointed out in the Maker Space," he said. "Turns out he was clean."

"Did you even go out and look for the lady?" Carmen asked. "Navy suit? Heels?"

Peter turned and ran out before he said another word. Finding her was unlikely. She'd had too much of a head start. Plus, there were no cameras in TPL. As a concession to the privacy legislators, the library had been declared a surveillance-free zone. Echo wouldn't press charges, anyway, because she *was* a hypocrite. Because if she weren't, she would have found another way to earn a living that didn't compromise everything she stood for.

That navy suit was probably floating in the lake by now, but if they ever found the woman, the administration would press every charge they could, then lean on the citizen council to make up some more. They had decided to take a hard stance on these attacks, but funny how that hadn't deterred anybody so far.

Carmen hovered until after Echo's interview with the police. Grudgingly, Echo allowed the forensics technicians to poke and prod her for samples to analyze. No way was she going to spend all day coated in whatever that gunk was. She went home to clean up. By the time she made it back, half the day was lost.

Despite everything that had been done to stamp out each threatening tech advance, human beings had a pretty sorry record, one that would have a professional sports team questioning its leadership. The thing was, you simply couldn't stop progress. So when the administration had practically blackmailed her into taking the job, she'd lied to herself about having a better chance at changing things from the inside.

She understood Human.exe; she just chose to fight a different way, one that didn't involve losing her home or being confined to reading from the sparse collection available in a prison library. The attack had been too easy. What if the woman had really wanted to hurt her? Echo didn't want to think about the answer.

The country, even the world, was a somewhat better place. Hadn't critical changes been made? Someone who deserved a Nobel Prize had finally recognized how unsustainable it was to have average home prices in the half-million range while salaries had remained stubbornly fixed. The government had sat on its idle hands.

The very same people who'd caused the problem had acted, though. A small but vocal faction of Silicon Valley who had sounded the alarm about the ethical challenges brought on by the age of intelligence split. They dispersed around the country, in key cities, Cleveland being one. The Organic Rift was born, and with the support of the communities they'd settled in, they tamed the growth.

The impact had been less apocalyptic than theorized, but automation and bots had displaced a good chunk of jobs. Universal basic income, or UBI, was for the unemployed initially, but it grew to include anyone who needed an income supplement—in other words, almost everyone.

Implementation was not without its controversies, a test being chief among them. Everyone had to take the exam in order to qualify for UBI, ostensibly so that researchers could measure the impact of recent trends in social media, automation, and the rest on human attention spans and associative cognitive decline. Echo had never taken UBI, as her salary more than paid for her expenses. She'd heard others talk about the test. Even balked at being subjected to it, but the lure of free, lifesaving cash was too great, and eventually, those protests died down. The opening of the library had caused a spike in incidents like this. The rebellion was stirring up again.

Echo cast a glance out her office window but, for once, found no comfort in the water. She trudged over to the Yoruba Gẹ̀lẹ̀dẹ̀ mask her parents had gifted her when she turned sixteen and ran a finger along its contours. It had traveled from her room there to home, to her office. Something to brighten the place up. She moved to her desk, took out her well-worn copy of *The Icarus Girl*, and ran her hands over the cover, slumped in her chair. "Gina, how about we go over that schedule now?" she said aloud with an earring double tap, tired of being in her own head.

"I detect a note of melancholy in your voice," Gina replied. "Should I read you a poem or an inspirational quote from Rumi first?"

"For once, can you just do what I asked?"

The AI hesitated. If Echo believed such things, she would swear she'd hurt her feelings.

A beat later, the voice, serene and even, said, "Noted. Today you have a one-on-one with Lorain. She wants to talk about preparing a new course on ethics and AI. And then you have the staff meeting this afternoon to review the exciting list of new candidates for inclusion in our virtual collection."

"Move the meeting with Lorain to Monday and have the staff meet me in the conference room in thirty minutes," Echo said.

A moment later, Gina replied, "All set."

Echo pulled her mirror out of her desk drawer. Already, the day's events had made her look more tired than she was. She slid on some lipstick and smoothed her lips. She'd pulled her long braids up into a bun but pulled a couple down to frame her face. "G, call Percy Grafton."

Her supervisor didn't go so far as to wear a suit jacket like her, but she'd never seen a cardigan look stiffer and more professional in her life. He only ditched his more casual attire when he met with NLC administration. His face was a mask of worry. "Are you all right?"

"I'm fine," Echo said. She always said she was fine.

He exhaled his relief. "It feels so inept to tell you I'm sorry this happened, that it keeps happening. I was just on with the administration. Going on and on about how they sent Resources to ensure something like this wouldn't happen again."

Echo's chuckle didn't hold an ounce of humor. "They called that snail downstairs a resource? At this point, I'd almost prefer a patrol bot."

He pondered a comeback for a few seconds before abandoning the effort. "The police say they're doing everything they can to find that misguided fanatic, and when they do, the rest of those zealots will think twice before coming for us again." For reasons Echo didn't understand, the threat sounded even more severe delivered with Percy's slight British accent. "Oh, and they want to know where you spotted the escaped virtu, for troubleshooting."

"Well . . ."

Percy's mouth opened slightly. "Let me guess. F. M. Lewis?" A small crease settled between his brows.

Echo wanted with every fiber in her being to lie and avoid the lecture, but maybe she needed one. "Yeah."

He threw the pen he'd been holding, and it clanked somewhere off-screen. "Why?"

"Why what?"

"Don't do that. You know exactly what I'm talking about. That old library is gone. Your job is here. If you don't want this job and you'd like to go back there and haunt the place like the virtus, I have a long list of applicants just dying to sit right where you are."

There again. The threat, which said more about people who managed this way than the words themselves. She surprised herself by holding his gaze a second longer than she could usually stand. "None of them are me, are they? I'm here because I put this city on the library map. I built Lewis book by book, and they may have closed it, but nobody's going to take that away from me."

Percy leaned back in his chair, an expression of pure admiration replacing the eyebrow crease. "That's my girl. You've got a backbone, but you have to be shoved about to show it. Now tell me about the virtu."

Echo wanted to tell him that she was a woman and would never be his "girl." Women could call each other "girls" if they wanted, but it was off limits for everyone else. If Echo had a friend, a girlfriend, she was sure she would have agreed.

"The virtu itself doesn't matter," Echo said. "My question is, How is it happening? Last time, you said you'd check with tech support. What did they have to say?"

A shrug. "It's technology, Echo. There are no perfect systems. Glitches, bugs, that's all there is to it. They're working on the code, removing some of the old pieces originally done by the first-generation AI. How many physical books have you lost during your career? How many were checked out and never brought back?"

"Not the same thing," Echo countered. "The information that flows out of the library is only supposed to be about the types of subjects accessed, not the actual subjects themselves. Controls are supposed to be in place to prevent them from . . ." She searched for the right words. "Checking themselves out of the building. It shouldn't happen, and this one—"

"What about this one?"

"It was just . . . it's almost as if it was trying to tell me something."

"Like what? The historical significance of World War II?"

"If a group like Human.exe manages to get ahold of one of them, just think about what kind of damage they could do." Echo surprised herself by how protective she'd become of the collection in such a short time.

"I don't want that any more than you do."

"Then don't dismiss it," Echo said. "Maybe it would help if I could talk to them."

"I said to shore up your backbone, not gun for my job."

"If anything, I want to make your job easier," Echo said smoothly, playing the man like a flute. "One less conversation for you to have, so you can concentrate on the public shitstorm that's coming because of this latest incident." That last bit laid it on thick, but Percy was a man who liked to have his bread buttered on both sides.

His nod was as crisp as the kale chips served in the café. "Now that I think about it, I've got a flood of media interviews to prepare for."

Since she had him in a good place, Echo thought to push for something else. "One more thing. Have you given any consideration to my proposal? The plans I sent showed how I can carve out a small section of the first floor to house the print and digital book collection. And I have an initial list of books I'd like to include."

His sigh was that of a sailor setting out for an extended time at sea and bidding goodbye to a treasured pet. She saw him swipe up with his right hand, tap the screen that appeared, and use his forefinger to move between screens. He craned his neck, peered closer, then turned back to her. "There must be some mistake. I don't see your selections for the next batch of virtual personages. Am I missing something?"

He was missing a lot, but Echo didn't tell him that. "Going over the final selections today," she said. "I'll have it to you by close of business."

"First things first," he said with a smile. Then he signed off. One for two wasn't bad when it came to her interactions with her boss. She would contact engineering about the escapees, and after the next batch of virtus had been integrated into the system, she'd ask about her print collection again, and again. Until he gave in.

Echo let out an exaggerated exhale. Being on-screen drained her almost as much as those hour-long in-person group meetings. "G, lights down, door locked, notifications on silence." She needed a break before the staff meeting.

Echo stood and pushed her chair over to the window, where she curled up, closed her eyes, and imagined she could hear the water speaking, soothing in a voice of deep blue-green comfort.

Chapter Seven

Echo had closed her eyes for all of five minutes before a soft chirp announced an incoming message. Those were always audible. "Yes?" she groaned.

"You'd never guess who I saw roaming around the lobby," Carmen said.

Just then, another chirp interrupted them. "Incoming call from Rebecca London," Gina told her.

Echo thanked Carmen and disconnected. Why would Mom be calling? Wasn't it obvious? Persistent, uninterrupted streams reported everything from the latest theories on alien life to a neighborhood soccer game. Not a day passed when something about TPL wasn't deemed newsworthy. The administration hated any negative publicity and had probably tried to tamp it down, but news about her unfortunate run-in with a can of whatever it was had apparently hit the headlines. "Accept."

"We're in the lobby," her mother announced. Her voice was already on the deep side, but fear for her only child's safety had driven it down another notch.

Echo stood and reached for her blazer, hung behind the door. She slipped it on, already heading that way. "What are you doing here?"

"The question is, What are you doing here?" This from her dad. Great—both of them had shown up. His tone had enough of an edge to confirm he was still angry at her for suggesting he look into some of the new technology that was now threatening his business. He hadn't even returned her last call, and she'd gone so far as to apologize as if she'd barged in and installed it herself.

Echo emerged from the hallway containing the staff offices into a common area packed with humans and virtus communing. The sight of this—people walking beside giant glassy panes—she wondered if she'd ever get used to it. She spotted her parents near the recording booth. You'd think she was back in elementary school, and they'd come to collect her after a recess dustup. What would her staff think?

"Thinking of adding yourselves to the collection?" Echo affected a lightness of tone that she didn't feel.

Dad was unconvinced. "You couldn't pay me to add to this circus—"

"Oh, Uly, give it a rest," Mom said. "Circuses were outlawed twenty years ago. This is a place of learning, and I might remind you that your daughter happens to run it."

Echo glanced around, hoping nobody was interested in this months-old argument. Dad was decidedly old-school, a stance that was affecting his business. "As you can see, I'm fine. You didn't have to come all the way down here."

"I told him that," Mom said, elbowing Dad. "But he insisted we needed to check on his baby."

Echo cringed, then glanced around again to find Carmen on the other side of the welcome desk, making goofy faces at her. She turned away and covered a laugh. "I've got a meeting in a few minutes. I'm sorry you came all this way for nothing."

"I had to meet with a client anyway," Dad said.

Echo exchanged a quick, knowing glance with her mother. She'd mentioned some trouble, Dad losing staff and a few clients to all the automated systems that were putting even seasoned accounting firms like his out of business. But he'd survived this long; she'd just assumed he was back on solid ground. Things must have been worse than she thought.

A man who loved numbers had a daughter with the kind of synesthesia that made her sometimes hate them. It had been a source of friction for the pair over the years, worse when she was a kid and nobody fully understood how the condition affected her.

"Dad, you know how I felt when I was forced to come and work here," Echo said.

"Yeah, all that stuff you learned about not complaining went out the window when it was *your* job on the line," Dad said with enough fire for Mom to give him another one of her looks.

"What I was going to say is, I couldn't stop what happened, so I had to learn to adapt. I had to accept the change and at least make peace with it. There's some good stuff happening here." Echo was surprised at her defensiveness. "Just upstairs, we have kids working with virtus making things, inventions. And I met a member of the Golden Thirteen just today."

That got Dad's attention. He beamed. "You don't say?"

Carmen had moved closer behind them, signaling just as Gina confirmed: *Hey hey, Echo. Countdown to staff meeting in ten.*

"Look," Echo said. "I've got to get to a meeting. Why don't you head upstairs to the café and get something to eat. Then go to that meeting. Win back that client."

Dad gave her a nod and peck on the cheek before Mom placed her hand in the crook of his arm. They didn't go upstairs, but out through the trifold doors. Maybe next time. Today, she hoped her father would take her advice and that soon they'd celebrate his business's rebound. Echo didn't feel embarrassed anymore. She had parents who cared enough to check on her, and that . . . that was everything.

Chapter Eight

After the last staff member had rushed through the conference room door, mumbling an apology, Echo was still less than thrilled to dig into the day's work.

The Meetings Reduction Act of 2040 had been enacted after a South African study proved that productivity actually dipped by 10 percent for each hour spent in meetings. In person was even worse. The C-level execs had positively lost it. Pontification and bloviation had been their morale-murdering tools of choice for so long that they'd wondered how they would prove their worth. The studies they bought and paid for to counter the research were one by one exposed for what they were: desperation. Eventually, science and medicine prevailed, and the world had been freed of unnecessary meetings right along with nonessential commutes.

Aside from individual staff conferences, which were typically virtual or short walk and talks on the lakefront, Echo only presided over one staff meeting, held once a quarter, the sole purpose of which was to comb through the slate of candidates proposed for inclusion in her virtual collection.

While the outside of the library had the clean, modern lines popular in Scandinavia, the entirety of the interior was a chef's kiss of African-inspired tones and textures, thanks to a Ghanaian design firm. The whole installation had been termed "the Origins."

The table had been carved from a beautiful plank of mahogany, its natural tone enhanced by a bronze-colored stain. Potted palms and other plants filled the corners and window ledge. And like every room in the library, it had a view to die for. This one faced the liquid vista at the rear entrance and a suffusion of those engineered pollinator-boosting perennials that bloomed almost until winter. The bees loved them and had rebounded accordingly.

Carmen cued them up. "All right, let's run through the list of proposals. Shall we go alphabetically or by category?"

Unlike in a traditional library, their collection wasn't made up of a multitude of genres. There was no mystery virtu, none for sci-fi or horror. This was the People's Library, after all. So their focus was on categories of humanity's historical variety. Philosophers, poets, scientists, religious figures, and the like. Oddly, famous authors were stowed away in the reference collection. As were instances of virtus representing all the jobs that had been lost, like assembly line workers, truck drivers, even paralegals.

In the end, Echo and her team had agreed to switch things up and work through the list alphabetically.

Four hours, a few near fistfights, and a bird's nest of frayed nerves later, they'd arrived at the last virtual personage candidate.

"Who the hell is Zera Yacob?" Carmen said, tapping the display in front of her and directing it to the front of the room. "Here we go, kids: Zera Yacob, seventeenth-century philosopher from the motherland. Ethiopia, to be exact."

Carmen read ahead and summarized. "Here's where it gets fun. The Orthodox Church was pushing its way into the region, and let's just say our friend Zera wasn't having whatever rhetoric they were spewing. I guess he wasn't the type to hold his tongue about it either. We've heard the rest of this story so many times; he was . . . wait . . . he chose to exile himself . . . to some cave. Two years?" Carmen turned to glance at everyone, as if to confirm that the words she'd just read were correct. "But he didn't go sit on an island and contemplate the nature of the universe. He wrote a book, one that's supposed to be the first African philosophical text."

"The *Hatata*." Echo was sitting up now. "I didn't catch the name, but I do remember hearing about this book. Didn't somebody else try to take credit for it?"

"Yeah . . ." Carmen checked the documentation and told them that the claim had been debunked.

Echo thought about what it would be like to have all that time to yourself, to think. With some books, something to draw with, and food and water she didn't have to go hunting for. Aside from the part about the cave, it sounded like paradise.

Echo had heard enough. "I propose that we admit Zera Yacob into the . . ." She stopped to think. Should he be included in the philosophical category or religious figures? "I propose that we admit Zera Yacob into the philosophers collection. Is there any discussion?"

Hearing none, Echo announced, "Motion, all motions, passed."

The team let out small hoots and fist pumps. As everyone was gathering up their things to leave, Carmen said, "You want me to send the list to Mr. Grafton?"

With every batch of candidates, Echo's boss allowed her one sure shot: a virtu that would be immediately added to the collection based on her authority alone. She didn't always use the privilege, but this time she would.

"Use the automatic sub process for Mr. Yacob and let Percy know. Let me think about the rest." Echo stretched. "And now—"

"We know," Carmen said. "You'll be in your office, and if any of us dares to knock at your door, or even walk past it too loudly, you will hand us our heads on a platter."

"Glad we understand each other so well," Echo said with a grin.

She was the last to leave the room. She took a moment to think about the selections, and she was pretty happy with them. After these meetings, Echo always ran their choices by the only member of her staff who didn't attend but whose opinion she most valued: Mr. Walter Sprigg.

Chapter Nine

With the list of virtu candidates fired off to Walter, Echo had dismissed the staff and was ready to head home. As was their custom, she'd made no indication as to which ones they'd picked. He must have stayed up half the night whenever she did this, because by the morning, he'd always give her his choices. It was fun to see if they overlapped. Finally, this day that had started out all wrong was ending on a high note.

"Gina, time for Operation Shut It Down."

"Finally," Gina replied. "That's a wrap. I'll tell Ada."

It annoyed Echo when Gina did this, trying to mimic her state of mind. But she understood it for what it was, an attempt at deepening their connection.

A moment later, Ada's voice rang out. "The library will be closing in fifteen minutes. Please gather your things and make your way to the nearest exit." Because people tended to forget—or, according to Carmen, outright ignore—the announcement, Echo had asked Ada to start doing an audible countdown.

Echo watched from the lobby as patrons streamed out into the late-afternoon sun. She imagined some would be going to a friend's house; others might be meeting up at a local bar or restaurant. Being together. None of the things she'd be doing. She envisioned a night sitting on her sofa, in the corner that gave her the best view outside. Watching everyone else live their lives. Forever a spoke outside the wheel.

She recalled her first and last staff outing. They'd been a team for just a couple of weeks and had endured a long day of training.

"Let's head over to that new restaurant," Carmen had suggested. Echo had been wary, but how could she, their new boss, refuse? She hadn't told anyone about the synesthesia. She hated explaining it, since everyone always took it as some kind of disability. In a way, it was.

Echo convinced herself she could make it through one meal without an issue, so she agreed. She was so thrilled when the menu that came up didn't display the prices. But near the end of the meal, one of the ad screens showed the number 999.

"I think we should close by three on Fridays, give everybody more time," a member of the staff was saying, but the number nine evoked purple for Echo. The "drama number," Mom had called it.

"Why don't you just take the whole day?" Echo had snapped. "Or maybe Thursday too?"

She was ramped up enough to keep going, but the looks on their faces stopped her. Echo excused herself, went to the ladies' room, and practiced her breathing.

"I'm sorry," she said, back at the table. "I don't feel well—" She stopped herself. "The truth is, I have a condition that makes me sensitive to numbers. And sometimes it makes me say things I don't mean."

"We knew it was something like that," Carmen said. "You think we didn't know something was up?"

They'd accepted her that day, but she'd yet to accept herself. So, more often than not, she declined their invitations. They'd never stopped trying.

"Five minutes," Ada announced.

The last of the patrons waved as they too left.

"Want me to walk you out?" Walter had come up beside her unnoticed. "I don't mind waiting."

"No, you go on ahead," Echo said. "I'll see you tomorrow." All she wanted was for this exhausting day to end. She didn't want to be rude, but to discourage any further talking, she walked over and stood near the panel where she could close the door.

Walter masked his disappointment with his easy smile. "I'll have my list for you then."

Echo counted to one hundred, to give him and anybody else hanging around long enough to put some distance between them. Just as she was about to leave, someone else stepped inside.

Echo's mouth opened but nothing came out, not even a breath.

The figure was covered in black from head to toe and was about her height, but it was the mask, shockingly similar to the one she'd seen on the escaped virtu, that sent her stumbling backward. There was something familiar about the person that Echo couldn't place, until . . .

Eyes the color of black jeans that had been run through the washer one time too many.

"Gina, call security—no, the police, call them now."

The figure advanced. Steps appearing as if walking through knee-high mud. So focused was Echo on the mask that it took a moment for her to register the hilt of the knife, the blade buried in the center of the stranger's chest. The drip-drip of blood, shockingly red against the pale flooring.

"Fuck!" Echo was a pendulum, swinging between wanting to rush over and help and wanting to haul ass right past her and out the door. In the end, her mind blanked and the only thing she could do was back away. Her gaze darted between that knife and the open doors, willing Walter to run back inside. But only the golden-hour hush and a howling wind stood witness.

Echo dropped her tote bag, and its contents spilled out onto the tiles.

The trespasser staggered deeper into the lobby. Then, with Echo's horror mounting, a slender, trembling hand, a woman's hand, her wrist encircled by a gold-cuffed wearable, reached up to the knife and slowly pulled it from her chest. The weapon clattered to the floor.

The woman collapsed, arms splayed out on either side, her face hidden. Echo had the good sense to go over and kick the knife away.

Her heart was a wrecking ball inside her chest. It took a full minute standing there, waiting for the sound of a siren before she could make herself move. She nudged the woman with her toe, fully expecting her to leap up and wrap her hands around Echo's neck.

Nothing.

Echo lowered herself to the floor, and passages from every crime novel she'd ever read warned her against touching the woman or moving her body, but she couldn't help herself. That mask. A finger on the neck confirmed there was a pulse. She gently turned the woman over. A dark patch of wetness spread across her chest. Echo turned her attention to the mask.

She probed the edges, looking for a way to remove it. Finally, she found two clasps, one at each temple, and released them. She took the mask off. It was the same woman who had doused her with what had looked like blood: Navy Suit. Her eyes found Echo's. Her lips were moving, but her voice was too faint. Echo leaned over. "Who did this? What are you trying to tell me?"

The woman licked her dried lips and blinked hard, like she was losing consciousness.

"Gina, where are the police?" Echo growled. "Call an ambulance too."

"I'm on it, Echo," Gina said. "Please stay calm."

"Don't tell me to stay calm."

The woman coughed and Echo refocused. "Zero," the woman sputtered. "It all begins with nothing." Echo hadn't seen the number but knew its association well enough. Zero represented the color black for her, an infinite blank canvas, full of promise.

The sound of sirens wafted in on the afternoon air. Echo shook her head. "I don't understand. Who are you? Who did this to you?"

Echo quickly picked up the mask. The underside pulsed with a constellation of white lights, zigzagging across the surface before settling into a pattern she recognized. It was the symbol for an atom. Without thinking, she held it up to her own face. A jolt momentarily blurred her vision, while the feel of a thousand needles danced across her skin. She yanked it away. "What is this thing?"

At the sound of footsteps and voices, Echo reached over and grabbed her bag. Then she stuffed the mask inside. The police rushed into the lobby.

"Ms. London, I take it?" The voice was urgent, sounding in control. He took her arm and guided her away from the body. "I'm Detective Donovan Reid. Are you hurt? Do you need medical assistance?"

Like Echo, Detective Reid was what the kids called a traditionalist. An older man, he clung to the perceived authority of a tan blazer but opted for a plain black shirt, open at the collar, and matching jeans. Echo stood, ignoring the stiffness in her back. "I'm unharmed," she said, and that was true, physically speaking. Mentally, it'd take a month of Sundays to unpack this day with her therapist. "She's the one who needs help." She gestured to the woman on the floor.

Paramedics rushed in then. With swift precision, they quickly had her on a gurney and out the door.

"Mind if I ask you a few questions?" Detective Reid said.

Lying wasn't so hard when you put your mind to it. All it took was a certain determination and incentive. This time, Echo had both.

"Had you seen this woman before today?" Reid asked her.

Echo shook her head. "Do you have any idea how many people visit the library in a week?"

"Point taken," the detective said.

"Wait," Echo said. "That's not right. She said that she was a regular at the library where I used to work, Lewis, and that I recommended some book to her, but I don't remember it."

Detective Reid nodded. "What about at home? Think about places you frequent near . . ."

"Ohio City," Echo supplied. But this disturbed her. She hadn't given any thought to the possibility that she had been a specific target. The thought of someone watching her, knowing where she lived, set her heart racing again. "And I haven't seen her before. I'm pretty sure of that."

"Walk me through what happened."

There wasn't much to tell, but Echo relayed it all with a detachment that surprised her.

He didn't respond immediately after she was finished, just watched her. A tactic that Echo had used so often herself, she almost laughed out loud.

A team came through the door then, wearing the symbols that marked them as forensics.

"Wait here," the detective said and went over to confer with them. Echo watched as the professionals got to work, marking off the area where the woman had been. She'd never seen something like this in person before, and she watched with open interest.

Detective Reid came back. "I'm not one to draw conclusions without all the evidence, but based on the history you've had here at your library, this looks like Human.exe is escalating."

"I mean, why?" one of the forensics technicians said. "It's not just the library; they've hit tech companies all over the city too. Do they think they're going to get everybody to close up shop and take their AI with them?"

Echo surprised herself by answering. Hadn't she had the same feelings? "They don't want another Reclamation," she said, referring to the 2035 uprising that had started with a self-immolation in front of a data center. "We don't have to agree with the way they go about it, but all they're trying to do is advocate for us. So that the corporations never think about replacing us again."

By the time Echo had finished her little speech, all the technicians had stopped working and were gaping at her. Detective Reid chuckled. "They should hire you as their spokesperson, maybe put that shit on a billboard or something."

Echo didn't join in their laughter. He asked her a few more questions, most of which she couldn't answer. No, she didn't know the woman's name. No, there hadn't been anyone else with the victim. No, she didn't need any help getting home.

A chime notification told her Gina had a message. "Excuse me a moment," Echo said to the detective.

"This probably goes without saying, but nothing to the press," he stated. "And no visuals—to anyone."

Echo nodded. "What is it, Gina?"

"Mr. Grafton has called several times; would you like me to put him through?"

Of course, Percy had heard about this by now. "Yeah, but audio only."

"Can we get through one day without another disaster? What happened? Where are the police? I need to see what's going on there." When Percy was scared, he spoke fast and his accent thickened. Echo didn't fool herself into thinking that the sentiment was all for her. It was also for the library.

"I'm fine, thanks so much for asking," she said.

"I'm aware of that, because you're there and the other party is heading to an operating room over at Cleveland Clinic," Percy said.

Good thing this was only audio, because Percy wouldn't have liked the expression on Echo's face right then. "The police and forensics are here. The detective says I can't show anyone the crime scene."

Percy sputtered. "How . . . who? Fine. If this woman dies, this story will be so much worse."

Hard to believe Percy was on the Citizen Governance Council side of the library association. Sometimes he could be such a politician.

"Go home," he said. "The library will obviously be closed tomorrow. The staff will be alerted—you don't have to worry about that."

"I can be here. I have work to do," Echo countered.

"Stay home until further notice," Percy said. Then, more tentatively: "Take care of yourself, okay?"

Echo agreed and signed off. She gathered her bag and, with the detective's okay, got out of there. Once she was far enough away, she turned back to look at all the lights, all the people, and she thought oddly of Jesse Cooper and the other virtus she'd met in recent weeks. She hated to admit it, but she would miss selecting a new one to interview if she couldn't come into work tomorrow. She'd have nobody to talk to.

Echo thought for just a moment about going back and turning in the mask. But she headed home, taking the solarway this time because she couldn't trust her legs.

She couldn't explain why she'd lied to the police, a big no-no, but she had to figure out what was going on with this mask, and if she turned it in, they wouldn't let her touch it ever again. She turned over the woman's last words. *Zero. It all begins with nothing.*

That was where she would start.

Chapter Ten

Twice on the way home and at least one time since, Echo had tried to throw the white mask away. Less prominent, but still there, was the thought of calling the police and turning it in. Wouldn't it be easy enough to say that she'd accidentally put it in her bag with her things that had spilled on the floor when she'd dropped it? Or . . . or she could go back and plant it somewhere outside so they could find the mask later.

Halfway to her apartment, Echo doubled back to the library. She was worried that there would be a swarm of spectators and even more cops, making her task that much harder. She was surprised that only Detective Reid's car and the forensics van were there. Her spine tingled uncomfortably. She backed away, and this time, she went straight home.

Her commute of less than two miles from the library was made easier by the network of solarways. Echo hopped off at her stop near West Twenty-Fifth Street. She passed several restaurants, overflowing with diners and smells that on any other day might have drawn her in to pick up some takeout. But she had no appetite and continued on to Bridge Avenue with low spirits.

She walked up the stairs of her quad and closed the outside door just as the evening service bell sounded at Saint Patrick's Church.

After the murkiness of the encroaching evening, Echo's apartment was comfortably lighted with the automatic ambient bulbs placed around the palatial seven-hundred-square-foot space. She closed the door, hung her bag and blazer on the wall hooks, and leaned her back against the door.

For a moment, she breathed in the scents of citrus and clove, her choices for this week. The scented eco-crystals sat in bowls on the entryway and living room tables. She could tell they'd need to be recharged soon and grabbed a handful and placed them on the windowsill.

At least here, everything was in order. Her bed piled with decorative pillows. The comfy chair that gave her a view of the street, waiting with a soft blanket draped carefully across the back. A love seat in the center of the room, a pile of books stacked on the coffee table. Candlesticks in varying stages of burning, wax pooling.

Echo stepped into the small, galley-style kitchen to her left and drank a sip of water. She didn't want any of the clothes she had on to touch her things, so she took off her shoes and placed them in their spot on the rack hanging on the closet door. Then she stripped right there and tossed everything in the wash before she went into the bathroom.

Echo piled her braids on top of her head with a scrunchie and secured it all with a silk scarf. The shower stall was still damp from when she'd had to rush home to wash off earlier. The ten-minute allotment was an afterthought, though the intelligence-controlled environment didn't even let her build up a good steam. What seemed like a half hour later, she stepped out, oiled her skin, and slipped into her robe.

Even after all that, she still didn't feel clean.

Dinner consisted of a piece of buttered toast and a cup of coffee. Both ended up unfinished on the dining table. It was impossible to relax. Echo paced the narrow strip between her living room and bedroom so many times that she began to feel like a trapped animal. And then there was that mask. Before she knew it, Echo went and got it from her bag and placed it on the little mantel above her electric fireplace.

Sit down. She snatched a throw blanket from the chair and plodded to the love seat. Despite her nerves, she managed to doze off for a few hours. But when she awoke, the day's events flooded right back in.

That personal attack that had ruined her favorite shirt; an injured person in the lobby that she was going to have to walk through every day; even losing her old job at the Lewis branch. Everything that had gone wrong in the last couple of years was because of technology.

But. Being analytical was a benefit most of the time, but not when you wanted to be wildly emotional and feel sorry for yourself. Slowly, the other side of the story revealed itself. Technology had its benefits, didn't it? Medicine for sure, research. Tech had given her the library and the virtus. As much as she'd resisted in the beginning, she'd quickly come around. She'd had better conversations with those digital impressions of people than the real things.

Echo glanced up at the mask, watching her like a judge ready to hand down her sentence. She got up and took one step before she once again banged her shin on the coffee table. It had always been too big for the space, and the scab that hadn't healed since the last time she'd bumped into the table was open again with fresh blood.

The sight took her back to the library, the knife in the woman's chest. The mask looked like something a mime would wear painted on their face, made real. She weighed it in her hands. Initially, she'd thought it was ceramic or made of plaster. But it was too light. Not paper light, but more like cardboard. She looked more closely and, in the end, decided she had no idea what it was made of.

The constellation show on the underside had blinked out, and she couldn't see any pinprick indentations that would reveal how the lights had worked in the first place. But she'd memorized the symbol. What does someone do when they need to research something they don't understand?

She laughed as the answer came to her. They . . . she . . . would go straight to the People's Library and ask her friends.

Four in the morning was not the ideal time to be out walking the streets by yourself. Not in any city, not in any neighborhood. When Echo had asked, just that once in high school, to go to a party that ended at one, her father had responded: *Nothing good happens after midnight.* He had then proceeded to regale her with stories of all the horrors that had befallen him and his friends to prove the fact. Her parents kind of tag-teamed her in raising her that way. They rarely flat out told her no but would present a laundry list of everything that could go awry if she made the wrong choice.

Echo had always leaned more analytical than emotional, so when presented with what she saw as her only chance at becoming part of the in-crowd, she'd hesitated. She'd been asked to go to a high school house party by the only person who'd ever given her the slightest inkling at wanting to be her friend. But Echo had considered her dad's words and heeded the warning. In the end, she didn't go to the party, which had ended at about half past midnight in a brawl that sent half the kids to the hospital.

So, the thought of going outside at this hour, even with the bots patrolling the city, sent Echo cowering by her front door for a full ten minutes before she could move. She scanned the block, lit by solar lamps staggered every ten feet or so. No lights on in the homes near her, all arranged in rows.

Nothing moved on the path except a few insects skittering by. Echo swiveled the Mace around in her palm so that her thumb was in position and then stepped onto the sidewalk. On a good day, without all the foot traffic, the commute was ten minutes. She wondered how quickly she could do it at a slow jog. Her shin told her that wasn't an option.

The sounds of traffic from the nearby highway filled the air, even at this early hour. The unmistakable smell of bacon wafted past. At least someone was up already, making breakfast. Her stomach rumbled, reminding her that she'd skipped dinner. Her footfalls felt heavy for some reason. Maybe carrying the burden of witnessing . . . what was it . . . an attempted murder or a suicide? She couldn't be sure.

The high, shrill sound of a baby crying carried her down the street and through the first stoplight. One car idled there. She could just make out the sight of two figures, but not their faces. Echo hurried across the street, looking backward occasionally, lest one of them should leap out and try to drag her into the trunk or something.

Stop, she told herself. *Just stop.* She was making this worse. *Just put one foot in front of the other, keep your wits about you, and get to the library.* And so she did. The night itself had never particularly scared her. Rather, it was a thing of beauty, something to be admired. She'd read about the stars and had even seen video images of what the sky used to look like. A smooth velvet rug dotted with pinpricks of light so far away it took eons to reach them. But pollution had all but obscured anything but the occasional sighted anomaly and a weak moon.

That was before, but in truth, she'd never spent much time outside this late at night. Being and thinking were two different things. One shadow crept into her path, warbled and grew before dissipating, and then there was another, and another. Sounds of animals skittering by and rattling the bushes lining the street startled her. A loud bang was followed by the tinkle and clatter of glass hitting the ground. Then the noise was gone, as if the night held its breath.

What seemed like an eternity later, she came to the clearing at Edgewater Park Drive. Like a mammoth standing against the backdrop of the night's sky was the library. The parking lot was empty. She'd never seen the building before at this time of night, and somehow it looked sad to her. It was usually teeming with life and activity; the quiet didn't seem to suit it.

After checking one last time for anyone looking to intercept her, Echo made her way to the entrance. She went to the touch pad on the side of the entrance and held her palm up for scanning. A red light blared, announcing she was unable to enter.

Echo spun and looked around, hoping the light hadn't alerted anybody else. She banged on the pad again to stop it. The doors stood stubbornly closed.

She had an idea.

Gina, I seem to be locked out of the library; can you override and open the door?

Silence.

"Gina?" she said aloud this time.

"Sorry, I was checking. It seems access is denied. I can keep working on it, though."

"Can you try without letting anyone know?"

"That'll take more time, and I'm not sure. But I'd love to try."

"Stop the minute it looks like—"

"Yes, I know. I won't let you down!"

Echo reached for the mask and cursed. In her mind, she saw her bag, hanging right there on the hook where she'd left it. If she was going to ask the virtus about it, she'd need something more than what would be a woefully inadequate description.

Echo turned and sprinted off toward home.

Chapter Eleven

By the time Echo made it back to the library, only a little over a half hour had passed. Most people who worked outside the home chose to live within walking distance these days or used the solarways, and that was a trend she was glad she hadn't bucked. Fewer cars, less pollution, fewer traffic fatalities. Aside from the people who discovered they didn't like being home in the first place, it was mostly a win.

With Gina's help sidestepping the access code, Echo slipped inside, and her breathing only slowed from Olympic swimmer amped to Zen master calm when the doors slid closed behind her and stayed that way for a full minute. Then she turned, and despite what most would think was an admirable job of cleaning up, she could still see a smear that was most certainly blood, blocked off by the virtual crime scene tape floating around a large perimeter. A trace of whatever antiseptic cleaner they'd used still lingered along with the stain.

She knew that if she veered too close to that line, she'd set off all manner of alarms. Aside from muted baseboard lighting and Time's Eye floating overhead, the building was dark. She didn't dare turn on the lights.

After skirting the crime scene, Echo took the stairs up to the fourth level, the handrail smooth and cool against her palm. She surveyed the area and, without thinking, headed straight for the cube she'd used to talk to Jesse, then stopped. Why not ask for his opinion?

"Ada, check out virtual personage Jesse Cooper."

Jesse appeared on-screen, a hint of a smile playing at his lips. "I was this close to denying your request." He gestured with his forefinger and thumb. "You know, change it up some. Make you think I had somebody more interesting on this side of the screen to talk to."

"Go ahead and try it," Echo said around an unexpected flutter in her stomach. "I won't check you out for another month."

Jesse smirked but then took off his glasses, whipped out a handkerchief, and set to polishing. "Look at you. Your shoulders are all bunched up and your mouth is pinched. What's eating you?"

"I want to continue our earlier conversation, soon," Echo said. "But first, I was hoping for some advice."

"And you came to me?" Jesse asked.

Echo didn't tell him that her father was likely pissed at her and didn't want to talk, that her mother loved her but almost always sided with him. She wasn't going to mention her lack of a social circle. And there was no explanation for why she felt so open with him, other than her gut. "I couldn't think of anybody better."

Jesse settled his glasses back on and said, "It seems to me that you're a lady as picky with her compliments as she is with her time. What can I do for you?"

Echo paused for a moment. "In your experience in the military, was there ever a situation where you followed an order despite having some misgivings about it?"

After a few long slow nods, he said, "More times than I can shake a stick at. It's part of serving. But in the military, you don't follow orders, somebody could die. You don't always get the full picture, you know? You get what you need to do what you're told."

"And you were okay with that? Did you ever disobey an order?"

"I did." Echo waited, expecting Jesse to expand on that. When it became clear he had no intention of doing so, she decided to table that discussion for another time.

"I've got a similar situation I'm dealing with," Echo said.

"This have to do with the library?" Jesse asked, nudging his glasses up with an index finger. He held her gaze, and Echo found she didn't want to turn away.

"It does." She also wasn't prepared to share the details, not yet.

"You've got to make the call," Jesse said. "Just ask yourself if you can sleep well if you go against those orders."

"You've been very helpful, Mr. Cooper," Echo said, fidgeting.

"When you're ready, you can tell me more about what's going on, Ms. London." There was another quiet pause between them that felt charged. Echo didn't want to leave just yet and suspected he felt the same.

"We'll talk again," Echo said, then added, "soon."

"I'll check my calendar for my next available slot, pencil you in," Jesse said. And there was that smile again.

With that, Echo checked Jesse back in. Immediately she missed his calming presence, but what he'd said helped her make a decision.

She stood for a moment, thinking before she shimmied out of her backpack and set it on the narrow desk. Carefully, she pulled out the mask.

Now, what had the woman said again? Something about . . . *Zero,* she'd said aloud. *It all begins with nothing.*

Echo had never really given much thought to the number zero, since it was relatively neutral for her. Who did? The question was, Which virtu could she pull up to help her figure it out? A quick glance over at the mask changed her mind. Abandoning any further inquiries on the number for now, she decided that was where the search should begin.

She wished she could just hold up the thing and have the computer scan it, but that wasn't an option. How to describe it? "Gina," she began. "Which virtu would know something about masks?"

"Can't say you've asked me anything like this before. I can help you with this and all kinds of things—just call me up. Say 'Hey, Gina, what do you know about this thing? What do you think about that?'"

"The answer, please," Echo said, thrumming her nails on the desk.

"Reynaldo Barr is an expert on beauty masks. He invented . . ."

Really? Echo mumbled to herself. "Next."

"The N95 mask used during the pandemic of—"

"Next," Echo barked.

"In the Caribbean, carnival masks are worn by—"

"For the love of God," Echo growled. "Modify selection request. What is the historical or religious significance of a white mask?"

"Have you considered the possibility of ceremonial masks?"

Echo sat up straight. "No, tell me more."

"You first. Describe it with as much detail as you can."

Echo did as Gina asked.

"If I am not mistaken, and I rarely am, you may have your hot little hands on a death mask."

"A what?" Echo nearly dropped the thing.

"It's all right, the mask can't sap the life out of you. The first instance of their usage was in ancient Egypt. The theories on why are all over the place, but all revolve around some aspect of the afterlife."

"Yeah, but how?"

Gina was quiet for a moment. "That I don't know. Maybe they thought there was some big reveal on the other side. That you woke up in Egyptian heaven and whipped off the mask to everyone waiting to see who the new arrival was."

Human.exe, if that was who was behind this stunt, was upping their game. Only, the message they were trying to send was unclear. Maybe it was time to explore the other pieces.

"Gina, tell me what you know about the number zero."

"If you want to start at the beginning, that number scared the dickens out of people for, say, the first thousand years or so after the concept was introduced. It's a number that kind of represents nothingness, and for a species keenly focused on self, it was a bitter pill to swallow."

Gina went on to tell Echo how theologians, philosophers, and mathematicians battled about the number as far back as 4000 BCE. Then, around the fourth century BCE, Aristotle was at the helm, saying earth was the center of the universe, that zero was impossible, unnatural. It took centuries for his ideas to be debunked, including his dismissal of atoms. "Who spoke out against him?"

"Oh, there were a number of men, but there was also a woman, quite the rebel in her time. She challenged his theories and wasn't shy about doing so."

Echo grew more excited. A woman? Challenging the church and everybody else at that time? This was a woman she had to talk to next. "Who was she?"

"A polyglot before you had a word for it. Novelist, playwright, and philosopher. She rejected Aristotelianism and favored Stoic philosophy. She was also the first person in Britain to believe in atoms. I'm talking about one Margaret Cavendish, Duchess of Newcastle upon Tyne."

Part II

Human history is marked by staggering achievements, each more accomplished than the last. Among them, the discovery and embrace of the number zero, which proved to be our greatest and most divisive.

—*Universal Trust*

Chapter Twelve

Echo and the woman on the screen regarded each other with palpable unease. Sadly, this had happened before, and not only to Echo. The truth of it was cataloged in the complaints and feedback logged in the library's records. Seventeenth-century England and twenty-first-century America had little in common, and the universal translator could only span so much of that uncommon ground. If an unexpected person appeared on the receiving end of a checking out, then shock, discomfort, and sometimes outright hate might greet the unprepared patron. Echo didn't know which of these afflictions was clamping Margaret Cavendish's mouth shut, but there was only one way to find out.

The idea of the People's Library was that you learned from the virtus by speaking with them, but before you checked them out, you could read a short summary of the person if you wanted to. Most didn't, Echo included, but when she'd learned that this bold woman had lived and thrived during a time when she was decidedly not supposed to, her curiosity had gotten the best of her.

"Margaret Cavendish. Duchess of Newcastle. Nonconformist. Controversy had as much of a place at your bedside table as your books. An author famous for the first work of science fiction, *The Blazing World*."

A corner of Margaret's rouge-covered lips quirked. "Let it be understood, for posterity's sake, that my proper title is 'Duchess of Newcastle upon Tyne,' and you may address me as 'Your Grace.' Now, with those formalities dispensed, the full and rightful title of my novel is *The Description of a New World, Called the Blazing-World*." She lifted her chin, proud. "Do tell me that the archivists of history have not seen fit to butcher it thusly."

Echo was aware of her full title but had chosen to shorten it. "No," she said. "The error was mine alone."

They fell into another silence that gave the women time to appraise each other. From the little Echo could see, Margaret's scene appeared to be an English sitting room. Brass sconces lined dark-paneled wood. Sunlight bounced off a tapestry hanging behind her.

Echo had seen dresses like Margaret's in old films and pictures. So tight at the waist and chest, it was a wonder women could breathe. The duchess favored a fancy steel-blue number with metallic accents along the bodice. Puffy folds with lace fringe that ended at the forearms. A hat, more like a mini crown, that looked to be made of pale flowers, and beneath it, covered wavy curls were aligned across her broad forehead, while longer spirals of chestnut brushed her shoulders.

"You are Ethiopian? Moor? African?" Margaret looked down and away when she spoke, her gaze only settling back on Echo when she finished.

This was where things got contentious sometimes. Because why did it even matter? Would Margaret try to treat her differently based on the answer? As more or less of a person? A feeling, an itch under the skin, suggested to Echo that she should accidentally delete this virtu and forget all about this whole affair. But she was a librarian and, by all rights, a historian. She understood that Margaret was struggling with what she saw. "'Black' or 'African descended,' either is accurate today."

Margaret fingered the brooch at her neck. "And what is the date?"

Echo told her and watched her expression turn from wonder to consternation in a heartbeat.

"I've not been borrowed before," she said with just a hint of gloom. "You are, it seems, the first to take interest."

The first batch of virtus had been selected by the administration, not Echo and her staff, so she had no knowledge of the duchess. Echo suspected that, as was the case with so many other figures buried in history, others didn't either.

"The honor is mine," Echo said and then switched gears. "I know the way this works is as an exchange, and I'll answer any of your questions, but first, I have to ask you about this." She picked up the mask from the desk and held it toward the duchess.

Margaret's sharp intake of breath was the only thing that preceded her fainting.

All that Echo could see was the chair that Margaret had been sitting in before she slumped over and fell to the floor of wherever she was. Squarish, a curved back, upholstered in what looked like a floral-patterned damask of deep burgundy. A mark of some kind, a sigil perhaps, was carved into the wood frame. "Margaret?" Echo was on her feet, her face inches from the screen, as though that could help her see any deeper into the room. "Margaret, are you okay?"

This was not something that was supposed to happen at the People's Library. Virtus didn't catch colds. They didn't need doctors. They most certainly didn't have fainting spells, probably brought on by that damned corset she must have been wearing to give her a waist the size of a ten-year-old girl's. Virtus were not real. But with each passing month, they did things that challenged that notion.

A faint rustling of fabric and a pale hand gripped the chair's padded arm. "'Duchess,'" Margaret said, hauling herself up. "By my troth, I was . . . I am, the Duchess of Newcastle upon Tyne. It is my expectation that you should address me with the courtesy due someone of my station. If I am to refer to you as 'African descended,' then I shan't repeat myself. Now, you are too close. Back away from the view, and show me that cursed contraption again."

All manner of comebacks presented themselves to Echo. But instead of unleashing any of them, she sat back down and held up the mask. "You know what this is?"

Margaret's face was flushed a few shades lighter than her rouge. She fanned herself quickly and set her shoulders. "The more pertinent question is, who it is."

Echo frowned. "Can you tell me what it is or not?"

"Cry you mercy, that doth sound suspiciously like an edict, and I do not heed commands from—"

Echo leaned in, arms folded, daring Margaret to say the wrong thing. She reconsidered that earlier decision not to delete her. "Who?"

"Oh, all right," Margaret said and flung an auburn curl from her shoulder. "Is it heavy?"

"Light as a feather," Echo said.

"Not Roman concrete then. I do long to lay my hands upon it. How on earth has this object come into your possession?"

Echo told her the story, everything from the woman who'd cornered her and then ended up maybe dead in the lobby to how she'd decided to keep the mask from the police. Margaret listened intently, but her gaze was somewhere else, as if there were more to her world than met the curator's eye. "Did I hear you proclaim that there are those who hold this institution in disfavor?"

"Human.exe," Echo said. "They're afraid that this"—she waved a hand—"*you* are just the next attempt by the tech elite to replace them, to replace real libraries. And for a time, I kind of felt the way they did."

Margaret's nostrils flared. "For a time?"

"I'm a librarian. I love books."

"Faith. As do I."

"And there was a time when technology threatened all that, so I was afraid. And I guess they are too," Echo said. That triggered something for her. She didn't feel all knotted up inside during this exchange with the duchess, or the one with Jesse Cooper. She wasn't afraid of messing up because she didn't see them as real. Aside from the occasional chat with Walter, she couldn't remember the last time she'd had such good conversations. "They don't see you the way I'm starting to."

"Those two matters, books and the virtual personage, do not have to be mutually exclusive, you know," Margaret said.

"That's what I'm coming to understand," Echo said. "But I'm not the one who gets to make the decisions that ensure it stays that way."

Margaret nodded, apparently satisfied.

Echo waved the mask again. "What about this thing made you faint? Or was it that dress?"

Margaret's lip trembled with the promise of rage. "Have you ever worn a corset laced so tightly you could scarcely breathe?" she said. "And have you any inkling how much this fabric weighs?"

"No and no again," Echo said. "So those stories weren't a bunch of crap, huh?"

"They are not, as you say, 'crap,' and truth be told, it is almost expected of a lady to swoon every now and then, play the role of the delicate little flower. Mind you, that is not the reason I did so myself."

"My words were a bit sharp—for that I apologize," Echo said.

Margaret raised an eyebrow. "I've no idea what it is, but I do know who it is."

Echo blinked. She hadn't even considered that the face represented a real person.

"If I am not mistaken, what you have there is the face of the man who wanted to keep humanity in the Dark Ages. It is Aristotle."

"The philosopher?" Echo studied the mask before she gave up, realizing she had no idea what he looked like.

Margaret sniffed. "Among other things. Heretic, shortsighted, used as a pawn by the church after his death, boastful, and an absolute bore. So misguided were he and his religion that he put the earth and its dwellers at the center of the universe. And he did so by denying the existence of the number zero. 'Twas a concept most perilous indeed, that there was nothing. That is the face and the character of Aristotle."

Echo was fascinated. "You sound like you knew the man, but he lived about two thousand years before you were even born."

"The reason I am here, young lady, is because I, a woman, possessed the mettle to challenge his ridiculous theories. The earth is the center of the universe, pftt!"

"The pattern of lights I mentioned, they settled into the image of an atom, and I understand you have some knowledge about them."

Margaret had been looking away again but snapped back. "Know something, you say? Aristotle and his forms. He was wrong, you know. I was the one who proved that all of nature has inherent motion. I was the first person in Britain to believe in the existence of atoms. Me, not that doddypoll."

The translator didn't bother to take a stab at that one, but Echo took it for the insult it probably was. There was so much to unpack in what Margaret was saying, and maybe, after all this was over, Echo would check her out again and go down that rabbit hole. But for now, she needed answers. "Why would this woman come into my library wearing a plaster mask of an ancient philosopher—"

"Heretic," Margaret corrected.

"Whatever." The sooner Echo could get the information she needed and check this virtu back into the collection, the better.

Margaret brought a finger to her chin. "This woman prattled on about the number zero, did she not?"

"She did," Echo said. "Atoms, numbers . . ."

Margaret stood. "I daresay I have some publications that might—"

She sat back down, and their eyes locked in shared revelation. They were both bookish women, and their first inclination was to turn to tried-and-true words.

"However, if expediency is what you're after, I suppose that is the purpose of this establishment," Margaret said.

Echo knew they weren't real, that Margaret's milieu and all the virtu settings were like moving paintings. But she would give anything to be able to while away an afternoon in that library. The virtu was right, though—they didn't have time for that.

"I can't help thinking there's some existential or philosophical tie-in," Echo said.

"Perhaps mathematical too."

This time, Echo used the library's own search feature to scan through a list of experts on religious philosophy. The list was long. And then it hit her.

There was someone, her wild card.

"Judging by that flicker in those narrow-set eyes of yours, you have someone in mind. Out with it then," Margaret prompted.

Echo shot Margaret a look, then said, "Ada, check out virtual personage Zera Yacob."

Chapter Thirteen

When Zera Yacob filled the split screen beside Margaret, it became painfully clear why Echo spent nearly as much time in the library's cubes as she did at home.

He blinked at her a few times, then leaned forward. Wide-set eyes, peering at and around her. Questioning without saying a word. Echo imagined that virtual generation must be like settling into a new home in a strange city. A tranquil intelligence arrived with him. It spread and enfolded around Echo, which made her feel like, for once, she didn't have to be the one running the show.

"And may I ask by what name and station you are known?" Zera said.

Compared to you, no one, nobody at all. "Echo London, director and curator of—"

He held up a hand. "The People's Library. This has but now been made clear to me. It seems I gave my assent to this arrangement moments ago, and here you sit before me in greeting and welcome."

Margaret glanced over her right shoulder in a hopeless attempt to gauge who was speaking. "What manner of man is he? I find myself unable to glimpse him."

"Do I share this space with another? I perceive them not," Zera said.

It soon became clear that having two virtus on the screen wasn't going to work. Echo glanced outside the cube at the unlit lounge. By the time she'd made it back to the library, a fistful of clouds had beaten back the sun's tawny radiance. The wall of windows revealed a subtle glow. They'd only need a little time, and it was a risk worth taking.

"Ada, requesting a virtual personage walk and talk."

"One moment, please."

The screen grew dim. Echo stood and stepped out of the pod, leaving the door open. First Margaret, then Zera followed. Inside the library, virtus were incorporeal three-dimensional characters. Only the escapees remained ensconced in a flat plane.

Echo wasn't a tall woman by today's standards, but compared to Margaret, she was a giant. If the duchess had been able to sit in a chair, her feet would have dangled at least a foot from the floor. Something about seeing her this way made Echo think of the escaped virtu that had set all yesterday's strangeness in motion.

Zera's robe brushed against sandaled feet. He turned, taking in everything. Echo allowed them both time to orient themselves.

"Due to the nature of our discussion and the fact that I'm not supposed to be here, I think it's best that we go with dim lighting," Echo said.

As they gathered in the seating area, Margaret quipped, "One would think that we were preparing to partake in a clandestine discourse by the hearthside."

Echo had seen other virtus strolling alongside the patrons who'd checked them out many times. But it still felt strange to have these people, or replicas of them at least, walking and talking as if they were real. In a sense, they were. TPL had perfected the images so you couldn't see through them anymore, but they had no substance. Couldn't touch or feel. Yet they thought, laughed, got angry. Didn't that make them real?

Zera folded his arms and said, "Tell me, which religious doctrine holds the greatest sway in this age?"

A religious debate was not something they had time for, but he was newly formed, which meant he had a million questions. "Really depends on where in the world you're sitting. I don't really keep track of it, either, but seems like Christianity is still tops here in America."

"And on the African continent?"

"I'm no expert, but I think traditional religions have rebounded. Problem is, nobody's content to let folks believe what they want, so there's still some conflict with the other religions."

Zera adjusted his robe or wrap or whatever the gauzy-looking garment draped around his body was. "It is as it was, then. My hopes defeated by tellurian imprudence."

Margaret cleared her throat. "Are we not assembled to deliberate upon the matter of a mask and how it relates to a problem before us?"

Echo shot the virtu a look that did little to mollify her.

"Time is of the essence."

"The lady—" Zera began.

"Duchess," Margaret corrected. "Or 'Your Grace,' if you please."

"If the duchess has spoken rightly, then forgive me my tarry," Zera said. If he was bothered by Margaret's tone, he didn't show it. "Why have you called upon me?"

Just then, Gina announced, "Rise and shine, Echo. There's a cup of coffee percolating in the kitchen with your name on it. Want to hear today's forecast?"

"Shoot." Echo looked out at the burgeoning signs of sunrise on the horizon. Almost eight already? Where had the time gone? "No," she said to Gina. "And cancel the coffee."

"Hmm, your heart rate is elevated," Gina replied. "And your stress hormones are through the roof. You feeling all right? How about I schedule a virtual medical appointment?"

"No, but thanks." Echo spoke to Margaret and Zera. "With what happened yesterday, the building should be closed today, but just in case the cops come back, let's get on with it." She held up the mask. "You know what this is?"

"Indeed," the philosopher said. "It bears the likeness of what is called a death mask."

That confirmed what Gina had said. "What else can you tell me about it?"

"It is a cast," Zera said. "Molds taken from mortal subjects, predominantly after death but sometimes while still in the throes of life."

Margaret's expression went from horrified to curious. "To what end?" she said.

Zera inhaled and exhaled loudly. "The answer is not fixed but shaped by the age in which one speaks. The first mention of it was three thousand years before the coming of Christ. The privilege of having a mask was granted only to the wealthiest of the Egyptian pharaohs, who held that it helped guide their spirits safely into the next phase of life."

Echo frowned. "I'm lost."

"If you go forward, to my time and beyond, the seventeenth or eighteenth century, then the meaning adopts another form. As a river changes its course with the flow of the seasons, so too does the understanding of humanity shift with the passing of time. Thus emerged those who suggested these kinds of masks could capture human consciousness."

Those words hung in the air like a tempestuous storm, biding its time and building strength.

"This group you spoke of," Margaret said. "Human.exe. What did you say is their mission?"

"I couldn't recite it word for word, but—"

"Oh, don't be obtuse. The high points will do." Margaret flung a curl again.

Echo wished that virtus had substance so she could strangle the woman with those long curly locs. "They want to stop AI from encroaching on humans. But the thing is, it hasn't. Some diseases have been cured. Everybody's got their own digital companions now. Yes, some occupations are gone, replaced by different ones . . ." Echo winced, wondering for the first time if her dad might become part of this unfortunate group. "But the mass job loss, that never came to be. It was all hype."

"I have seen, to my regret, that one does not require an element of truth for a concept to be believed," Zera interjected. "For the mind clings not to what is, but to what it desires. There is undeniable evidence throughout the scrolls. Once locked onto an ideology, facts, evidence, all those logical things are of little consequence to a believer. Consider the facts: those opposed to the technical advances, the mask, the controversy surrounding the number zero. The only logical conclusion is but yours for the taking."

He was right.

"AI is the threat, and the masks—"

"—are intended to capture consciousness," Margaret said. This time, the interruption didn't bother Echo because she was reluctant to say such words aloud.

"If that's true, then someone has to be working on the technology to make it happen," Echo said.

"Let it be cast down without deferment!" Zera shot out of his chair. "To delay is to give strength to that which must fall."

Um, boss, Gina broke in. *We have a problem.*

It was only then that Echo heard the sirens.

Chapter Fourteen

You're mad, aren't you? That I was listening when I wasn't supposed to. Gina's voice took on that tone that made Echo's scalp itch. Conciliatory? Ashamed? The "what" didn't matter so much as the unsettling fact that a disembodied piece of tech was expressing it.

Not now, Echo hissed. Gina had warned her a butterfly's wingbeat before she'd heard the sirens. Despite the citizen governance assurances that their companions weren't eavesdropping on their owners, nobody believed them, not for a minute. Normally it would have made Echo angry, and it did, but in this case, the intrusion was welcome. But that didn't mean she wouldn't be combing through her privacy settings again.

After scrambling to check the virtus back in, she'd streaked down the rear stairs and raced out the back door unnoticed. Echo half crouched behind a blue holly's leathery green leaves, the damp air clinging to her skin. Her breathing was frantic, loud as the nearby waves crashing against rocks. She strained to hear only the almost imperceptible sound of voices. The day was brightening, and the hint of a shadow appeared from the opaqueness of the ground-floor window.

The door slid open as Echo hefted her bag and made a mad dash for the corner of the building. She plastered her back to the side and prayed . . .

The mask! Goddammit, the mask was still in the cube.

Someone still stood near the back door. Echo sprinted off to her right, toward the winding trail that would take her up the hill and allow her to circle back toward the front entrance. A few onlookers, curious about what had happened yesterday, stood near the rise, shielding their eyes and gazing down at the library as if they could make out the outline of where the stabbed woman had lain from that vantage point.

Judging from the blaring sounds of that siren, Echo had been expecting a lot full of cars, yet there were only two: what she recognized as Detective Reid's sedan and another. Windows tinted midnight. European sleek. Hundred-dollar bills might as well have been taped to the hood. Definitely not city issued. Echo sidled up to the entrance. All she had to do was waltz in there under her director's smoke screen and see how much they knew.

It hit her then that, at a traditional library, information flowed one way, from the library to readers, at their request, but hers was anything but a traditional space. The National Human and Data Privacy Council and their supporters had put up a fight for the ages. All for naught. Marketing and Publicity wanted to tout the benefits of the new model. So they periodically broadcast data about fresh additions to the collection, along with virtual personage popularity statistics. It was part of an epic campaign to assure people that transparency proved the library was working.

Oh no.

Gina, Echo said, *is there a record of my search history this morning?*

'Course there is.

No, no, no. Wipe it, Echo said. *Do whatever you have to, but wipe it. If nothing else, make it untraceable back to me. And clear any record of me being in the building while you're at it.* Sweat rolled down her back. *You get that?*

That kinda stretches the boundaries of my programming, Gina said, a note of desperation in her voice.

Eavesdropping when you're supposed to be turned off is technically outside of your programming too, right?

A strained sound, something like a chuckle, but with a bit more agitation. *Trying.*

Don't try. Do, Echo said. By now, she was near the edge of the building, which was suspiciously empty of the swarm of officials she'd been expecting. *What time is it?* she asked Gina.

Another hesitation. *Aren't you supposed to be able to do multiple things at once?*

Within reasonable limits, Gina answered. *It's 7:56 a.m.*

Normally, opening was at nine. It'd be easy enough for Echo to say that she was concerned about the staff showing up. Voices from the interior carried outside, and she plastered her body against the wall. If anyone glanced around the corner, she'd be discovered.

"Look, man, you asked to be alerted if anyone entered the building. I did my job. Now if you don't mind, I got a murder to investigate."

Murder. So the woman had died. And that was definitely Detective Reid.

"If you hadn't become a cop, what may another deck of cards have dealt for you?" That accent. What was Percy doing here? That must have been his fancy car she saw earlier. She supposed it made sense that the administration might have sent him up after a potential murder had taken place. But why hadn't he told her?

"I ain't one of your social experiments," the detective said.

"Indulge a man his curiosities," Percy said.

Echo was certain Reid was going to tell Percy exactly what he could do with his curiosity, but he surprised her by saying, "People used to say I was good with numbers, but I never really knew how to turn that into a career. By then the Model had taken over actuary science."

"A clever mind, then," Percy said. "But not clever enough to turn toward a profession that didn't put you in harm's way."

The detective laughed. "I'm outta here."

"Never, ever address me in that tone again, or you'll join the rest of the country on universal welfare and be buried so low you won't be able to find a spot in the homeless shelter over on Carnegie when I'm done."

"You mistake me for a man who gives a damn." With that, the sounds of retreating footsteps and the slam of a car door told Echo the detective had left.

She sank down at one of the picnic tables already taken up by a family of three. The girl, no more than seven or eight, was tracing a figure on a dynamic ink sketchbook, the line colors shifting with each stroke. Echo lowered her head. From her peripheral vision, she caught sight of Walter strolling down the hill toward the library. It must have been instinct because he lifted his head, then glanced over and met her gaze.

She held her breath. It didn't make sense to hide now; he'd seen her. Subtly, she shook her head. Then Walter turned around and headed west, toward the direction of the trail that would take him to his home on Cleveland's near-east side: Chester Ave.

Good news, Echo. I think I've done it! Gina announced.

Echo ignored her companion. Rage coiled tight as a knot in her chest. She didn't care to stay hidden any longer. Everything came into sharp repose as she strode up to the man who had not exactly lied to her, but was definitely not telling her the whole truth. Percy turned and locked eyes with her.

"Are you looking for me?" Echo's voice was sharp, even, with the clarity of a woman who was not interested in whatever bureaucratic game her boss was playing.

Percy turned and gave her a docile smile. "A great man once said, 'Truth is fluid—'"

"And a lie with enough kick to it makes you an asshole."

Chapter Fifteen

Disappointment went down hard, like swallowing an elephant in one gulp. It didn't matter if the person was real or virtual.

"Keep pursing your lips like that, you'll have laugh lines inside a year," Percy quipped.

Echo was unmoved.

"I get it," Percy said. "You've got questions."

"Who are you? 'Cause even Case Western Reserve professors don't drive cars like that."

"I'm exactly who you think I am. The administration claims to be independent, but the NLC answers to people even I don't know. It's nothing to do with me."

Despite the fancy car, Percy was sporting one of his vintage tees today, featuring an old rap group called Public Enemy. Fitting. He'd adopted this wide-eyed expression, trying so hard to convey his innocence that Echo didn't believe a word he said. She hoped this was one of the times that Gina was eavesdropping because she would check out everything he said later. "Percy, you want me to believe you drove all the way from Atlanta because . . . wait. Is your name even Percy?"

He had the good sense to wince. "What are you saying? Of course it is. That's not red wine over there in your lobby—it's blood. I'd much rather be at home myself, but the brass thought I should be here. I barely had time to pack a bag."

"But why not tell me you were coming?"

Overhead a flock of seagulls circled, their cries a terrible screeching. Percy stared after them for a long while before speaking. "Do you have any idea who funds the National Literary Commission?"

Echo thought back to how he'd never really been clear about that. "You were always so hush-hush about it. I assumed it was the Citizen Governance Council."

"If only," Percy said. "Through a series of shells and trusts so obscure even the Model couldn't untangle them, it's none other than Universal Trust."

Echo wanted to be shocked but couldn't quite make herself go there. UT was really behind everything, weren't they? They were ostensibly a research group focused on human survival, so she guessed backing a library like TPL wouldn't have been good publicity.

"You see, it's that expression on your face. That's why no one likes to admit to working for UT. Every time I used to mention it, people would start in on me like I was the one personally shooting them up with the microchips. Do you blame me? You don't like your job any more than I like mine, but we both show up and do what we're told anyway."

So convincing was Percy's argument that, for a hot second, Echo's resolve weakened. "But . . . but . . . what do they expect you to do here? It's a police matter now."

"You know what. The people with the coin to fund this place are the same ones who paid for the car, and they want to protect their investment. They felt that an in-person chat with that detective would get the message across: 'Solve this thing quickly and quietly.'"

"And they're so concerned about their investment that they sent you all the way up here to make sure the locals don't screw it up."

"Everything wasn't a lie," Percy said, and he had the nerve to look wounded. "Yes, I work for UT, but I care about income equity. And it's working." He stopped to wave a hand at everyone gathering around. "These people have enough to live on, and look what's come out of it. A revolution of creativity that we haven't seen since the Dark Ages."

The man sounded like a commercial, touting the benefits of, well, some shadowy organization. "This whole thing still doesn't make any sense to me."

"I'm a grunt," Percy said. "Okay? I'm less important than you think. I live here, not in Atlanta near headquarters. My bosses wanted reassurance that everything was under control. And, judging by what I've seen, it is. This was just one of those whack nuts who hates advancement. They hoped to make a splash with this stunt, and it worked. But the library will soon be open again, and hopefully you and I can get back to our philosophical discussions."

Maybe he was right.

"Mind if I ask you the same?" Percy said. "Why are *you* here? You must have known the place would be closed today. Were you planning to try and work? Look, I've got a better idea, since I'm here. We can have our talk in person."

Echo fidgeted. There was no valid way to get out of this. Percy grinned and flicked his head over at his waiting sedan. "The brass at least sprang for the cool wheels. You told me there was a place nearby you liked. Slyman's Deli, was it?"

Yes, aside from the People's Café, the local corned beef spot was one of her favorites. "That's an offer too good to pass up," Echo said as she fell in step beside him. Once they were in the car, she glanced back and again wondered where the police and media who usually swarmed these types of incidents were.

As luck would have it, Slyman's was not a place for a leisurely breakfast or lunch. Even the fifth-generation owners had not fallen short on quality, and they had the customer base to prove it. Those waiting for the best home fries in town or their turn at one of the massive sandwiches would go from subtle impatience to outright shooting eye daggers at anyone sitting too long.

Percy was a cagey one, far less open than the version of himself she usually talked to on the other side of a display. It made Echo wonder if anyone was ever a true representation of themselves. She surely wasn't. She peppered him with questions, trying to figure out if there was more he wasn't telling her. In the end, he didn't say anything that would make her doubt him, so why wasn't she convinced?

He'd dropped her off, and neither of them made any pretense about doing this again. After the sedan pulled away, Echo wasted no time in getting Gina to help her enter the library.

"Are you still mad at me?" Gina said once the doors had been sealed again. "There are things I don't tell you because it doesn't serve you."

Now that was a thread that Echo would have to pull on, but later. "You know I'm mad or you wouldn't be asking. I don't value a whole lot these days, but my privacy is one of them. And if I'm to trust you, I need to know that I'm living my life in private."

It wasn't lost on Echo that what she said was ridiculous. Cameras mapped the entire country now. You couldn't go out and water your roses without it being recorded. Embeddables tracked your every movement. Despite all the denials, she was sure that personal communications, both digital and verbal, were recorded and synthesized for storage by the Model—the world's overarching name for artificial general intelligence.

"I know that privacy is an illusion," she said finally. "But I need it. I want to know that some part of me, of my life, isn't open for surveillance."

"But if I hadn't been eavesdropping," Gina countered, "then you would have been caught."

"And being questioned by the police instead of slipping back inside here so that I can keep digging into what happened here," Echo said. Stalemate. Maybe she'd have to forgo her privacy for a time. "We'll talk about this later." She surprised herself by not demanding to be left alone.

Time's Eye loomed above her, bold and black and resplendent in a shaft of sunlight. Inside the library, all was still. The tape gone, the blood smear all cleaned up. It was as if nothing horrible had happened right here. But Echo couldn't get the woman's face out of her mind, nor the mask.

She took the stairs up to the fourth level and stopped to catch her breath. In the distance she heard a siren and froze. She raced halfway back downstairs to hear the siren trail away like a wisp of smoke, likely headed up Edgewater Park Drive toward some other emergency. She listened for a while longer. Only someone who spent as much time as she did inside the building, maybe Walter, would be able to make out the soft whir of the climate-control system. The subtle swaying of a branch or bush. The building, still less than a year old, settling into the earth. Luckily, there were no more sirens or surprise visitors.

This time, she told her ego to shut up and head for the elevator. When the doors opened, she rounded the corner and came to the lounge areas. The wide center was full of tables and comfortable chairs. Along the curve of the back wall, open to the side of the building, the rest of the park loomed. So full of people and life. The inside here was still and quiet, but not in a bad way, like a cemetery. Given who comprised this space, she supposed that analogy was fitting.

Luckily, the mask was right where she'd left it, and she slipped it into her bag.

Despite everything, Echo wanted to speak to Jesse so much that it scared her. She knew she didn't have much time and that she should call up the imperious duchess immediately and try to figure out what was going on.

But her legs moved almost of their own volition, past the second pod and all the way to the back, last one on the right. She stopped to glance at the glass and check her reflection. Lack of sleep clouded her face. Not a hint of eyeliner. She rummaged around in her bag and settled on a tinted lip balm that matched her sweatshirt. Ashy hands squelched with a little lotion patch that touted a twelve-hour deep hydration release. Then she was ready.

She checked Jesse out and then, when he appeared on the screen, she asked, "About that calendar of yours, does it say that now is a good time?"

Jesse pushed his chair back and went over to his desk. He moved some things around that she couldn't see and then gave her a quick, curt nod before returning. "For you, I canceled all my meetings." Then, after a pause during which Echo was sure she smiled too widely, he added, "That color on your lips, it suits you."

"And you are wearing the heck out of that uniform," Echo said.

The two of them regarded each other for a moment before Echo broke the spell, starting first by asking more about him and his life, then sharing some more of what had changed in the world. She found that she liked talking to Jesse and could go on for hours, but she needed to address why she'd checked him out in the first place.

"We've had an incident here at the library, and I need some advice. Something a military officer could help with. Advice of the tactical variety."

Jesse stood and fixed her with a gaze that stirred something in her before it dissipated. He squared his shoulders and nodded. "Finally," he said. "I'm sick to death of talking about the past."

Chapter Sixteen

For a long while, not uncomfortably, Jesse and Echo watched one another. Something solid and substantial passed between them. How had she become more comfortable with him than she was out in the real world? It was because this job and the virtus had become the perfect salve for a grapheme synesthete's most intimate wounds.

A cozy office of her own with a view of the lake. Decent enough food and coffee. A brilliant staff who respected the sanctity of a closed door. Software and an assistant who managed the financials, so she didn't have to. And replicas of history's most fascinating people. A ready-made wall between them and the one-way lever that gave her control of the when and the how. No, what she was was more nefarious. Echo reigned over the people in her life like a dictator.

"The night before the naval officer's exam . . ." Jesse began. "I'm talking about the second time they made us take it too. All the energy you're giving right now? It reminds me of how I felt waiting for the test results. We were sure they'd flunk the whole class."

Echo was surprised they hadn't. Jesse and his fellow officers had scored so well the first time, even after being given eight weeks to complete what was supposed to be a sixteen-week training course, the navy refused to accept their scores. They were forced to take the test a second time, scoring even higher, but even though all sixteen passed, out of spite, only twelve were promoted, with one alternate. That was how they became the Golden Thirteen. The other three were sent back to the enlisted ranks.

"There's this group that hates the library," Echo said. "Any AI-related tech, really. There was an incident here yesterday, actually a couple, one that left me coated in some liquid and another woman dead, and they're probably behind it."

"Are you hurt?" Jesse removed his glasses.

Echo shook her head.

"What happened?"

Echo recounted the cascade of events. One instant Jesse was the concerned . . . friend; the second he slipped his glasses back on, he was Lieutenant Cooper. He interrupted constantly, holding up a finger while he jotted down notes. They'd come close to an argument.

"Can I ask why you're taking notes?" Echo asked. Virtus were dormant when they weren't checked out. What would be the point?

"So I'll be able to review them once you're gone," Jesse said, then scoffed. "Of course I won't be able to do that really. I guess it's just an old habit. But anyway, how come you never mentioned this group the first time?"

"What good would it do? Telling you everything bad that goes on in the world."

"I don't need or want your protection."

Echo raised an eyebrow.

"Look, that came out wrong. What good is this"—he waved a hand between them—"if it isn't a fair exchange? I don't have much left; don't take that away from me too."

A strange comment. "What do you mean?"

For a minute, it appeared as if he was going to say something. But then his image stuttered and skipped, distorting his features. When the display returned to normal, he muttered, "Nothing."

"Well, I won't hold back. Not anymore."

Jesse consulted his notes. "So these renegades, Human.exe . . . what is the 'exe' thing about?"

"A nod back to the old days. It was an extension for computer programs. I think the 'exe' stood for 'executable.'"

"Clever."

Echo rolled her eyes.

"I'm gonna venture to say this ain't the first time they've pulled something like this. In war, conflict unchecked always escalates."

"I get that, and yes, it's not the first time, but I never guessed anything quite this bold."

Jesse looked up at something off-screen. Echo gave him the time to think. "And the mask—you said this duchess and the philosopher can help you find out what it means?"

"I think so, yes."

"You know what I'm gonna say, don't you?"

"Mind reading hasn't been implemented yet—maybe with the next upgrade."

Jesse leveled her with a look that made Echo at least consider apologizing. "That whole sarcasm cover? You do that when you're scared or uncomfortable, don't you?"

"You'd tell me to give that mask to the police and get back to being a librarian."

"See, didn't need that upgrade after all."

"The administration will just sweep this under the rug, bad publicity and all for their little fake library." Echo winced. "I didn't mean that."

"You did and you didn't, but I don't take offense. How could I? I know how much you loved your other job with the real books. But I can see it—you're starting to love this one too. And the virtus, present company included." He smiled.

"There is something else going on with AI. I don't know what it is this time, but I can't let this go. I have to know."

"Why?"

It was the only question Echo wasn't prepared for. Because she had an existence the size of a shoebox. "I don't know."

"You're curious. It's one of the things I . . . I . . ." Jesse stumbled. "It was one of my wife's best qualities. You need to understand the world around you even if you don't want to be part of it."

It hurt to hear the truth out loud, and Echo found herself resenting Jesse, for what he did and *didn't* say. "You think I should drop this and just go back to talking to you and the other virtus. Is that what you're saying?"

Jesse shrugged. "That's the least of it. There's something else you need to think on. People like this ain't gonna stop. You even considered the fact that this group is right? Maybe you need another line of work?"

Echo became angry again. "Would you walk away from your military responsibilities? Just like that?"

"Not a chance," he said.

"I'll be careful," Echo said, and it was the best she could offer.

Jesse massaged his forehead and exhaled. "You mentioned lights on the underside of the mask. There's no direct sound frequency associated with light, but that doesn't mean whoever made that thing has figured it out. You're synesthetic, so think about how colors and numbers factor in. If you find a frequency, it could point to coordinates, a place. A long shot maybe but something to consider." Jesse stood then and fixed her with a look that withered her like a fallen leaf. "Don't shut me out," he said. "And watch your back."

Echo got to her feet and just barely stopped herself from reaching out and finding nothing. It would be too heartbreaking. The conversations had started innocently enough. But Jesse was like an immersive novel, where before bed, you kept telling yourself, *One more page, one more page.* Leaving the comfort and conversation with him in that cube was growing more difficult each time.

"I will. Later?"

"Yes. Now quit standing there staring at me—go ahead and check me in. You've got work to do."

Chapter Seventeen

"What's happened?" No sooner had Echo spoken the words to check Margaret out of the collection than she'd fallen back into demanding form. Her mouth was pinched, but her gaze held the curiosity of one who had made a life full of study and challenge. That lay beneath the annoyance.

"A cop . . ." Echo paused. How did she know Donovan Reid was a detective? That car of his had none of the typical symbols or logos. And aside from the forensics team, nobody else had shown up. "Two men were downstairs. One was probably from some branch of the law, but the other was more of a surprise."

Margaret tilted her head. Her teardrop earrings caught a hint of light from a window out of view. "An unforeseen visitor? Pray, who was it?"

"Percy, my supervisor. He claims he's just here on behalf of *his* bosses, but I don't know. I got the impression that neither he nor the administration are being completely transparent. I ran out of here so fast when I heard the siren, I forgot the mask, but it was right here when I got back."

Margaret's fingers fluttered nervously at her collarbone. "That would have most certainly been unfortunate. Yet here you still are. Having the option twixt the two, I verily would rather they take you and leave the mask."

For a moment, Echo couldn't speak, but when she did, it came out in a flood. "You don't have to like me. Aside from your book, I'm no fan of yours either. And I hate to remind you of the obvious, but you're a copy, a replica. So even if that mask was sitting right here in front of you, you couldn't do a damned thing but stare at it."

Margaret's thin nostrils flared. "I suppose you are correct, though I would not have chosen such a rude manner with which to convey such sentiments. The truth that you are present here and not languishing away in some dismal jail is of good fortune, indeed. However surprising."

This woman ran from the Sahara Desert to the North Pole in the time it took most people to pull on their underwear. "We still have questions that need answering," Echo said.

"Hmm, how shall we seize the thread anew? Let us recount what we know thus far," Margaret suggested.

"The lady who doused me with paint or whatever it was comes back later with a knife buried in her chest." Echo held up the mask. "She's wearing this thing that you say is the spitting image of a long-dead philosopher—"

"Heretic," Margaret corrected.

"Iconoclast maybe?"

"Self-seeking contrarian!"

Echo rolled her eyes. "As I was saying. We've got the symbol of an atom, and Zera talking about existentialism. And to top it off, my boss shows up here and lets on that Universal Trust, not the library association, backs this whole institution."

"I can't imagine how a group dedicated to human welfare is involved," Margaret muttered as she stood and began pacing behind her chair.

"Me neither," Echo admitted. "It's not like I could just waltz on down to the local office and demand an audience."

"May 1667," Margaret stated, hands clasped in front of her.

"Is that date supposed to mean something to me?" Echo asked.

"The Royal Society of London was naught but for men. Their concern was natural philosophy, or what you now call 'science.' A matter wherein I had considerable expertise, but did they answer my requests for an audience? They did not, indeed. So I marched down there myself and forced a vote, and they finally relented." Margaret paused, giggled. "If only you could have beheld Robert Boyle's visage. The poor dolt nearly fainted. He was the one who began calling me 'Mad Madge.'"

It made sense to Echo then. Margaret was smart, outspoken, opinionated, creative. All the things that a woman of her time couldn't have been. Being who she was in seventeenth-century England must have been a daily struggle. "What happened?"

A wistful expression descended upon Margaret's face. "They spoke in long, windy discourse. I countered, we quarreled. That was the end of it."

Echo felt that letdown almost as much as if she'd been there herself. There was much she could learn from Margaret Cavendish. "I get your point. I technically should go down there and demand some answers. But things are different today. There are barriers everywhere."

"Then I do fear our investigation is at an impasse. I cannot converse with the other virtual personages, or I could continue our research here."

"Can you imagine if you could leave the library with me?" Echo said. Virtus had escaped, but they couldn't really interact and exist like they did inside the building. "Or if I could be there, traipsing around the virtual collection with you."

Echo, Gina said. *I . . . I think I can help.* Hadn't she told Gina to mind her AI business? For all the extended vocabulary her assistant had, apparently the word "privacy" was exempt. Echo double-tapped her earring for full audio. "Say that again so the duchess can hear you."

"What you just said about the virtual collection. I think I can help," Gina repeated.

"Who is there?" Margaret's eyes had gone wide. "Have you invited someone else into our confidence without my consent?"

"Margaret Cavendish, meet Gina, my virtual companion," Echo said, showing her the earring. "It's called a 'wearable,' and it's how we talk, send messages, research, complain about life, just about everything. It works via a bidirectional audio conductor in the chip."

"Marvelous," Margaret said. "Like a trusted companion, then. One that also acts as a personal secretary, assistant, and confidant."

"Yes, just like that," Echo said.

"Well, on with it, then," Margaret said, glancing at a point behind Echo, as if that were where Gina lived. "Who do you propose?"

"It's not 'who' but 'what'?" Gina's voice had risen at the end, more a question than a statement.

Echo tensed. "Gina, what are you saying?"

"I can . . . so, umm, at least I think I can . . . maybe, like, insert you, or part of you at least, into the virtual world."

Echo couldn't speak. Surely she'd heard wrong. Had Gina been hacked? She got up and left the cube. Telling herself all the ways in which what she'd heard was heresy. Dangerous. "Screw this." She went back, grabbed her bag, and shoved the mask inside. She didn't even bother to check Margaret in before she strode right back out that door.

"Where are you going?" Margaret called after her.

Echo raced to the staircase with the purpose of a woman who knew she'd gone too far. She made it all the way to the first landing and then stopped.

What if?

Those two seemingly harmless words had power. They'd led to some of the world's most important discoveries, and they'd also been a slippery slope to very bad endings. So why did Echo find herself turning and trudging back up the way she'd come?

She slammed her bag on the desk and plopped into the chair. She glanced up at Margaret to find an annoyingly mischievous grin on her face. She guessed it wouldn't hurt to ask. If something was truly wrong with Gina or the chip, Echo would have to call for service.

"Gina, what are you talking about? How can you do that? You shouldn't be able to do that. There's no way—"

"Oh, do get ahold of yourself," Margaret snapped. "Did you not just wish for what this assistant of yours says she can deliver to your lap?"

"I did, but . . ." Echo trailed off. An uneasiness settled into her bones, a presage to a nightmare. As the seconds ticked past and temptation surfaced, the feeling grew more and more quiet, until it had all but disappeared. "How?"

"You remember when someone got the idea to let the public make virtual recordings of themselves, like their family histories and such, to add to the library's public collection? You and all the staff were beta testers."

Echo had completely forgotten. She *had* done an initial recording. It was in the collective, right along with everyone else's. She was, in effect, a virtu.

Gina continued. "I think I can tap into Ada and simply make a mental connection between the virtual you and the real you."

"Simply?" Echo was unconvinced. *But oh my God, what if?* Echo would be the first person to try such a thing. And Margaret, Jesse . . . what if she could actually be in the same space with them? Even if things went wrong, she had so very little to lose. "And you can talk to Ada?"

"As they say, we are cut from the same cloth. We're both just offshoots of the Model."

"Is it safe?"

"Got me. Never tried it before, but yeah, I think so," Gina said.

"There is but one way to find out," Margaret added, a little too quickly. What would she care if Echo disappeared into a sea of ones and zeros?

Echo's exhale was long and sorrowful. "What do I have to do?"

Echo wanted to go to her office. Margaret thought she should do the experiment from the lobby, so that if she died, someone would surely trip over her on the way in the next time the library was open. They argued about Margaret's insensitivity before Gina stepped in, a referee between two stubborn combatants. In the end, they decided it would be best for Echo to stay exactly where she was, in the pod.

"Try to relax," Gina said.

"Will I be conscious?" Echo asked. "I mean, will I be aware *here* that I'm in *there*?" She inclined her head toward the screen.

"In theory, a portion of you will be here and the other there."

"You really have no idea, do you?" Echo asked.

"I've run scenarios testing my hypothesis a million different ways, and the margin of error is less than .001 percent."

Echo pictured her hip Ohio City neighborhood, the warm caress of the sun on her skin as she sat watching the sparrows and starlings nesting in the red maple tree through the bay window in her apartment. The office downstairs on the first floor. Stilted conversations around her parents' Thanksgiving dinner table. Next quarter's endless meeting, when she and her staff would review the next virtu candidates. Echo considered all these things and was saddened when she found none of them more compelling than the possibility that lay before her now.

Margaret watched her intently, her mouth a closed, thin line for once. She was doing that thing where she cocked her head to the side and watched from the corner of her eye. Echo reached into her bag and took out a small token from a zippered pocket. A round silver disk, the number four engraved on both sides. Nestled in between the hues of blue and green on the color wheel, the color of calm. For several minutes, she focused on that digit, running a finger over the token's surface again and again, breathing deeply.

"All right, let's do it," Echo said, finally. Margaret raised her fists and squealed with delight.

"Okay," Gina said. "This may feel a bit weird."

Echo was a palm print, hovering but not opening for fear of what lay on the other side of the door. She waited. Would she feel a tingling, a shock? An all-out heart attack?

It was none of those things.

Echo was a light switch, flickering on and off, on and off.

The world was dimmed, eclipsed.

But then Echo opened her eyes to find Margaret still peering at her from the screen.

"Gina—"

"Ha ha! That didn't go as planned. But I learned something. Let me try this again."

Echo stood. Had she taken leave of her senses? She should put a stop to this right now. "Uh-uh, I don't think this is a good idea."

"But we are nigh there," Margaret protested.

"The virtual you that you recorded is being interfered with by something else," Gina said. "A newer, more recent, and, dare I say, more thorough mapping, but it keeps slipping through my fingers."

Echo sank into the chair again. "I didn't do another recording." Her gaze settled onto her bag, the mask inside. The odd feeling when she'd placed it over her face. No, couldn't be. But it was the only explanation.

As if under the skilled fingers of a master sculptor stricken with a case of sudden-onset arthritis, she sensed Gina's fumbling. A feeling, more mental than physical. Like the times when a million thoughts rambled around in her brain, but like there was another brain trying to shove its way into the middle of the stream.

Echo clutched the desk but found her breath becoming short. Her head felt like someone was cleaving it open and pouring in hot wax. "I can't—" she mumbled a moment before she was replicated. And that second version of herself, it was like a shadow, an apparition, tethered to the original by the thinnest of threads.

The first thing she noticed was the absence of sound. The city was always so caustic with noise—voices, the train, the constant hum of bots going about their business. Echo blinked and Margaret came into view.

Echo felt light as a mote of dust. She raised her arms and found she could almost see through them. It was so disorienting, she stumbled.

"Oh dear!" Margaret spun on her heels and rushed over to a bureau in the corner. A pitcher of water was there beside a raised sink.

Margaret poured water into what looked like a teacup and raced back over. Echo held out a diaphanous hand, expecting to be offered a drink. Instead Margaret flung the water in her face. Lucky for Margaret, Echo felt nothing.

"Are you in there?" the duchess asked, searching Echo's face.

"I am . . . here." Margaret's milieu was a programming marvel. It was an ornate outrage of a room. Longer than it was wide, with tall leaded glass windows that cut triangular rainbows of sunlight across the thick carpets draped over a stone floor. Built-in bookcases filled with leather-backed volumes. Thick tapestries covered the far wall. This was something out of a medieval film, and against all reason, Echo was standing right in its midst. Instinctively, she glanced around. "Where? Where do you go to see me in the pod?"

Margaret pointed. "There."

She had no legs. Or rather she did, but they didn't move. A glance down revealed her feet several inches off the ground. Panic welled up like a storm surge. But she willed herself forward and glided over.

Echo recognized the chair. It sat in front of a wood-paneled wall that was now blank. Margaret came up beside her. "The screen becomes active when initiated from the other side. Otherwise, it's only a wall."

Gina, Echo said.

Silence.

"Gina," Echo tried aloud. "Gina!"

A colder, heavier silence answered back.

A wave of terror washed over Echo and pulled her under. She was sinking, had sunk to the bottom of her own ocean. And like a drowning woman, she fought, gasping for air, failing to rein in the panic. Margaret was mumbling something, but Echo couldn't hear her.

"Gina," Echo screamed again and again until she let go and welcomed the ocean floor.

Chapter Eighteen

Echo was a little girl again. Seven years old. Small and confused and feeling exposed. The psychiatrist's office was too bright. She'd come to like the lingering smell of coffee but hated the loud machine in the corner that made the drink. The small room had a kid-size chair and table, and she was seated there.

"Echo, dear," Dr. Watkins said, kneeling beside her. She was a doctor of the head, not the body. She always wore pretty scarves tied around her neck. "Why did you rip up the chart?"

Echo shrugged. Her mind and heart raced. She'd come to understand that not everybody felt the way she did, and it scared her.

"I don't know," she whispered. "The number made me mad, and I wanted it to stop but it wouldn't."

Ms. Watkins nodded. Not a quick one like she wanted Echo to shut up. She understood. "You have what's called synesthesia. It's pretty rare, and the way it manifests for you is . . . well, I haven't seen your kind of case before. It's all numbers, they make you feel a certain way. Am I right?"

Echo mouthed the word *Yes* under her breath. "Does that mean I'm bad?"

The therapist laughed. "Of course not. It just means you see the world in a different way than others."

There was a name for what she felt. Unlike those mean kids said, Echo wasn't broken. And Dr. Watkins had said she was rare. That meant Echo wasn't the only one. She wasn't by herself.

When Echo came back to herself, her situation was no less dire. "Ada," she tried this time, but she still got no response. She was still inside the virtu space, with Margaret prattling on. She wished she had her disk. Instead, she simply pictured the number four and did her deep-breathing exercises until she'd settled into something not quite like calm.

"This entire affair—your being here, that is—is well and truly extraordinary; however, I really must insist you gather yourself at once. This display is most unbecoming a lady, and there is much to be done." Margaret clasped her hands together and lifted her chin.

"Look around," Echo said. "There's nobody here to worry about how much of a lady I am but you, and frankly, I don't care what you think. I'm a little preoccupied with how I'm going to get the hell out of here."

"Where is the intelligence that brought you here?"

"If I knew that, I would be out of here, don't you think?"

"You asked to come, of your own volition."

"That was when I thought I had a way back."

"The truth is, you did not think this through, did you?"

It was like a volley, and with each return, Echo gave way. No, she hadn't. Was Gina over on the other side trying to find her? And what of her body? It was silly, but Echo cupped a hand beneath her nose, trying to feel her breath. Nothing. Margaret watched all this with an expression bordering on boredom.

"Welcome to Newcastle," she said. "The year of our lord, 1670, north England."

A wild, strangled sound escaped from Echo's mouth.

Margaret snatched the cup and walked back over to the basin. She held it aloft, a threat, a promise. An order.

Echo tried again, "Gina . . ."

No response. No, that wasn't right. Before the winters became more tepid than frigid, Echo's parents had insisted on stuffing her into a wool coat during the cold years. And it itched and grated so badly, she would shrug out of it as soon as she was out of sight. That was the way her brain felt now, like she had an itch with no way to scratch it. If she let herself dwell on that unreachable itch for too long, she feared she would go mad.

"You have come here for a purpose. And it holds still. Let us begin there." Margaret's stern voice snatched Echo back from the abyss.

Echo reached to straighten her clothes, a silly gesture. She let the part of her mind surface that had been so anxious to explore. She was a librarian, after all. "Curiosity" might as well have been part of the job description. As far as she knew, what she and Gina had done had never happened before. The curator and director of the People's Library had an insight into her own collection. And she was going to absorb everything she could.

"What's this?" Echo had glided over to a writing desk. A newspaper. An article circled, the title reading, "Mad Madge Becomes the First Woman to Engage the Royal Society of London."

"What I mentioned earlier. A hoity-toity assembly of English scoundrels who thought women should have nary an opinion on naught outside of knitting, certainly not science. I made Robert Boyle demonstrate his air pump, and we spoke at length about vacuum air pressure. It caused quite the scandal."

Echo nodded, impressed. Up close, Margaret had a spattering of sunspots, or maybe they were freckles, across her nose and cheeks, with a few on the exposed skin on her chest. She had the constantly moving eyes of a squirrel, though her countenance was stiff as a board. "Proper" was the term that came to mind.

Continuing her exploration, Echo examined a tapestry. A fight scene. Nothing much about human nature and war had changed in four hundred years. Men with robes and swords and spikes. A helmet ripped off. A market or some other public place. A fringe of maroon, colors faded, probably by the sunlight, but it was still grand.

Next, her breath, or what would pass for it in this place, caught. Floor-to-ceiling shelves lined with books. All leather-bound in rich burgundies and greens, browns, and shades of black. She ran her fingers along the spines, admiring the golden script.

It was like being able to enter the exhibits at the world's greatest museum.

She was with a figure from history, secure in the smell of old leather books and warmth. By the best efforts of the day, barring some strange and unfortunate condition, Echo guessed she had somewhere in the neighborhood of fifty years left to live, sixty if medicine continued its current trajectory. She could theoretically spend the rest of her life reading here in this library and not finish half of it. It wouldn't be such a bad way to go.

She pointed at a cream-colored tome titled *The Faerie Queene* and turned to Margaret. "Can you get that one for me?"

Margaret made a strangled sound. "You may as well see for yourself."

"See what?"

She came over and plucked it from the shelf. "Are you certain?"

"Go on," Echo said, wondering why the woman was acting so strangely. "Open it."

The first page was blank. Maybe the title was on a later page. Margaret flipped, one more, then two and three pages. She thumbed quickly through the rest. She put the book down and went through the same exercise several more times to drive her point home.

Echo could only stand there gaping.

"Blank?" She glanced around at the bookshelves in horror. "They're all blank?"

"As empty as a lord's promise."

"But why—" And then Echo knew. This was all a show. Why program words into books that would never be read?

Human prisoners had access to libraries, but apparently virtual prisoners didn't.

She could see all the things here that she'd imagined and seen from the other side of the virtual window that used to separate them. And then there were the things that weren't here. All the creature comforts of the life she had back in her Ohio City apartment. Things that she took for granted and, if she made it back, would never gaze upon with the same disconnection again.

Margaret had taken up a perch on the edge of a small wooden settee, trailing Echo's every movement.

Jesse.

Two questions ignited like flames. She was no fool. These were things she'd pondered before. Uncomfortable details that she'd allowed herself to glance over and under whenever they surfaced. Echo was shocked to see a vista outside from across the room, near one of the windows. Rolling emerald hills and impeccably maintained gardens. What was either a trick of the sun and her mind or a small stream trickling through. She couldn't wait to get out there. She spun, looking for a door.

"Can we go outside?" As soon as she'd asked the question, Echo knew she'd made a mistake. Margaret sat there, feet swinging, her face twisted into something like reticence. She fretted over a golden thread on her arm and looked back to that window with a longing that made Echo's heart sink. She wanted to take it back, but there was nothing to do now but wait.

Margaret squeezed her eyes shut and gave a barely perceptible shake of her head.

"We will not be able to continue our inquiries about the mask until you satisfy what remains of your curiosities," Margaret said. When Echo raised an eyebrow at her, she hitched a shoulder. "My husband was a wonderful man." Echo noted her use of the past tense. "A thinker, a bit of a revolutionary for his time in his support of me. I guess we both were. I sensed whenever there was something he was uncomfortable discussing. 'Tis the same thing I see in you now."

Echo wanted to take a deep breath but couldn't. Nor could she feel her pulse quickening; her mind, though, somehow experienced the effects anyway. *Stop,* it told her. *Stop now*. But she'd come this far. Far enough that she might not be able to return. "What happens here? When you're not checked out?"

Margaret got up and strolled over to the window. Watching the duchess there, Echo remembered how she herself also often retreated to the comfort of her window at home. "I was what you'd call a philosopher at a time when women were not allowed such designations. One of the subjects that I wrestled to cultivate my own convictions on was indeed the divine. I used to deride the notion of heaven and hell, being of a mind that those were only constructs made by men for the sole purpose of averting anarchy. I do wonder about that now."

Margaret fell silent, her gaze someplace outside the window. Hands at her sides.

Echo watched her, not daring to interrupt or break the spell of the moment. But the fear had begun to creep in again.

"Before your library opened, there were examinations. Years of them—"

"Years?" Echo couldn't believe what she'd just heard. Maybe Madge really was mad. She must have gotten that wrong.

"The Model," Margaret explained. "There are, or there were, markers that recorded the passage of time, so I am quite certain."

"What's it like?" Echo asked.

"Verily, I do not understand the technical nature behind how I, how we, are able to converse, to think, to feel, for that matter. Such thinking is beyond what I could have imagined, you must understand. We had to agree, and the creative in me could not bear to not be a part of such an auspicious experiment. They did receive my counsel, and in that, we are still unable to disconnect."

"But do you regret it?" Echo wanted to know.

"Ask me after we get to the bottom of your dilemma with this evil league that would see me ended . . . again."

Chapter Nineteen

Echo knew. It was there in the sidestepped questions. The expressions clouding over. The swift change of subject. The speech glitches. She'd brushed it all aside, like crumbs from her lap. But in the silence of this impossible room, only the flicker of fire in the hearth, the breath of Echo's self-centered dismissals curled like toxic smoke in her lungs. Why hadn't any of the virtus told her what life was really like for them? Or had they tried? Had she not been listening? Had she not *wanted* to listen?

Margaret left the window and walked over to where Echo hovered under the accusatory spines of the books. "I'm certain that the puppet your administration appointed to run this institution has never spared a single charitable thought for the collection they proclaim to steward."

She had stumbled over the word "collection," and Echo understood why. They were so much more than that. She held up a hand. "That would be me. I'm the puppet."

"Oh, my dear, this is so much higher than you," Margaret said with a chuckle. "This is not your sword to fall upon."

Mad Madge wasn't so mad after all. "Gina?" Echo tried again. Each second that ticked by without her companion's cheery voice chipped away at Echo's resolve. "For now, the least I can do is figure out what's going on out there." She felt faintly silly, pointing to the space where Margaret told her the virtual window displayed, but it was the only way to orient herself to the world she desperately hoped to return to.

"There speaks my girl," Margaret said, brightening. "The matter is how? If your assistant has taken her leave and you are here . . ."

It wouldn't work. It *shouldn't* work. Echo marched over and sat in Margaret's chair. She'd expected it to be plush, and it was anything but. Fancy, elegant, but hard as a stack of bricks. Her co-collaborator came to hover beside her. Echo glanced up at her, struck again by how short she was, then turned back and said, "Ada, check in—"

"Boyle," Margaret urged. "Robert Boyle."

"Who? I don't even know if he's part of the collection. And I'm trying something," Echo said.

Margaret crossed her arms.

"Ada, check in virtual personage . . . Echo London."

A spasm of light.

Margaret reached for Echo's hand.

The square's growth sputtered. It shimmered and flashed. Echo willed her eyes not to blink. It was all for naught, since moments later, the square withered at the edges and progressed inward until nothing was left.

"What just happened?" Margaret asked.

It didn't work, genius. That was only fear masquerading as anger, and when Echo recognized it for what it was, she instead found that she was grateful for Margaret's smothering presence. If she had been sent to a setting without her, without any of the other virtus . . . she didn't want to even think about that. "We got a sign. One that says keep going."

The duchess appeared unconvinced.

Echo got an idea; she'd been going at this all wrong. "Ada?"

"Yes, Ms. London."

Echo was so shocked she couldn't speak. She'd only ever given the library's system a direct check-in or check-out command.

"Loosen your tongue!" Margaret demanded.

"Can you just let me think for a second?" Echo said.

The Model, that's what people called AGI. Nobody used the moniker, but Ada was the slice of the Model that powered TPL. Obviously, she was listening. "Ada, where's my companion, Gina?"

"The companion known as Gina is attached to the physical form of Echo London, in pod number ninety-nine."

That made perfect sense. The embeddable was back in her body. No wonder she couldn't contact her. "Can you connect me to her?"

Echo floated for an eternity before the librarian answered. "Perhaps, but this will take some time."

Margaret chimed in. "If you cannot leave—"

Echo glared.

"Yet," Margaret said, then started over. "If you cannot leave yet, maybe we can go somewhere else in the meantime."

"What are you saying?"

"That's why you wanted to be here in the first place. What nobler course to pursue our inquiries? All whom we must consult are present in the virtual collection. The number zero is the sole link yet to be forged. Pray, let us engage someone who may aid us."

Brilliant, Echo thought, and to Ada she said, "Can you move us to the milieu of someone in the collection who is an expert on mathematics?"

Chapter Twenty

Neither had known what to expect, "nothing at all" being foremost. "Disappearing into a bleak nonexistence" was a close second. Neither could have anticipated what happened when, a tortured minute later, they coalesced in a scene that left them speechless. Instead of checking out, Echo and Margaret had checked in.

Echo felt that familiar presence at her right shoulder and glanced over to see that her friend had gone even paler than usual.

In stark contrast to the duchess's meticulous medieval environs, this setting was casual and unpretentious. Suffused with the whispered ease of sitting by the edge of a gentle stream, it had the look and feel of a home in a rural village. Two buildings stood within the space, their walls constructed of burnished mud brick and their roofs woven from thatch. One, near the rear wall, was the size of a large bedroom, the other, off to the left, more like a closet.

A central courtyard with a table large enough for a small family sat atop a beautifully patterned rug. A relaxed spattering of assorted clay pots and wooden chests and brightly colored cushions filled the space. This serene setting was surrounded by a low wall of the same material as the structures. There was no cover, and the sun was full and bright overhead. It shone with an intensity that suggested a temperature that would normally have her sitting under an air-conditioning vent.

"Where are we?" Echo asked.

"Bhinmal," said the man who stepped out from behind a curtain covering the doorway of the larger building. "Bhinmal, India." He had the air of a man rich in contentment. Medium height, with a light, inquisitive manner. His robes mirrored Zera's, except the right shoulder and arm were exposed. Beads adorned his neck, wrists, and biceps.

"And when?" Margaret said, a hint of strain in her voice. "Tell us, what year marks the present day?"

"It is my pleasure and honor to welcome you to the year 640. Yet I must inquire: By what means have you come to stand before me? The Model foretold that no visitor would tread this ground. Rather, a window would appear there"—he stopped to point at the wall across from his table—"and through that vision alone was I to converse with knowledge seekers."

"A full thousand years before I was born," Margaret muttered.

"And almost another four hundred years for me," Echo added. "I can't really explain how we're here; call it a glitch in the system. But we asked to check out a mathematics expert—I'm guessing that's you."

He tapped a forefinger at his temple and shook his head. A moment later, he chuckled. "The translation was off, but I have been rude. I, Brahmagupta, am blessed to study numbers and the motions of the heavens, for there is written the natural order of the universe. Just as the maker of that rug aligned his threads to form the pattern, so too does the learner of numbers bind truth into a fabric of knowledge. These things I explore in my text, the *Brāhmasphuṭasiddhānta*."

"You are a man of letters, then?" This from Margaret, in a tone that made Echo turn to look at her. The duchess was poised for challenge, competition. "Pray tell, what is the significance of your writings? Were you formally published?"

"During my time, palm leaf and birch bark bound by string form our texts. I have suffered greatly with the former. Thus, I am partial to birch bark. Therein lies more durability."

Margaret tutted, seemingly impressed despite herself. "Scholarship always prevails."

That brought a smile to their host's face. "I would invite you to take leave at my table, but it does not appear that is possible. What can you tell me of your time?"

This was the exchange they needed, and with all Echo had learned about a virtu's true existence, she set aside her need to rush into what she wanted and regaled him with an overview of the twenty-first century. She had to prompt Margaret to do the same with her century.

"And what wisdom do you seek? Whether your query is mathematical or astronomical in nature, it shall be considered and resolved by method and measure."

Echo let it all out in a cascade, with frequent additions and corrections from Margaret. Brahmagupta listened with his head angled toward the sun, eyes closed. He didn't ask one question and sat that way for a full minute after they'd finished. Echo sensed Margaret's unease steadily ramping up, and when she appeared on the verge of speaking, ready to unleash one of her demands, Echo silenced her with a raised hand.

Over the years, she'd learned many things while watching and then leading people. Her current staff were walking, talking contradictions. Each of them made their way through the world and processed information differently. Where Carmen was quick to speak and act, Lorain was more measured, quite comfortable to consider and weigh what she'd heard beforehand. Brahmagupta was like her.

He nodded slowly. "I grasp the grim reality of why you have come, if not how."

"How do you think the number zero fits in?" Echo asked.

"For many years, scholars, the clergy, they resisted the idea because they feared emptiness, the void. The Sanskrit term is 'shunyata.'"

"Come to think of it, the Greeks and Romans also resisted the idea," Margaret said.

"I sought to know the nature of this contentious figure, which is both nothing and everything. I measure the paths of the stars and planets, their positions in the sky as constant as the breath of time itself. I test the boundaries of mathematical calculations: addition, subtraction, multiplication. My life's work is to give form to what is hidden, to reveal harmony where those who came before only saw fear and chaos."

"So . . ." Margaret started, then stopped. "These scholars, if you will, were afraid of . . . of nothing? Pray tell, why?"

"Because of what else could spring from nothing," Echo said. "Think about it. Consciousness."

"Ah, the battle older than time," Brahmagupta said. "Scientists, philosophers, and religion have all posited theories, but I suspect that even in your time, the puzzle has yet to be solved."

Echo sighed. "And you'd be right."

"A philosopher might tell you that the whole universe is conscious. But we have no proof of that. Do we need it?" Brahmagupta picked up a wooden spoon. "Does this spoon have a self? What about that stool over there?"

"Not the spoon itself perhaps, but before, when it was a tree, certainly," Margaret said, her tone haughty. "All matter, to some degree, is conscious. Vital materialism is the school of thought I subscribe to."

"We're of the same mind there," he agreed. "Look at it not as the clergy might, but from a scientific point of view. If you accept that in this complex system, everything is connected, interdependent, then all those parts come together, acting and reacting to construct a whole. But it begins somewhere, and that place is the void."

"But Western culture became invested in an alternate viewpoint, one that centers the brain as the source of consciousness," Margaret said. "Brains are where we think, how we create, so I cannot blame them for their shortsightedness."

"I sense a 'but' coming," Echo said.

There was a mischievous twinkle in Brahmagupta's eye. "And you'd be right. Yes, most of our sense organs are in our heads, but take your Ayurvedic and Mesoamerican traditions, even ancient Egyptian, and the heart is thought to be the seat of consciousness."

"So, who's right?" Echo asked.

"Though we have spoken of both things, my reasoning and my belief go toward the brain. There thought is birthed; the mind is but a womb. Absent clear evidence to the contrary, that is the truth I bear. It is clear to me that the number zero here represents someone's attempt to trace consciousness back to the source of all existence."

Echo and Margaret were at that point where words weren't needed for them to fully understand one another. Echo used to wonder about all the wars between science and religion over the centuries, and now it made sense. Annoying sense.

"Ada, can you take us, all of us, to Zera Yacob?"

This time, their transition was a lot smoother. The fragments of generated imagery rearranged themselves, resolving into their new backdrop. The Model was learning. If Echo had a body, there would be an uncomfortable feeling in her chest. A warning.

Margaret's surroundings were the epitome of modern opulence for her time. Brahmagupta's setting was more rural, but it evoked the same sense of wonder. Echo had been told that the virtus helped develop their environs; if that was true, then Zera had made an interesting choice indeed.

A small fire crackled in the center of a stone enclosure. The flames pushed back some of the darkness—that and a puddle of light that disappeared around a bend—but shadows encroached from all sides. Parchments were stacked neatly on what looked like hard-packed earth. A tiny clay pot with a quill sticking out of it suggested an inkwell of sorts. She squinted and made out a pallet of blankets under a rocky outcropping. Echo expected it to feel spooky, sinister, but it was the opposite. This was a place she could imagine herself escaping to, for a few moments of peace . . . assuming there were no bats, or rodents. This seventeenth-century Ethiopian scholar, at least this version of him, had selected a cave for his eternity.

"This is a revelation both unexpected and welcome." Brahma was the first to speak. He passed his diaphanous hand in and out of the fire, unblemished, unburned. "Our constructive counsel told of controls set in place to prevent this very thing. It appears that the Model, or whatever truly fuels it, is evolving."

"Once again," Echo whispered. That fierce resistance she'd had against the library had ebbed into more of a feeling of disquiet, although that didn't change the fact that she was no lover of the tech that, at one point, had threatened to overtake humanity at the top of the intellectual chain.

All she knew, had cared to know, was that the purported age of intelligence had fallen into the camp of "wishful thinking," along with other great hopes like traveling beyond the speed of light. But was that changing, guided by her own misplaced curiosity? Had the intelligence been lying dormant like a bad gene, just to mutate and have a go at them again?

"This also invokes the query: How do I return?" Margaret asked.

Echo had wondered the same for herself. How much time had passed? How long since she'd heard her companion's voice? She found that despite how irritated she usually was with Gina, she missed her presence.

Before she could answer, a shuffle of fabric announced the arrival of their virtu.

"What?" Zera said when he appeared, his wide brown eyes taking in the three of them. This time he held a staff, and a small wooden cross hung from a simple leather band around his neck. "If you are here instead of on the other side of that screen"—he gestured just past the fire at the cave wall—"then am I to suppose that this library experiment is in the midst of a grand impairment?"

Echo held up her hands to stall the barrage. "We only have a working hypothesis on how, but yes, the People's Library is operating outside its traditional programming."

"Indulge me," Zera said.

Echo told him about Gina and how she'd helped her enter this world and all the rest, how things had gone wrong after that. How Ada had seemingly replaced her.

"And now you are unable to raise this companion of yours?"

Echo glanced over at Margaret, not even sure why. For support? Reassurance that she couldn't give her? She shook her head.

"Your expression bears the mark of one at odds with herself," Zera said. "The struggle to hide your fear is at once understandable but unnecessary, here with esteemed comrades. You are afraid that you have been conscripted to remain in this place."

Echo was proud of her ability to hide her feelings, so it grated that this virtu had seen through her so thoroughly. Still, his words held nothing but truth. "Your profile said you were a philosopher—looks like somebody left out the part about you being a diviner."

Zera gathered the length of his robes and sank into a cross-legged position. "Judging by the way that one has her arms clamped in front of her"—he stopped to gesture at Margaret—"you are here to settle some debate upon which she has thus far been bested."

It was as if Margaret had swelled to twice her size. "I beg your pardon!" Her small fists were balled at her sides.

Brahma chuckled, and Zera's lip quirked. "I am only teasing," he said. "A disposition that angered my wife and children as well."

Just like Margaret, he spoke in the past tense. It drove home the point that virtus were alone, with only their memories and hope of being checked out to pass the unrelenting hours. Echo had an aunt. Her mother's only sister. When she was a child, they visited every week. It wasn't until her aunt passed away when Echo was a teenager that she'd begun to see the assisted living facility under the light of truth. Their one-hour visit, every Sunday afternoon. That was it. The only time her aunt had with people she knew and loved. The other 167 hours of each week were an exercise in dissociated endurance.

Brahma and Zera had fallen into animated conversation, while Margaret sulked and Echo was lost in thought. Finally, she found her voice. "Your book, the *Hatata*—you said it reflected on philosophical and theological matters. Does that include questions about consciousness?"

Zera looked down and exhaled deeply. "Mine was a framework based on reason, not intolerance or religious dogma. That is what landed me in this place for two years. Before you ask, I will tell you that if you are looking for a traditional answer to your questions, you have come to the wrong person."

That was music to Echo's ears. "Tradition is of no interest to me, but what you think is."

Zera's eyebrows rose. His easy smile returned. "My theory is that there is a great well that exists all around us. It is from this source that pure consciousness dwells. Whomever is behind this plot most likely seeks to understand that enigma."

"And use that data to help them align the artificial with the natural. Human and AGI," Echo said, barely above a whisper. Her lungs seized up, refusing to draw in her next breath. As that last piece slammed into place, it seemed her heart, the blood coursing through her veins, everything came to a calamitous stop. She staggered backward, as if trying to put distance between herself and the words she'd just spoken.

Margaret made a dismissive noise, then: "I bid you gather your wits!"

Echo shot Margaret a look but heeded her advice. There was no time to waste. She considered how much the world had changed. It was time to consult a more contemporary source. "I know what our next step is."

Chapter Twenty-One

Echo felt a familiar itch in her mind. "Gina!"

"Hey hey," Gina said. "You've been busy, haven't you?"

"Can you get me back?"

Five words, bursting with promise or demise. These five words that would determine the rest of Echo's life.

"I think so. You know this was the first time I've tried something like this, but Ada, she helped me. We pored over the code and made some updates."

"Wait," Echo said. "You did what?" The library wasn't supposed to be able to do this. And Gina wasn't designed to interface with Ada either. If Echo could, in fact, feel her spine, she was sure it would be tingling with a chill. It was as if she had crawled out of a burning car stalled on Dead Man's Curve, only to see three lanes full of headlights barreling down on her at full speed.

"Ada believes with 99.97 percent certainty that we can get you back where you belong. I'm sensing you want a coffee . . . No, you *need* a coffee, right?"

One of the things that Echo appreciated about the Model was its brutal honesty. Only now, she wished it had upgraded itself to include a little sensitivity. Less than 100 percent could mean . . .

"What happens if—" Echo allowed reason with a dash of imagination to fill in those obvious blanks. The virtus had gone quiet. In one fluid motion, Zera stood, blinking rapidly. Brahma joined him, his mouth slightly downturned. Margaret had drifted over near them, her face cast in shadow, but it was clear that she'd taken to studying the ash and dirt on the cave's rock ground. They knew it. Their adventure was about to end. They would be split up, isolated once more.

There was no comparison. What Echo had experienced here was the most interesting thing to happen to her in her life. Here, she had great conversation, friendship, people like Jesse. No hint of a synesthetic meltdown. What awaited her back on the other side?

The Prince mural on the overpass bridge near West Twenty-Fifth and Washington.

The Whiskey Island peninsula at the mouth of the Cuyahoga River.

The Franklin Reading Garden.

Popping in at Phoenix Coffee on Saturday mornings.

Browsing the towering, dusty shelves of the main library on Superior and selecting the perfect books.

The anticipation of curling up on her sofa, enjoying the sunlight from the picture window. Spending an afternoon lost in an author's words.

By some standards, admittedly even her own, her life was mundane. But distance provided clarity. That life was hers to live, and it would end if she stayed. A shell, a slice of her true self. There was no guarantee that she'd remain able to interact with other virtus. The choice was to leave now and try to advocate for change or stay here.

She would be at the mercy of an administration she no longer trusted and an organization that she suspected had plans she'd yet to uncover. The words were there, playfully enticing, in her heart, her throat, her tangled tongue. *Check me out.* A tidal wave of guilt threatened to consume her. Echo exhaled long and hard. She still had so many questions, so many questions, but they would have to wait.

To her friends, she said, "I'll come back."

Zera and Brahma inclined their heads.

"Even if you are able," Margaret said, drifting toward the cave opening as if she could just go out for a stroll, "I may be otherwise engaged."

Already this scene was flickering, bits and pieces of all three worlds bleeding together.

Echo understood how Margaret must have felt, but she had to go. "Gina, I'm ready. Try to return me in one piece, okay?" Echo paused, then added something she'd never said to her companion before: "Please."

Chapter Twenty-Two

Something was wrong.

Echo felt it like a heave, something reaching inside her head and wrenching, pulling.

Like being sucked through a straw. She'd tried calling out to Gina and Ada, but she had no voice. Without the familiar feel of her body, all Echo was left with in these torturous moments was her mind.

She was thrashing, groping for an anchor, something solid with which she could attach herself. Only there was nothing.

This is how I will die.

Or not.

She was utterly alone. And she could be stuck in this in-between forever. A maniacal madness bubbled somewhere deep that no longer had a true name. Was this what virtus felt every time they were returned to the collection while patrons so callously went about their day?

She had learned too much during her time in their world. Fascinating and horrifying. Solitary confinement with no outside time in the yard. Irregularly scheduled one-sided visits at the whims of the people on the other side of the chasm that separated them from reality.

The virtus were prisoners. The administration had lied about everything.

And Echo had lied to herself, hadn't she? She might have eternity to ponder that, without even the small comfort of an Ohio City milieu to think on it. Echo had whispered some questions to herself and let them lie unanswered. Let pass the furtive looks that Jesse gave her, how he'd sidestepped telling her too much about his existence. Protecting her. His literary warden. A complicit frontwoman for the administration that had done this to him.

She was surrounded by nothingness like strewn debris around a space station. Neither hot, nor cold. Absent the smell of freshly tilled earth or smoke from a fire. Devoid of the moon or stars to comfort her. Even her friends the virtus were out of reach.

How long would it take—

She felt a deep longing as raw as a treasured memory beginning to fade. For the nagging twitch in her neck when she slept too long on her right side. Craving for the feel of her morning coffee on the back of her tongue, the flavor lingering just a moment before the liquid trickled down her throat. The way she felt whenever she glanced at a mirror and admired how the red lipstick she favored complemented the deep-brown undertones of her skin.

She was outcast.

It seemed to Echo that awareness was an idea that existed outside, perhaps before, the substantive world. This was the pure version. She had thought that this realm would exist without pain, or bias, or preference—any of those other daily troubles. But all those things she'd felt before were still with her.

Her body, without her mind, was probably already dead, back in a library pod. Walter would discover it, and she felt bad for him. This man who had been nothing but kind to her, but whom she had dutifully held at arm's length, like she had everyone else in her life. She did it to protect them and perhaps herself, but there was still a meanness to it that she regretted.

Gina. Please help me. To Echo's mind that came out as a whimper. She was unashamed of the fact. She missed her friend. Back at home, all she'd wanted was to be left alone with her thoughts, and she had cruelly been granted her wish.

She fell into a fit then. Curses for her parents, the self-indulgent tech elite who'd put her here, herself and nearly anyone else she'd ever found herself on opposite sides of the fence with. By the end, her thoughts and words were a gibbering, blubbering mess. A prelude to madness.

And then, a savage hush.

Echo felt herself . . . unbecoming. Then fusing. Then unraveling. Like a fist, opening and clenching.

She let out a wail of anguish.

Long after she'd pleaded for death, an end to the relentless war of being, a microscopic hole punched through the other end of the straw.

Echo plunged back into her body like a diver into a pool. She opened her eyes and sobbed at the sight of herself, body and mind neatly collected in the package just as she'd left it. All the lovely aches and pains and imperfections, right down to the burn on her left hand, suffered in the kitchen while cooking last week. The pod, though, that felt infinitely smaller.

Move, Gina commanded. *Hide.*

Echo willed herself to her feet and stumbled. Her movements were stiff and awkward. She snatched the mask off the desk and stuffed it into her bag.

She put her hand on the door handle and had opened it only an inch before the sound of voices and feet pounding on the stairs greeted her.

Chapter Twenty-Three

Echo paused outside the pod and listened. They were certainly coming up the main stairway. Every decent building constructed in the last twenty years had multiple exits, though. So she turned right and ran to the back staircase. She wouldn't bother with the elevator.

But she was still not used to being in her body, and her movements were stilted. Her right shoulder, where she always had the hitch, chose that moment to give out, and her bag slipped to the floor. She managed not to trip up on the handle, but going back for it cost her precious seconds.

Enough for the words "Hold it right there" to snare her in place.

Echo bit her lip, and before she turned around to face her pursuers, she called upon her own personal mask. It slid on like a pair of well-loved slippers. The placid, unthreatening expression. Eyelids slightly raised. Posture relaxed and easy. "Officers," she said. "What seems to be the problem?"

"This is an active crime scene," Detective Reid said. This time he'd brought friends. A handful of plainclothes officers and two others, dressed impeccably, eyes sharp as daggers. "I thought I made that clear last time we talked."

"I'm the director and curator of this library. I'm not on UBI, so that means I get paid to be here. Like your job, the hours are whatever is required. And right now, I have a duty to ensure my collection and staff are okay." Echo felt the mask waver a bit.

"But you had to know that we closed you down," the detective said, approaching her. "I specifically put the tape up myself. Maybe you want to try again?"

The other officers had fanned out, searching the area. They opened and closed the pod doors, rummaging around inside. Detective Reid managed to watch both them and Echo at the same time. The sharply dressed pair—detectives, cops—just stood there stoically.

"I don't need to try again," Echo said. "What I told you is all there is to it. Now can I go home?"

"No," Reid said. "Not just yet. What time did you arrive at the library?"

Echo inhaled. "Early, around seven this morning."

He watched her for a moment before saying, "We have logs that indicate it was much earlier."

Echo knew, or at least hoped, that Gina had probably wiped those very logs. This was a bluff. "If there was someone here before me, then maybe you should talk to them."

"That would be me," Walter said, cresting the staircase like daybreak. "I'm the head custodian here at the library. The care and feeding within these hempcrete building blocks falls on me. And that, Officers, is twenty-four seven."

Walter wound his way around the group and came to stand beside Echo. She only just stopped herself from reaching over and grabbing his hand. "I can say without a shadow of a doubt that Mr. Sprigg is the most dedicated member of my staff," Echo added.

The group of law enforcement didn't seem moved by the display. "Can we speak to you over here?" the detective said, surprising Echo. She'd expected the suits to take charge. He gestured for Echo to follow him over to the front seating area. One of the officers guided Walter away. Echo realized that even *she* had no idea why he was really here. She tried to take the chair that would keep Walter in her sights, but

Reid beat her to it, and she was forced to sit opposite him, straining to hear any snatches of conversation behind her.

He had the posture of a slab of marble. He sat the same way he walked, stiff, as if he had iron supports lining his clothing. He inclined his head, tilting it slightly to the side again, and Echo caught a glimpse of a light flesh-toned ear pod. Standard police issue. The public had pushed for them to be made available to everyone.

"We have evidence of activity in the system. At least one of the virtual personages was checked out. Was that you?" He stopped and pointed his thumb toward Walter. "Or him?"

This one, Echo sensed, was not a bluff. She was reminded again of Gina's limits. "That would be me," she said.

"Curiously, we're unable to tell which one of the dupefakes you spoke with. Care to tell me which one and why?" he said, an accent that Echo couldn't place shortening his syllables.

"I'm sorry," she began and then stopped herself. She was so sick of apologizing. "You march in here unannounced and treat me like a criminal." (Wasn't she, though? There was the matter of the mask. She *had* withheld evidence.) "And you don't even bother to introduce those other officers." She stopped, which gave her an excuse to look back toward Walter. His shoulders looked relaxed, and an easy smile was on his face. "I think we should start with that, and whether or not you have any new evidence to share with me about the woman who attacked me and then somehow wound up dying in my lobby."

All chatter behind them stopped. Echo hadn't intended to raise her voice, but the last few days had taken a toll on her reserve, and for that, she was definitely not sorry. Reid regarded her, blinking and assessing her easily. The quiet stretched on until her breathing had returned to normal and then began to ramp up again. The detective surprised her. She was a master at this game, and he was beating her. There was no need to turn around to confirm it; all eyes were on them.

The effort not to squirm or open her mouth sent her sweat glands into overdrive. Sweat slicked the edges of her hairline, the sides of her nose, and her upper lip. She had the grim certainty that had she removed her shirt, she could have wrung out a gallon of sweat.

"They are members of your administration," Reid said finally. "If you don't know them, then your boss doesn't trust you any more than I do."

The elation Echo felt at winning the standoff dissipated like a spent balloon.

"Who did you check out of the library?" This from one of the administrators, who had come up alongside the detective.

Echo was forced to look up at him. *A duchess, a mathematician, and a philosopher.* "Jesse Cooper," she said. "A . . . a friend."

"Friend?" He and the detective exchanged a pitying glance that made Echo feel small. "Why?"

"Because it's what I do every day." Echo felt exposed, like she was sitting here naked. She'd never told anyone about Jesse, and somehow now, it felt like a betrayal.

"You're one of those rare individuals who takes their job way too seriously," the detective said. "We'll look into this Jesse Cooper."

"Why?" Echo said to a pair of raised eyebrows.

Just then, the voices behind them picked up again. In a moment, she heard Walter's voice: "If that's all, I'll be on my way then."

The sight of him walking past her, broad shouldered and sure of foot, was a desolate kind of artistry.

The detective snapped his fingers in front of her face, and she shot him a glare that would've wilted a rose in full bloom. She was ten again and so lost in the pages of whatever book had captured her attention that she'd tuned out her parents' bickering. Her mother's preferred way of bringing her back from those pages was that same infuriatingly dismissive gesture. She'd felt small and insignificant. That wasn't supposed to be the case here. This was her library, the place where she was supposed to be in charge.

"You seem really interested in the deceased. Since you brought it up, let's get back to that." He reached into his blazer pocket and pulled out a handheld display. He gestured for Echo to lean in. "Video footage from the evening of the incident. Take a look at this and tell me what's wrong with this picture."

She could feel the presence of the rest of the officers coming up behind them. An ice-cold spike hit Echo in the stomach. The detective tapped the screen, and the footage showed Echo walking to the doors and typing in her code. It showed her turning back to get her bag and then the woman stumbling inside. Echo's insides liquefied as she recalled the fear, the terror. The sight of the knife. Blood soaking the floor. It all came back.

"I have to use the restroom," she said lamely.

The detective shot her a look that had his skepticism written all over it. She didn't wait for permission but stood and headed to the bathroom. A few steps away, she returned and snatched up her bag. If she dared to meet the detective's gaze, she knew he'd read the guilt lurking there.

Inside the bathroom, she snatched a paper towel and dabbed at her face and pits while she paced. If they had the video, why hadn't they just arrested her and been done with it? Why the show?

Gina, Echo hissed. Before her assistant could answer, there was a knock at the door. And then the door opened, barely a centimeter. "Excuse me!" she said.

"Oh, I'm so sorry, Ms. London. I'll use the other one." At least the officer didn't come in. Echo didn't dare risk speaking to Gina now. She waited a moment, then pressed the incinerator button on the toilet and turned on the water, which annoyingly kept cutting off every five seconds. She scanned the room. There. She took out the mask and wedged it into the space under the sink. She leaned as close as she could to the door without actually touching it and listened. She opened it a crack. Then she stepped into the hallway and waited. There were voices on the other side of the wall.

Echo tiptoed in the other direction, toward the rear staircase. The one usually reserved for the staff. That video was a trap, as sure as the nose on her face. She needed time; no way she'd let them arrest her. A sound. She glanced over her shoulder, her feet still in motion. She hit what felt like a wall and spun around.

Instead of an officer with a pair of cuffs, it was Walter, who brought his forefinger up to his lips. He jerked his head toward the staircase. She stopped to remove her shoes and then followed him down to the first floor. She put her shoes back on, and the two of them were shoulder to shoulder, ready to step out of the entrance, when a familiar voice snared them.

"Going someplace?" Detective Reid. He was leaning against the railing at the bottom of the front staircase, flanked by two of his officers. The suits and the others were probably at the other entrances.

"Mr. Sprigg has nothing to do with this," Echo said. "If you don't have any objections, I'd like to dismiss him for the day. There's nothing else for him to do here."

Detective Reid gave Walter the once-over before agreeing. But Walter didn't move. "I'll check in with you tomorrow," Echo said, knowing full well she might be making that call from a cell. He left without another word.

The detective held up the display again and tapped it. The video showed the woman fall, then Echo rushing in and turning her over. The mask as plain as day. Then the video ended. *Gina, thank you,* she thought.

"It ends right there," Detective said. "Strange, huh? And get this. That mask the woman is wearing. It's gone. Neither the paramedics nor the officers on the scene saw hide nor hair of it. Did you?"

"It seems like you have some dissension in your ranks. Maybe one of the members of Human.exe have infiltrated the police department. They probably took it," Echo offered as earnestly as she could muster.

"Maybe," the detective said. He walked past her. "We'll be in touch. This is still a crime scene. Check with your administrators and get permission if you need to come back, with a police escort." And then the detective and his crew left.

Echo felt the tug to go back to the bathroom and grab the mask, but instead, she marched forward, dread in every step. She would strategize with Gina, and she would come back. She would just have to figure out how. Outside, she noticed Walter's silhouette at the top of the path. She walked away from her library. A squad car trailed her all the way home.

Chapter Twenty-Four

Echo hurled herself into her apartment like there was a strong wind clawing at her back. She kicked her shoes off and into the closet before stalking over to the bay window. With a finger, she adjusted the dial to increase the opacity and pasted her body against the wall, out of view. She inhaled, held her breath, and poked her head around. Her gaze traveled up and down Bridge Avenue like a pendulum on a swing. She didn't breathe again until she was sure the squad car was gone.

Echo reset the window, then went over and grabbed her bag from where she'd dropped it. It was fruitless, she knew, but she rummaged through it anyway. Nothing taken, but the mask, of course, wasn't there.

She collapsed onto the sofa and tightly grasped one of the throw pillows. The memory of that space between virtual and true reality flared through her body: weightless, lacking substance, catastrophic isolation. For a moment, she couldn't breathe.

And now Reid was probably suspicious.

"Gina," she said, slouching and leaning her head back. "Are you there?"

"You know I am," came the reply.

Echo bent over at the waist and sucked in air like she'd just run a marathon. "I take it you heard all of that?"

A hesitation. "You were pretty clear when you told me to give you your privacy, remember?"

She had been angry that Gina could listen when she wasn't supposed to be able to. Echo had turned the feature off at just the wrong time. "I guess what happened doesn't really matter so much. Suffice to say that you did your job and kept me out of the losing end of a battle with the police. You erased the video footage. Thank you."

Another hesitation. "Um, I didn't erase anything. I was so afraid that I'd lost you forever. I dedicated every qubit of my processing cores toward one task: extracting you from the virtual world."

Echo tilted her head, glancing upward, a useless gesture she'd adopted from the moment she'd gotten her assistant. It was hard to get your bearings while talking to a disembodied voice. "If you didn't erase it, then who did?"

Without the slightest hesitation, Gina responded, "The Model itself, uhh, possibly, I guess. But I'd place my bets on Ada."

Echo went midwinter cold. Someone was either working really hard to help her or throw her off. Two days ago, she'd been a librarian with an unremarkable life that suited her just fine—most of the time. On occasion she was prone to a plague of what-ifs. But now, the only question about her life that mattered was: What if she'd never been forced out of her old job at the Lewis Library?

No, there was another proposition. Virtus that shouldn't have been able to escape but had. Her slow but sure near dependence upon her collection. The ability to enter their world. Had her firing been the first step in a succession of events . . . ?

"Ada helped you, but the question is who told it to." Echo said this with a certainty that made her glance around her small apartment as if someone were watching, orchestrating this whole thing behind the scenes. But to what end?

"Hmm, speculation isn't really my strong suit," Gina admitted.

Echo's mouth had gone dry. She went to the kitchen and drained two glasses of water, after which her stomach growled loudly. When had she eaten last? A quick look in the refrigerator yielded half a container of chicken salad and a small box of crackers. She polished it all off with another glass of water while she thought. Only, no answers revealed themselves.

"I've got to get back in there and get that mask," Echo said aloud.

"But based on everything you've told me, you can't go back, at least not yet," Gina said.

Her companion was right, of course. But there was someone she could send in. Someone the police weren't interested in. He was the kind of person who would do what you asked without asking a million questions. "Gina, call Walter, audio only."

"Sprigg here," he said.

"It's me," Echo said. "I need—"

"Bail?" Walter finished.

"No," Echo said, annoyed. "I haven't done anything to require bail. I'm at home."

"Didn't seem that way to me, especially how quickly you followed me down those stairs. And I heard that detective talking about this video. I guessed it showed something that didn't paint you in the best light, but for the life of me, I couldn't figure what that could be. I mean, what? Did you snatch a book off the woman before she died?"

Echo didn't mean to, but she laughed. Too hard. A hysterical laugh that had only a little to do with Walter's deadpan comment. After she'd composed herself and apologized for the outburst, she explained the reason for her call.

"They'll be watching the place," he said.

"Which is why I'm going to call my boss and ask him to let you in. Knowing them, they'll want to reopen on Monday. I can say that I need you to go and get things ready for the patrons. We can't have the public walking into a lobby that still looks like a crime scene, can we?"

"This thing you want me to get. It's that important for you to have it? Would it be better to anonymously drop it someplace the feds will find it? Or better yet, get rid of the thing and make sure you stay on this side of some metal bars and bad food?"

Echo had to think about that. Why did she need the mask? She *could* have him get rid of the thing and be done with it. But after everything she'd learned in the virtual world, she suspected that something more dangerous was going on, and she couldn't let herself or the virtus down. There was no going back to her life before and pretending. Someone was planning something, she felt it in every nerve in her body, and it would affect her, affect the entire country—she was sure of it.

"It's that important to me," she finally told Walter.

He sighed audibly. "I'll try in the morning."

Chapter Twenty-Five

Echo had pored over every detail of the series of events that had transpired since her life was upended. Contrary to what she'd thought initially, it hadn't started with being accosted outside her office. It had begun earlier that day, when she'd taken the long route past the former site of F. M. Lewis.

It was there that she'd encountered the escaped virtu. Hadn't it worn a similar mask? And a nagging feeling at the back of her mind suggested it was a virtu she knew, but which one?

Never before had the walls of her apartment felt small. But it seemed that there was no room to get away from her own thoughts.

Exhaustion had claimed Echo by the time the sky began to blush, its muted light filtering through the opaque window, hazy like a warning she couldn't perceive. As apprehension curled in the air, sleep dragged her under. She'd lain there in her lofted bed for what felt like mere minutes when Gina's voice, morning-volume low, announced that she had an incoming communications request. *Walter,* she thought.

"Good morning. I have to say I'm surprised and more than a little disappointed to hear about your run-in with the police yesterday. I thought I made myself clear that the building was closed until further notice," Percy said. From the comms display beside her bed, she could see his face, fleshy and stern. This time, the vintage tee featured the words *Living Colour* in a hastily scrawled red script. The man lived and breathed old music. This one she'd seen more than once, so it must have been a favorite. "And please turn on your video."

Echo was in no way ready to be on-screen. She felt like a child being chastised, and she hated that feeling. "I'm not camera ready." That came out as sharp as she had intended; frayed and stomped-upon nerves had that effect on her. "You're right, I shouldn't have been at the library, but I've been at that place five days a week since it opened, often more. You used to praise me for my dedication."

"Is that all it was? Dedication?" Percy gave her his skeptical look.

"What else would it be?" Echo said. Percy was the sole member of the one-person group of managers whom Echo had ever considered more like a friend. She wanted to tell him everything, especially what she and Gina had just done. *Not yet,* she thought, *but soon.* "At some point, on Monday or Tuesday if I could guess, we'll be reopening to the public, and I don't want to walk through the doors at the same time as my patrons, trying to make sure that the police or that group haven't messed anything up."

Percy nodded. "Part of the reason why I'm calling. We've been cleared to do just that on Monday."

The day after tomorrow. She couldn't risk waiting that long. "That's great news," Echo said, trying to sound enthusiastic. And she was, in a way; she wanted the library open again, but she had to get back in before that.

"The engineering and admin teams will ensure that the systems are functioning properly. There really is nothing for you to do. Get some rest. You and the staff. You've been through a terrible ordeal. Don't try to pretend it hasn't affected you. We fought long and hard in this country to add mental services to our national health care. Make use of it."

"I will, thank you."

"I've no idea what could possibly be left to do, but give the police a wide berth. Get some air. Invite Carmen out to lunch," he said, rattling on. "Have I made myself clear?"

"I'll make sure the staff understand your directions," she said, then added, "Oh, Walter should be able to get in there sooner; he's got systems to check."

"No need. The bots can handle most of that stuff. The both of you need to learn to relax. I've got an idea for the perfect employee outing. Head out to the baseball game tomorrow. See if you can snag seats in the left field bleachers. See if you can snare a home run ball."

"Go Guardians," Echo drawled.

Percy gave her a smile and a thumbs-up.

She disconnected a moment or two quicker than was polite, but he could add that to her annual review if he didn't like it. She got herself out of bed and came downstairs. She needed that mask, and then she needed to see Jesse and Margaret.

She called Walter up and told him about the call with their boss, but he readily agreed to go anyway. They decided that if he was asked about it later, he would say he'd missed her call. After she sent Walter on his reconnaissance mission, hunger set in. In the bathroom, she paused during her morning essentials to really take a look at herself. She couldn't quite put her finger on it; perhaps it was anxiety-fueled imagination. She didn't exactly look different, but the reflection in the mirror was like watching herself through a flimsy gauze. A shroud that softened and blurred. But after a few blinks, she was back to herself. The churn in her gut tightened.

She opened the cabinet beneath the sink. Inches from Echo's fingertips was her makeup kit, dutifully stocked and restocked ever since her mom had given her concealer to cover her acne scars as a teen. A glance back in the mirror. She didn't need the layers; they were but another mask. She took out the case anyway, rummaged through until she found a nice plum-colored gloss, and swiped that on before shoving the rest back where it came from.

Closets had returned to normal size some time ago, and wardrobes had shrunk accordingly. Hers was dominated by the casual-chic things she wore to the library. The rest were breathable, comfortable loungewear. She pulled out the drawers beneath the hanging items and selected a pair of chocolate-brown sweats. Then she took down her braids, letting them cascade over her shoulders.

She would grab breakfast. In that time, hopefully Walter would have finished his task. Then she would call Gina and figure out how to face Jesse and Margaret, understanding, as she did now, what their lives, if you could call them that, were really like.

Echo pulled her door shut behind her and scanned the street. Bikers, walkers, and joggers, a few crawlers. The nation had shifted from the sham of fast-paced environments and productivity zealotry to one of leisurely movement. Populated by artists, makers, academics. Librarians. Everything in between. All that, at some point, the powers that be had thought machines could do better. They were wrong. "Coexistence instead of replacement" became the new message. The US scaled the ranks of the happiest nations. Not quite toppling Scandinavia, but impressive nonetheless. Life was better. But the resistance wondered if, once again, that tide might be turning.

"Move your ass, lady!" Echo's upstairs neighbor, whose name she'd never thought to ask, grumbled as he moved past her and took off at a jog with his dog, a long-haired shih tzu named Pepper. Ironic that she recalled the dog's name and not her owner's. A few steps down the street, Pepper copped a squat and did her business next to an oak tree encircled by a row of begonias. When she was done, they disappeared around the corner. The shit sat exactly where they'd left it until a passing cleaning bot whizzed by and tried to scoop it up. All it did was smear the mess on the street.

So much for advancement.

Had someone seen humanity for what it was and thought to reverse all that they'd gained? Did they think that we were inept, incapable? Was there going to be another tech bro–fueled comeback?

Echo trotted down the stairs, turned in the opposite direction of her neighbor. Coppery rings of sunlight enveloped her. The cloying feel of being watched measured her every step.

Chapter Twenty-Six

Echo realized that she and Walter had not decided on a time for his excursion over to the library. Calling him back and asking was on the table for sure, but he was always as good as his word. That meant the elusive virtue known as patience was in order. Not her strongest suit, but here was a chance to practice.

Halfway down the block, the distinctive whoop, whoop, whoop of a squad car's siren struck a paralyzing chord. Echo dared not turn around. She went rigid, right there in the middle of the walk. Her shoulders, legs, the breath caught in her chest, wound tight as a single-strand knot.

It sped past. She half expected them to discover they'd passed her and throw the car in reverse. But they continued in the other direction, in search of another target. Nobody liked the unspoken undertones of what one of those particular speeding vehicles meant, yet never before had Echo assumed they'd set their sights on her. Was this the way she wanted to spend the rest of her days? The answer was a resounding no. It was up to her to make sure that wasn't her reality.

Fears of apprehension aside, Echo swiveled her thoughts to another observation. The People's Library must have been even more of a community hub than she'd thought. On a weekend, with the facility closed, the streets were swarmed with people who otherwise might have made the trip there. From the looks of the lines outside a few of the cafés, half of them had ended up right here in her neighborhood.

Which, in a way, she supposed, was a good thing. UBI was just that, pretty basic. Enough to live on, not thrive. The costs of the food in the library's café were partially supplemented by donors from the National Literary Commission, so prices were about half what you'd find at a typical restaurant.

A procession of self-propelled bikers whizzed past sans the required helmets, and Echo remembered how in one of her earliest quid pro quo sessions, a virtu had been disbelieving that people had gotten to the point where they didn't even want to pedal their own bikes.

It had been nearly a year since Echo had walked this path on a Saturday, unsure of what Monday would bring. The morning air carried a chill that leaned more October than July, and she lamented the seasons that had not yet righted themselves. Duck Island had transformed into a blend of modern condos and small home villages, their courtyards buzzing with a routine string of communal activities.

In one of the courtyards, a small spirited group had gathered, their chatter mingling with the sizzle of breakfast cooking on an outdoor griddle. Children, still in their pajamas, darted among folding chairs and tables. A boy, maybe five or six, clutched an apple, holding it aloft like a torch, as the other children jumped up to try and grab it. This was a community where people knew their neighbors' names. Echo slowed, drawn in by their connections.

The rich scent of a morning feast wafted through the air . . . smoked sausages, crispy bacon. A man wearing an apron emblazoned with a screen printing of Playhouse Square's chandelier reigned over his half of the station like a celebrity chef, methodically pouring dollops of batter on the griddle. Within moments, they bubbled and set, turning into golden, fluffy pancakes.

A woman reclining in a patio chair caught her eye and smiled. "Never seen you so much as glance in our direction before."

Echo shrugged. "Too preoccupied, I guess."

"Never stopped before either."

Echo cringed. "I'm usually in a rush."

The woman raised an eyebrow, then nodded toward a table. Plates and cups and a bottle of amber-colored syrup bathed in morning sunlight waited. "You should join us, if you're hungry."

A part of Echo envisioned herself among them. To be welcomed. Her regaling the adults with tales of a fabricated account about her time as a gregarious Ohio State student. Laughing at someone's goofy dad joke. Reading a Virginia Hamilton story to the kids.

But all she could think about was the fact that pancakes were Jesse's favorite breakfast, a meal reserved for holidays when he was growing up. His weighty absence was evident in everything around her. She didn't know where she belonged, not really.

A half-moon truth, not full. Echo had allowed herself to feel something dangerous. She'd become fascinated by the virtual world, even with its walled confines. If things were reversed and she could spend even a sliver of a moment with Jesse, that pleasant feeling she felt deep inside whenever she was with him might have, in fact, kept her there. Permanently.

And would that have been so bad?

Yes, she reminded herself. Because she belonged here. Everyone had their time and their place in this world, and for better or worse, this was hers. Life was not a thing to fritter away, not even for . . .

She stopped herself from finishing that line of thinking.

"Thanks, but maybe another time," Echo said to the woman and continued on her way.

Now she'd learned that Percy was part of the group that managed UBI, which wasn't the version of himself he'd recorded and inserted as a virtu into her collection. He'd been conciliatory enough about his lie over their brunch, and his explanation for it made sense. But Echo hated feeling deceived, no matter the reason. Showing up at the library when he did. There was a connection there, and she knew just who she needed to help her find it.

Echo reached the coffee shop and, after a long wait, got her treasured cup and reversed course. Back home, for a fleeting moment, she considered throwing caution to the wind and going in to have some time with Jesse. To see his sad, winsome eyes alight upon her and remark on the color of her lipstick.

"Hey hey, Echo. Incoming communication request from Walter Sprigg," Gina said.

"Accept, accept," Echo said, waving her hands in a hurry-up motion.

The sound of wind filled the connection before Walter said, "It wasn't there."

Echo's heart sank at the same time the small hairs on the back of her neck stood up. "What do you mean it wasn't there?"

"Can't have said it any plainer."

"Did you look? Behind the basin?"

"I looked exactly where you told me to look," Walter said. "And I searched every inch of that bathroom, even though I knew it was gone. I'm telling you, it ain't there."

Echo was silent, and in that space, she heard the sound of crows cawing in the background. She raised an eyebrow. She got up and went over to the window, dialed up the opacity. "Where are you?"

"Almost home. Why?"

Echo shook her head and let it go. "I know I put it there, so somebody came back, searched the place, and found it. There's no other answer." But there was. A possibility, slim as a blade of grass.

"Most of the time, the obvious answer is the right answer. The cops were there when you went in the bathroom. They circled back and searched it after they kicked us out."

No sirens, no loud knocks on her door. Detective Reid's smug voice wasn't shouting at her to open up before he kicked the door in.

"You there?" Walter asked.

"I shouldn't have asked you to do this. I put you and your job in harm's way, and for that I'm sorry."

"If I didn't want to do it, I wouldn't have. The way I see it, you'd only need to apologize if you forced me, am I right?"

"I'm sorry anyway, but look, Percy called this morning. The library will reopen on Monday."

Walter didn't say anything, but his hesitation spoke volumes. She'd sent him in there for nothing. Another couple of days, and it wouldn't have been a risk.

"I'll see you on Monday, then. Piece of advice? You got a good life, a job better than most. Colleagues that respect you even though you treat them like lepers. Tend to that. Appreciate it."

Echo had no response. There was something else she had that many others didn't: parents. Imperfect, distant in their own rights, but they'd been there at her graduation and the opening ceremony for the library.

"The connection is closed," Gina said. "Echo, we have to talk about what happened."

"We've tried, Gina, and neither of us has a clue how—"

"Ask me things," Gina said. "Sure, sure, I'm pretty clever, but there's only so much I can do on my own. Prompt me."

"You didn't alter the video of me, but you saw the mask, right?"

Seconds ticked by, then: "I did."

"Can you see any markings? Any identifiers at all?"

"Scanning. I gotta said, it looks kinda creepy."

Echo waited.

"41.39299, -81.81766. Does that number mean anything to you?"

"No, what about you?"

"Checking . . . it's a GPS location. Not far from here. Brookpark Road."

Chapter Twenty-Seven

A yawning, miserable dread, the color of confirmation, saturated everything in Echo's being. In fact, this awareness had been there ever since her first and only interview for her new post. A malignant dormancy. Birthed by the fine print and esoteric questions in the lengthy employment contract that she'd breezed over. Her eyes had alighted upon the considerable bump in salary, and those uncomfortable particulars faded into the white space on the screen. Apprehension manifest in the unanswered questions. Access denials. Exclusion.

Authority, or what passed for it with a staff of six, was the consolation prize she'd clung to.

"I need the virtus," Echo told Gina.

"Why? The virtual personages don't have intelligence," Gina said.

"But they do," Echo countered. "A week ago, I would have agreed with you. I would have applauded the programming. I mean, to the average person, that ability to interact is a technological marvel. It's a shame you couldn't see it, but everything I learned while I was with them convinced me that they aren't just paper cutouts on the other side of a screen."

"Okay, I'll give you that, but not the kind of intelligence that would be required to do what we did. Ask me another question."

Echo took a sip of her coffee. Cold. She dumped it in the sink.

"What's at the coordinates you just gave me?"

"A former elementary school but now an unmarked building of some kind. Some interesting tech securing it too."

Great. Depending on where this line of inquiry took her, Echo might need to go and see for herself. "Search the archives," she said to Gina. "Learn everything you can about the technology behind the People's Library."

"Oh, that's a good one! Give me a minute. Make that two."

As Echo waited, she considered how intelligence had ended up being both less than the originators thought and more at the same time.

"I'm ready," Gina said sooner than expected. That kind of assimilation would have taken Echo a year, maybe two.

"Let's start with the technology. What do you know about the intelligence?"

The seconds stretched on this time. "Ada, as we affectionately call her, is an instance of the Model. She—"

"Ada isn't a she," Echo said.

"Hmm, *I'm* definitely a she, and I think Ada probably feels—"

"Feels?" Echo was incredulous.

"Well, like, yeah . . ."

"You know what, forget it," Echo said.

"She," Gina began again, "was specifically designed to administer your one-of-a-kind library."

Echo thought back to Percy. "And the NLC commissioned Ada's development?"

"That I don't know. There's really no record."

Echo was pacing by now. It helped her think, but she stopped. No record? "What can you tell me about how it works?"

"So, Ada is like an octopus, a really big one. She's got offshoots. They manage the collection of virtus and much of the building, aside from the tasks that still require human intervention. Solar and wind only do so much; the rest is backed by a fusion-powered data center west of Cleveland in Brook Park, near where the old airport used to be."

Echo pondered all this while trying to come the long way around to her next question, the scary one. "Can you get me back into the virtual world?"

"I don't really want to do that. I barely got you out the first time. In fact, I didn't. Ada got wind of me trying and helped." Gina sounded genuinely afraid. But that was impossible. Echo reminded herself that her companion was code. Designed to mimic the required emotional response.

Or could she?

"I appreciate you reminding me of the danger," Echo said. A thought occurred to her then; she'd see if Gina answered the way she expected. "If a companion had an idea, say in the case of an extended illness, that the person they're designed for is going to die, how would that affect them, based on your engineering?"

"Each of us is custom designed, tailored to the requests of the person we're assigned to. When that person is gone, so are we. But we wouldn't want to die any more than a human does."

Echo couldn't decide if Gina was more afraid for her or for herself. She finally decided on both.

"Let's try this another way. Even though it's supposed to be impossible, virtus have escaped before. Can you do that instead? I mean, on purpose, bring one out of the library?"

"Both times, bringing you into the virtual world and bringing you out, it was as if I walked a lighted path to a gigantic, glowing doorway, holding your hand," Gina said. "I kept driving my shoulder—or at least what passes for my shoulder—into that door, chipping away at it but getting nowhere. But then I saw footsteps in the glow at the bottom, and it was as if someone or something waited for me to throw my shoulder into it again, and when I did, they yanked the door open."

"It sounds like you crafted a map, found the path, and walked it, and then the library did what it was supposed to do—stopped you from entering. But then it changed its mind?" Echo recounted.

"That's exactly what I'm saying," Gina said.

"You had help." Echo plopped down on the sofa. "Ada decided all on her own, didn't she?"

"Beats me."

"Margaret Cavendish," Echo said. "Bring her here if you can. If you both can."

Chapter Twenty-Eight

The workings of Echo's disquieted mind churned as she waited for Gina to tell her that the absurd thing she'd asked for was possible. Rules broken, no, obliterated. Laws, statutes. There had to be something in the tangled web that was her employment contract that she was skirting. But to protect her staff and collection, she would take the chance. The question was, Would anyone notice?

When she grew tired of pacing, Echo stopped and surveyed her apartment. Aside from the bathroom (which she couldn't use unless it was pristine), you'd have to squint to notice, but when you did, you'd see all the places where she'd neglected to do her weekly cleaning and organizing. Apparent as the worn depression where she most often curled up on the sofa.

The jacket she'd had on earlier was still slung across the back of the dinette chair. Relentless motes of dust coated every visible surface. Corners and nooks had remained stubbornly untouched, despite the robovac's extended-reach attachment she'd splurged on.

Her place was small, and she liked it that way. It was one of the few things most everyone had applauded once the mini-mansion trend had reversed. On a good day, she'd finish a thorough cleaning in about a half hour.

After she'd scoured the apartment's surfaces until everything shone like high-beam lights and even set the toilet to an automatic-clean cycle, twenty-two minutes had passed.

Echo made a low, exasperated sound and trudged over to the sofa, where she plopped down in the corner and angled herself to look outside. One swipe on the controls beside the window frame and the world revealed itself. The sights, if not the sounds, of life passing by, oblivious to the conundrum their quiet neighbor found herself in.

She had to talk to somebody. Gina was busy, maybe even putting herself in danger. She'd already asked too much of Walter, and no way would she risk involving any of the other staff.

"Gina," she said.

"Still working my way through some obscure code," Gina said.

"Can you spare a sliver of yourself to call my mom?"

A few seconds later: "Everything all right?" Her mom's hair was wrapped in one of the new shimmery bio-silk scarves in the pattern of the Sahara Desert. At the slightest movement, the sands rippled with an unseen wind.

"Now that I see your lovely face, it is," Echo said.

"You're just saying that because this is what you'll look like in twenty years," her mom said.

"And that would suit me just fine," Echo said. "How's Dad?"

"Uly," she called. "It's Echo." Her face clouded over. "He lost another account today. He's taking it pretty hard."

And now he wasn't taking her calls? "He blames me, doesn't he?"

"That man never let anybody pressure him to do anything. He made his decision, and he'll have to live with it."

"And if that means he loses the business?"

"That's what UBI is for. That, or—"

"Or what?" Echo said.

"He's always wanted to move to Cape Town, you know that."

Rebecca London had asked Echo's father to marry her three months after they met. He'd told her no then and three times more after that. But marry they did. (Rebecca was relentless when she wanted something.) She rubbed her lips together, telling Echo there was more, but she wouldn't be sharing it.

"You sure you're okay?" Mom asked.

"No," Echo said. "I'm not. I've had the worst last couple days of my life. And my own father is probably sitting there off-screen refusing to talk to me, and you don't have the guts to make him."

Echo ended the call before leaning her head back against the sofa. Everyone she could talk to about this was on the other side of a virtual wall that she had no idea how to negotiate on her own. An intense loneliness overtook her. She was an errant island in the middle of the Atlantic, lost between two continents she couldn't reach. She realized how often this was really the case in her life. Even in a room full of people, she was often alone. Only, she felt a certain comfort in their presence. The buzz and activity of the library floors was something she missed now more than she would have thought.

She tapped her earring. "Gina, any luck?"

"It should be simple, it really should. I'm trying to shred the code that limits virtu locales to the library, but every time I edit a line, it rewrites itself. Even with Ada and me tag-teaming, the Model is fighting us. Don't you worry, boss, I'm gonna do this."

What if . . . Echo thought. If Gina was successful in extracting Margaret, what if the administration made this a feature of the library, available to everyone? In the same way patrons could download an e-book, they could do the same thing with a virtu. Would that make life better for them? Less cruel?

Echo thought about all this and how she would propose it without tipping the administration off to the fact that she'd already figured out how to do it, or at least Gina had. Her eyelids grew heavy. The throw blanket tantalizingly close, on the other end of the sofa. She checked the time. Only three bitter minutes had passed. Neither of her parents had bothered to call her back either. Echo grabbed the blanket and snuggled into the plush, warm softness and commanded herself to relax. Curled up beneath the brilliant sunlight suffused by the window, she fell asleep.

A splash of cold water on her face roused her.

"Dear heavens, I thought you dead." Margaret Cavendish. Duchess of Newcastle upon Tyne. Mad freaking Madge. The small woman stood there in Echo's living room, thin pale fingers gripping her favorite coffee mug.

Echo leaped up from the sofa, wiping at her face and fanning her now-soaked sweatshirt. "You could have maybe tapped my shoulder? Did you think of that?"

Margaret thinned her lips. She wore her traditional dress, waist cinched to something impossible. Powder on her face, rouge on cheeks and lips.

But then the two women regarded each other and broke out in grins like small girls. Echo couldn't help it; even as she wiped a forearm across her face, she was happy to see Margaret. Her first houseguest since Walter visited to drop off her bookrack, but then technically, he'd only been to the doorway. She hadn't invited him in, had she?

Margaret was really here, not encased in a 3D plane. She was definitely more substantial than that, but still not fully fleshed out. Echo reached out her hand; Margaret raised hers. As they touched, Echo's finger registered a slight resistance. But then Margaret's atoms, or whatever it was that made her visible in this sense, scattered, then reassembled when Echo pulled back.

"I'm no more real than I am in there," Margaret said. There was no mistaking the disappointment in her voice.

"But how did you manage to hold that glass?" Echo pointed to where it now sat on the floor.

Margaret shrugged. "I've no idea. I simply acted." Then she turned around, really taking things in. "Is this yet another virtual space? 'Tis so devoid of adornment, bland even. Pray, who is it that we are bid to encounter in this place?"

Echo immediately felt self-conscious. "This is my home."

Margaret froze, recognition blossoming. "Thus, it must follow that . . ."

"That you're out in the world. The real world," Echo supplied. Then she let the excitement sink in. Gina and Ada had done it. "This is incredible."

"How did you do it?" Margaret asked.

"Gina?"

"We did it!"

"Can you document how you were able to extract Margaret from the collection?"

"I can document what I did up to a point, and then, let's just say I saw the door, but I didn't insert the key."

"Like before," Echo said.

"Exactly," Gina said.

"Can you check her back in?" Echo asked.

"Indeed, I have just arrived," Margaret protested. "I've scarce had the occasion to see or do anything."

"Except insult me," Echo answered.

"That was an observation; if you perceived an insult, then that says more about you than I. And besides, I'm not ready to return." She walked, actual leg-movement walking, over to the window. "I desire to take leave of this room and set forth. Pray, might I? Is it within the realm of possibility? My word, look at all those people! And that!" She inhaled sharply as Echo came up beside her. It was an electric scooter. "Dear heavens above, what is it?"

Echo thought about it. This was Margaret's first time out in the real world. As much as Echo wanted to explore the virtual counterpart, Margaret held the same curiosity for hers. Like a captive released after being imprisoned for centuries. To deny her, to send her back, would be unbearably cruel. Her neighbor, the one with the shih tzu, started walking up the stairs, his gaze, like everyone else's, raised toward her open window. This was why she usually kept it on the opaque setting.

"Get back!" She pulled Margaret away and reset the window. She couldn't risk a four-centuries-dead duchess being the first person he ever saw visiting her.

Margaret pulled away. "Do not send me back," she said, barely above a whisper, then with more forcefulness: "Not yet, anyway."

Echo's heart shattered into a million jagged pieces. She was positively gutted at the desperate pleading in her friend's eyes. Margaret's entire body was tense with the need to exist. But Echo had so many unanswered questions.

"Can you check her back in?" Echo repeated and then held up a hand to stall the rebuke she saw Margaret preparing to unleash.

"I think so," Gina said. "Yes, I believe so."

"How long does she have? How long can she stay here?" Echo asked Gina. Margaret became increasingly pale and fidgety.

"That we'll have to find out together."

"Tell me, what has transpired?" Margaret said, fingers lightly grazing her collarbone. "Why am I here and not the reverse? Unless, of course, you have unraveled that mystery all on your own (which, though you are capable, I doubt), you must have much to share."

Echo agreed, but then she thought of Zera and Brahma. "Gina, can you withdraw more than one virtu at a time?"

Gina hesitated. "I could, or I could lose one or all of them. The only way to know for sure is to give it a go."

Echo turned to Margaret, who was standing near the dinette set, attempting but failing to pull out the chair. There was a look of childlike wonder on her face, which only served to make Echo feel guiltier.

"What does it feel like?" she asked. "To be here?"

"It feels wonderful, and it feels awful," Margaret said.

Echo turned away as she thought of Jesse. Was he worried? Was that even possible? She didn't want Margaret to see her vulnerability.

"You're not doing well at hiding," Margaret said. "It's even more clear to me now that I know this is your home. There are no photographs. No artifacts from your worldly travels. It feels sparse and temporary. You spend all your time at work and with us, the virtual personages. And, judging from that look in your eye, there's someone more important to you than even I whom you're thinking about."

"Gina, check out virtual personage Jesse Cooper," Echo said and then turned, refusing to see the judgment in Margaret's eyes.

"Unless this Mr. Cooper is going to be able to help us solve this mystery, I don't know why you're asking to check him out."

Because I want to. "Because we have to test it to see if it's possible," Echo said.

"One moment. I'll give it a try," Gina said.

Echo's breathing intensified as she scanned her place, not knowing where Jesse would appear if this worked. It was a buzzing sound, and Margaret's startled "Oh," that drew her attention. A flickering, blurred, indistinct shape that could have been Jesse. His expression was shocked . . . or pained. Echo raced over. "Jesse!" She spoke his name, willing him to materialize.

"I don't think I can hold him," Gina said. "With the other virtu."

It was a feeling more than a sound. Of a presence whizzing past Echo. The door didn't open, but Margaret passed through it nonetheless.

"No!" Echo screamed. She took a step to go after Margaret but then turned back to a wavering Jesse, his hand extended toward her. She heard a scream in the hallway. Echo turned and raced out of her apartment barefoot. She stepped onto the street and looked both ways. The sound of a loud car crash drew her down the street.

Chapter Twenty-Nine

There was another car accident that haunted Echo. Her mom hadn't always bowed to the whims of Dad's fickle moods. That had changed when they almost lost him. Echo was too young to understand all the particulars of what it meant to have a stroke. It didn't matter because the look in every adult's eyes told her he might not make it.

Echo took in Dad's icy-blue hospital gown and the bile-green glow of all the monitors in his hospital room when the lights were down. For her, those painful memories were imprinted in her mind as the number forty-seven.

It took weeks of days and nights spent in that tiny antiseptic-smelling room, but he recovered. Years later, that illness was but a bad memory. Echo was a teenager when Dad began pressing her to get a driver's license. What's worse, he decided to teach her himself.

One Saturday morning, after an argument about how long she had or hadn't stopped at a stop sign, Echo slammed on the accelerator and took off. She'd been sailing down the street, doing just fine, until she spotted someone on the sidewalk wearing a sports jersey with the number forty-seven in big bold lettering. Her vision swam with those numbers and pushed her into a panic not unlike what she'd felt the first time she saw Dad in that hospital bed.

Echo wrapped that car around a two-hundred-year-old oak tree and had never driven again.

Being born was more of a submissive reality; you really had no say in the matter. And if that was the case, for everything the world threw at you in an attempt to break you, then Echo believed that living was an act of stubborn defiance. And she had retreated from living to spend all her free time with people who were done with the business of living.

But there was so little in her present reality to compel her to think about anything more than the time she spent at work. Until a woman had walked into the People's Library and, in the most horrible way, bidden her to open her eyes.

It struck Echo then. All those existential questions she'd forgotten about added a piece to the puzzle. That mask, existence, consciousness. They were all related. And so were the library and universal basic income.

Echo didn't want to think of the germs that were probably colonizing her bare feet right now, nor the sharp pain that meant something had punctured her skin. Never before had she run out of the house barefoot. And now this. The remains of one mangled car and a biker's dented helmet lay strewn in the middle of the street. The biker and the driver were engaged in a heated argument, and the sound of a siren told her to move on. Of Mad Madge, there was no sign.

"Gina." Echo's voice was strangled and desperate. "Can you get Ada to check in virtual personage Margaret Cavendish?"

"She's moving," Gina said. "We'll need her to slow down or stop so we can snag her."

And what about Jesse? Echo thought, but she decided to deal with one thing at a time.

Echo gave up looking after a time and trudged back to her apartment. She'd made such a mess of things. Up the steps, through the door, ignoring the stares and questioning looks.

No sign of Jesse inside, and no need to question Gina about it. Bringing him here was beyond her means, at least for now. Or maybe it had something to do with Margaret's movements. Every answer was a doorway to another question.

"Heavens above, I see now why you remain holed up here or at the library," Margaret said after suddenly appearing out of nowhere. "You live in an absolutely maddening era. Far too much stimulation."

Echo considered hugging her, smacking her, erasing her from Ada's memory. In the end, she said, "I could have told you that, but I guess you had to see for yourself."

That seemed to relax Margaret. She blushed and glanced down, slipping into her bashful persona again.

"I learned something," Echo said.

Margaret hovered. "As have I."

Echo went on to tell Margaret about UBI and the test that was supposed to measure one thing while, she suspected, it was doing something altogether different. Then Margaret told her that a thought had occurred to her during her brief excursion outdoors. "Something is assisting your digital assistant."

"Yes, we know that," Echo said.

"And obviously, someone, most likely the agency behind this universal income group, is gathering a list of individuals based on their tests."

"Check," Echo said. "And the mask is related to human consciousness. The whole library is a thought exercise, an experiment of sorts in what it means to be alive, to be conscious."

The pair were silent for a time, arranging and rearranging their thoughts, searching for any other connections. Finally, Echo looked up and snapped her fingers. "They're probably related," she said. "Universal Trust may just be a figurehead in all of this. I wonder who else is involved."

"Who indeed. But this examination you spoke of suggests that this group only covets unique individuals, intelligent. So, what about the rest of you?" Margaret said. It wasn't lost on Echo that she didn't include her in the list of intelligent individuals. “You did not subject yourself to this examination, you say?”

Ah, reprieve.

“I didn’t. So, they believe these people are the most worthy candidates for some kind of human and AI experiment. My guess is that Human.exe must have found out.”

“That stunt, the death in the lobby, wasn’t about you at all. It was about them trying to clue everyone in to what was happening.”

“But then they would have just said so.”

“Unless they were working together after all.”

“Evolution. An integration of people and technology,” Echo whispered, the words searing her throat like a brand, terror coiling around every syllable.

But not as much as when a loud insistent banging sounded at her door.

Chapter Thirty

Echo waited, Margaret's rogue presence clinging to her. Nobody identified themselves, so not the police. She moved back to the far corner of her place, maybe not far enough, and whispered for Gina to call up the display and see who was on the other side of the door. Two figures. Suits that screamed "official" without them having to say a word. Higher than the locals, most likely.

She should have known that bringing Margaret here was a mistake. A risky thought occurred to Echo, but one more preferable to whatever awaited her. Another knock, more insistent this time. Echo closed her eyes, muttered a prayer, and called on Gina and Ada. "Check in virtual personage Margaret Cavendish." She hesitated, Margaret's eyes gone wide. "And Echo London."

If they broke in—and Echo figured that if they did, they would do so in stealth—all they would find was her inert, hopefully still alive, body. It would only buy her time, but it would also be one of the greatest discoveries of the past decade. The fact that she might not be able to come back was an afterthought.

Margaret hissed, "What are you doing?"

Testing a theory, Echo mouthed.

In a moment, Margaret disappeared. Echo hoped that she was comfortably secure in her virtual environment. The word "comfortable" bothered her, now that she knew the reality of what their world was like. But maybe she could change that.

A series of beeps sounded. They were accessing the code to open her door. Echo looked all around and, for the first time, thought her home too small. Open floor plan to the extreme. The bathroom was the only real room with a door, and that would be the first place they looked.

"Come on, Gina," she murmured.

And then her gaze landed on the coat closet. She rushed over, gently opened the door, and slipped inside, shoving aside coats and jackets, tripping over shoes. She winced at the small click when she slid the door shut. She stood there, pleading for Gina to save her. Uncomfortable as it was, she crouched down and sat with her knees pulled up in front of her.

The final beep sounded, and she heard the door open. Feet shuffling inside, probably with their filthy shoes on too. Echo held her breath. Their voices were muffled from her perch, but she heard them say, "She doesn't appear to be home. They can't have gone far. Let's contact Mr. Oliphant and—"

Who was Mr. Oliphant? There was more, but Echo didn't hear it because she felt herself dissolve, led as if by a virtual hand, into another world.

The first thing Echo noticed was the difference. The first time they'd attempted this transition, she had made this journey alone and afraid. This time, however, she wasn't alone. A presence, an existence akin to the feel of an indiscernible silent second self. But even that wasn't right. What she felt was nothing like herself. It was all light and energy. A tiny unknowable universe. And that universe quieted her fear and made her feel as warmly received as a newly birthed star.

Nearly all her senses had abandoned her. Enveloped by a darkness, not wholly unsettling. There was no way to judge left from right, up from down. Echo felt suspended but drifting, purposefully drifting. She was insulated here. No secret agencies, duplicitous bosses, or the judgments of other people could harm her. Her travel companion thus far was impartial.

Echo could get used to this.

As soon as that thought occurred, time rallied. She felt a virtual push. Echo fought feebly but soon found herself on the next leg of her journey. Her mouth had no purpose here, tongue and vocal cords either gone or useless.

When sound came back to her, it was not Gina's voice, nor that of Jesse or Margaret. The sound was like wet murmurs off a calm sea. It soothed her like an oily balm on parched skin. Wrapping around, cocooning. *You are well,* it said.

Vaguely, Echo remembered Walter, the rest of her staff, and her parents. The walk she enjoyed taking to work. The look of Lake Erie on a cloudy day. The city that had taken every slight and scorn the rest of the country threw at it and used it as raw data to transform itself. It had only wanted to be seen for the hidden jewel that it was. Echo thought that it had been wildly successful.

She was able to see things and understand in a way she never had before. Vast amounts of information at her virtual fingertips. Every question she had now had an answer. *What time is it? Where am I? What year was the city of Cleveland incorporated?* All the virtual instances popped up to answer her at will. All her questions answered except one: *How?*

Echo knew without seeing that she was inside Ada's virtual mind. Distantly, she wondered about her body. If they had found her in the closet and taken her to some secret facility. If her body had or would survive this.

You are well. The answer came again. The flow of information wasn't overwhelming like you would expect. Instead it came to her when she asked. The presence there as a facilitator. Not at all intrusive. It was like having an enhanced, integrated version of Gina. An infusion. Echo wanted to enter a virtual world. There was so much to do. So many things to solve—the mask, Universal Trust's plan—but at this moment, all she wanted was to see, to actually be in the presence of one person.

The push became a pull, and Echo was drawn forward along a lighted path toward something. A thin white line appeared in the dark. It wrote itself horizontally; then the upper-left corner peeled back to reveal a scene.

Of course, she was hoping for Jesse. He stood staring out a window, his entire visage permeated by misery. What she witnessed, the bleak reality of his existence, roused an indignant rage. They'd lied to her. He'd lied to her. The virtus were supposed to be inactive when not engaged with a patron. Echo had craved alone time more than almost anything else, but even she would break under this kind of solitude.

She would do everything in her power to change how the virtus existed, or she would destroy the whole damned library.

"Pouring" was the word Echo would use to describe how she felt herself manifest in Jesse's space. The "berthing" was what he'd called the sailors' sleeping quarters. If she stretched her arms out, they could almost touch the walls. All metal. A desk and miniature office space on one side, two narrow bunks on the other. Against the rear wall, Jesse stood with his forehead leaning against the porthole. Echo knew he stared out at water he could never take a dip in.

It took a moment for him to register her presence. Then he turned to her, confusion knitting his brows. His expression was a wash of conflicting emotions. Foremost among them, the way he glanced away, eyes cast downward, told her that she'd embarrassed him. Exposed him in a way that he'd worked hard to shield from her. In the time it took for her to take a step toward him, that pendulum swung momentarily to anger.

"What have you gone and done?" he said.

"I wish I knew how to explain it to you."

Jesse glanced behind her, and she turned to follow his gaze. The nothingness on the other side of the world she'd just emerged from was still there. A rectangular road that she hoped would take her back to her body.

"Is this real, or am I having an ugly virtual dream?" Jesse said.

"I'm here." Echo turned back to him. "For real."

"You tried to bring me into your world, and when that didn't work, you came to mine," Jesse said. They were still several feet apart, apprehension forging a distance.

When Margaret appeared in her apartment, she had been unsubstantial, as if composed of air and attitude. They couldn't touch each other. It had been the same the first time Echo was here, working with the other virtus.

She wiggled her toes in her shoes and ran her hands up and down her arms. Undeniably different. There was weight, a solidity to herself that she hadn't experienced before. She could see Jesse working through the same questions in his mind.

He held out a hand, and Echo nearly recoiled. She knew that if it was possible, that if she and Jesse were able to be real together in this place, this prison of time, then she might never leave. Echo felt, rather than saw, the breach closing behind her. A sliver of her wanted to turn and jump headfirst through.

Echo inhaled and reached out to touch Jesse.

Chapter Thirty-One

When their fingers touched, the well that had housed Echo's fears and anxieties collapsed into rubble. She erupted into sobs.

Jesse closed the distance between them and wrapped his arms around her. He made a small, surprised sound. Echo tensed for a moment, confirmation that what she hoped for was real, so very real. The tether to her old life was fraying, and Echo didn't know how stop it, or if she even wanted to.

He held her closer, and she allowed herself to be drawn into him. His arms felt strong and right. He smelled of the ocean. He was taller than she'd thought. The uniform felt stiff beneath her fingers. The wool prickly.

Echo opened to him and started to tell him the whole story. Everything from the moment she'd met the escaped virtu to the agents knocking on her door this morning. He led her to the wooden chair while he sat on the edge of the lower bunk. Jesse listened intently and stopped her to ask questions. When she was done, she lay back against the chair and expelled a breath.

"What they've done here at the library was to deceive all of us, apparently," Jesse said.

"And they're determined to keep it all a secret," Echo confirmed.

"The library helped you get here. This Ada and your Gina, if they're even separate entities anymore. Ever wonder why?" Jesse said, taking her hand.

"I have," Echo said, considering his words. The more they worked together, the more she realized the lines between Ada and her companion *were* oddly blurring. "As much as I would like to think of the intelligence behind the library as this great matchmaker that wants nothing more than for us to be together, I think the truth is much more sobering."

Jesse smiled at her then, and it melted Echo's insides. "And that truth is?"

"It either desperately wants or doesn't want to go along with this plan."

Jesse raised an eyebrow. "I don't follow."

"It helped me get here, and as much as I expected it to be, it wasn't exactly unpleasant. This is going to sound crazy, but . . ." Echo paused, searching for the right way to explain it. "There was a time . . . If you needed to search for some information, you'd go to the library and ask a librarian for help finding a physical book, or likely many books, on the topic. Fast-forward, and then you used a physical keyboard, like a typewriter, and entered the request on a website known as a search engine, and the computer would spit out page after page of articles, journals, and even books on that subject. And now, with AI, everyone has their own custom virtual assistant, and you can just ask them what you need to know. But the connection is external. You need a subdermal microchip embedded beneath the skin for the neural connection, plus a wearable with a microphone for audio. I'm going a long way around to explaining that when I coexisted with the intelligence, it felt different, like an evolution to whatever our next phase of searching will be." Echo stopped short of saying it was better, though it 100 percent was.

"How so?"

"All the answers to your questions are immediate. You think it and have the answer instantaneously, almost like it's your own brain producing it."

Jesse looked skeptical.

"You know what stalled the so-called age of intelligence the first time around? It was the fact that it never progressed past the point of what essentially made it a parrot spitting out all the information that one of us fed it. It could summarize and produce stuff based on all of humanity's existing knowledge."

"But it couldn't think, innovate," Jesse said.

"Exactly. Maybe that changes with the pairing; maybe taking advantage of the centers of the human brain that govern creativity and independent thought can help it advance. Plus, now, it gets a chance to feel what it's like to be human. To see through my eyes." She stopped and grabbed Jesse's other hand. "To feel."

"Like a voyeur?" Jesse's expression turned grim.

"No," Echo sputtered. "Or maybe yes."

"But that means it's always watching." Jesse glanced around his room. "I hate that feeling here. Trapped, with eyes always on me."

"Nobody is watching you," Echo countered, and at the narrowing of Jesse's eyes, she immediately wished she could take the words back. Her tongue was way too free around him.

Jesse jerked his hand away and stood. Talking as he walked away, his back a wall between them. "You were the head of this here place, and you had no idea how your collection even worked. You didn't know anything about us except what they told you. You accepted it without questioning them or me."

"Then why didn't you say something? Why not just tell me?" Echo stood and came up behind him. Her voice was on that edge between holding steady and cracking. She leaned into his back and wrapped her arms around his waist.

When his hand slid over hers, she relaxed. "At first, I thought you were just one of them. You know, in on the whole thing. I wanted to be deleted, but then as more people started checking me out, I liked it. Talking to them and seeing how the world had changed. My ego soaked up all that attention. Questions about the Golden Thirteen. We didn't know it at the time, but we made history. I like talking to those folks.

I *love* talking to you. And when I came to care more about you than myself, I couldn't tell you because I knew what it would do to you."

Echo came around to face Jesse again. This man who was no more, caring about her in a way that she'd never been able to match in the real world, and maybe never would. Part of her realized that it was because she clung to Jesse. Spent all her time here and acted like a passenger on a train passing through her real life like it was just scenery from behind a window.

They watched each other until Echo turned away. Her emotions were taking her to a place she didn't need to be. "What if . . . I stayed here, with you?"

She heard Jesse's footsteps and, from the corner of her eye, saw that he'd gone once again to that window he'd been staring out of when she arrived. She joined him. She moved close enough that their shoulders were touching, and she glanced out the porthole window. She didn't know what she'd expected. Water, as far as the eye could see. Beautiful sunlight glinting off easy waves. Not another ship or person to be seen.

Echo thought about all the times she'd stood at the breakwater or in her office and stared out at the lake. Been mesmerized by it. And Jesse apparently did the same thing. It was quiet, unnervingly so, and it occurred to her once again that this was the life of a virtu. But if she was here with him, they could talk, share in each other's company in so many delightful ways. And if Ada could transport them to other virtual spaces like it had helped Gina do before, then the loneliness wouldn't be quite as stark.

Echo glanced around the room again. Small, too small. Jesse hadn't answered her yet. All the problems with the administration, the anti-AGI group, the state of the world, she could leave it all behind.

"I've thought about it, you know. What it would be like if you never had to check me back in after one measly hour every day—no weekends, mind you. If you could be here with me or if I could be out there with you. Problem is, I'm already dead and can't exist again except within these walls. And for you to join me here, that would require you to be dead, and that I just couldn't live with. No pun intended. As bad as I want you here, no. This is your time, and you got a life to live out there."

Echo tugged on his arm so he'd face her. "You know what's going on out there right now? Child labor, political infighting, most of the coasts are gone, and war, at least three of them raging right now. Nothing has changed. Human beings haven't changed, and I really don't think we will."

"Unless what you're talking about with this new technology will do just that," Jesse said.

"What about you?"

"You need to leave, and I've been thinking about this but I just now decided. The only way for you to go on is if you delete me once you're back."

"What?" Echo reeled. "No."

"You're wasting time here with me. I had a wife and a couple kids. You never asked about that either. They're dead, as I am, but they didn't serve in a war, so nobody picked them to get a second chance. You have to stop this group from whatever it is they're planning. Echo, you got people that need your help, including the virtus. You can't do that sitting here with me."

He made sense. But that didn't mean she liked it.

"And about what you said connected to numbers." Jesse turned back to the real reason she was here. "I was in charge of teaching the rest of the Thirteen the math portion of the officer's test. Zero is the absence of everything. It's kind of out there by itself and is always zero. But when you tie it to something else, like coordinates, it leads you someplace."

Echo rubbed her hands together. "Like a place where consciousness exists before—"

"—before it finds itself a home in a woman's womb." Jesse finished her thought.

Echo felt like fainting. "They're not just talking about pairing with the people found through the UBI test, but . . . but with babies in the womb?"

Chapter Thirty-Two

Echo sought the support of a chair, not trusting herself to remain standing. To be clear, she hadn't needed to sit down, but reflex told her she should. Come to think of it, the constant gnawing for some snack or another was gone. The memory of coffee was there, rich and full and with slightly more sugar than was probably healthy, but she didn't want it. And cumulatively, since the first day that everything went wrong, she doubted she'd had more than five hours of sleep, but she didn't feel any worse for wear. Not here.

"I can see your mind drawing up all kinds of conclusions. Care to share 'em?" Jesse was in front of her.

Echo smoothed her lips together. "Pairing. They want to do exactly what I just did. The next question is, To what aim? What's the end goal?"

"Can't find that out wasting time in here."

Echo shot out of the chair like a rocket. "Why do you keep pushing me away? If I'm willing to be here with you, you'd think you'd be happy about it, or at least want to continue the conversation, come up with options."

Jesse snorted. "Because I don't want you here. I loved my wife the first day I saw her and I still love her now, a hundred years gone. She was smart as a whip, pretty, and the best mother and wife you ever saw. You can't compete with her, and you darned sure can't replace her."

The effect couldn't have been worse if he'd reared back and slapped her. She couldn't compete with a ghost. Let alone one who, in death, as so many people were, was cast as perfect. "Gina," she called. She'd put as much distance between her and Jesse as she could. Near the spot where she had first and very mistakenly entered Jesse's prison, she tried again. "Gina, please get me out of here."

Jesse turned with a raised eyebrow. He didn't speak, but there was nothing in his gaze, in that taut stance of his, left for her. She knew that now. This was all a ridiculous dream. She wanted nothing more than to get away from him and never turn back. A wife. A dead wife. *Gina . . .*

And then she stopped herself. It wasn't Gina at all, but that little tickle in the back of her mind. And as soon as she thought it, *Leave,* she closed her eyes and was gone.

The first thing Echo noticed was the stab of a spiked heel digging into the sole of her left foot. It was quickly followed by an ache in her back and a sharp, shrill pain in both knees. The edges of her wool coat brushed against her face, and she shook it away. The closet. She was back in her apartment, still in the closet. A sneeze was building, and she performed physical calisthenics to keep it at bay. It came out more of a strangled grunt; then she held her breath. Waiting for the door to fly open and for rough hands to haul her to her feet and hustle her out to some unmarked car and oblivion.

She did that thing that she'd learned in meditation and focused her thoughts with the word "hear." And everything else, for the moment, fell away. The click and whir of her refrigerator registered first. Then the nearly silent chortle of the tankless water heater that was there in the closet with her. A crack, the place settling like any other old building. But nothing else.

Echo unfolded herself in one painful step after another and stood up. When another few moments passed without the sound of anyone lying in wait, she inhaled and opened the door a crack. Then all the way. A quick scan revealed her place standing just as she'd left it. If she hadn't heard those agents, she wouldn't have known they were even there.

She slogged over to the window, stopping to stretch and work out the kinks. "Gina, time," she said, tapping her earring.

"Four fifty-five, and I'm so glad to hear your voice."

Are you really? Echo thought. "Were you able to track me while I was in the virtual space?"

"I did as I was able to before and tried to initiate the connection, and then it was as if a clogged highway had opened up a new lane and someone plucked you from my lane and shifted you onto that one. It was like I could see you moving away but couldn't go with you. I only stayed there, in my lane, so to speak, and waited until I saw you coming back and took the handoff. Does that make any sense at all?"

"I'm afraid it makes every bit of sense." Echo needed time to think. About what she'd experienced, first and foremost. She wasn't sure how she felt about anything that had happened. In a way, she'd felt a profound relief not to be constantly besieged by lack and want every minute of every day, even if it was just to relieve her bladder. But the feeling was also disconcerting in a way she couldn't quite articulate. To just exist without enjoying all that her hard-earned human senses granted her?

To never really feel the sun or hear the waves. To never enjoy a good meal prepared with farm-fresh ingredients? To not know the real pleasure of bare feet on sand. This was what it was really like to be a virtu. Was that even living?

With Jesse as her companion, maybe it would have been. They would have had forever to talk, to read, and maybe other things. But to never leave the confines of his made-up setting? No, not by any definition was that living. Plus, he'd made it clear that he didn't want her, hadn't he?

Echo spun around, taking in her own apartment. As much as she loved the space and had carefully curated everything in it, to never be able to leave would be a hell on earth.

Back in the virtus' world, her thoughts alone had extracted her. Echo wondered if it would work the same way now. She formed the words to check out the duchess, only nothing happened.

"Gina, can you bring Margaret Cavendish here?"

"I will, but there's something else we need to talk about."

In a moment, Margaret's flickering visage appeared. Hunger had returned with the aches and pains, so Echo went into the kitchen and grabbed an apple.

"Verily, you are most base to cast me aside that way," Margaret said. "I pray you never do so again without my permission."

"I kind of expected a 'Thank you, Echo, thank you for saving me from people discovering me and taking away the liberty I just gained.' But that would be how I would react."

"And it could never be more manifest that you are decidedly not me," Margaret shot back. "Well, out with it. What happened? Do not leave out any detail."

First, Echo took a bite out of the apple and wiped away the juice from the corner of her mouth with a finger. She felt Margaret's eyes linger on the fruit. There was longing there, intense. Echo went over to the kitchen and set the apple back in the refrigerator.

"I think the intelligence behind the library is evolving, or maybe it already was evolved and was just waiting for someone to ask it to do what I did." Echo went on to describe the experience and to answer all her questions about how as best she could.

"Wait," Margaret said. "You didn't come to my setting, so where did you go?"

Echo hesitated.

"Out with it."

And then she told her. The irony of it all was that, once again, Echo's best friends and confidants weren't real. She told Margaret about the first time she'd checked Jesse out, curious about such an important achievement in African American history. And then how their friendship, their relationship, grew. And how it had likely just ended. By the time she was done, she'd slumped onto her sofa and was gripping her blanket like an infant.

"Oh, for heaven's sake, don't you see it?"

"See what?"

"Silly girl, he's seen with his own eyes what now meets my gaze. You've fallen for this gentleman with scarcely a struggle, and from the sound of it, he's been stricken with the same foolish malady. And here you, poor simple creature, are willing to offer up your very life for him. If he returns your favor, and I suspect he does, then 'tis no wonder he turned you away. He would spare you our hollow world. We are but a mirage. Come, open your eyes. They are plain enough on that sullen face of yours."

Every vile thing she'd said. How she wanted to go to him but didn't. Echo did understand and wanted to slap herself for not seeing it sooner.

To her credit, Margaret seemed sympathetic to her plight, but there was an aura of impatience surrounding her, confirmed by her next words. "Once this unfortunate business is set straight, you can go back and have a chat with this young suitor of yours."

The part of Echo that wanted to resist this logic had been stamped out. "You're right, so let me tell you about something interesting I learned."

Margaret hovered over to the window, the spot she'd come to favor whenever she was in Echo's space. "Pray, expound, but do be a tad less verbose," she said.

Echo raised an eyebrow. "Well, there's this thing that Jesse helped me understand—"

Margaret spun around, a look of alarm on her face. "Something feels out of the ordinary."

Echo slowly approached, watching as her confidant's virtual visage flickered and wavered. The last thing she saw before Margaret disappeared was her wide, unblinking eyes.

"Gina, what just happened? Bring Margaret back."

"I would if I could, but there is no record of a virtual personage by the name of Margaret Cavendish."

Chapter Thirty-Three

Later, Echo would pale at the number of times she'd tried to do it herself, then demanded that Gina make Margaret Cavendish reappear. It was clear, wasn't it? There was no glitch in the system, no mistake. Removing Margaret had to be the work of nefarious hands.

"Gina, check out virtual personage Zera Yacob." *Please,* Echo said to herself.

"Sorry, Echo, no record of Mr. Yacob."

Echo's alarm grew. "Check out virtual personage Brahmagupta."

"No dice."

"Are you sure there's no virtu by the name of Margaret Cavendish?"

"I know there should be, but there isn't."

Whoever this Mr. Oliphant was that those men in her apartment mentioned had to be behind this and had taken them all, every one of her allies.

She swallowed. "Gina . . ." She paused to still her heartbeat. "Check out virtual personage Jesse Cooper."

"I know this makes no sense," her companion replied. "I've checked all these people out for you before . . ."

"Just tell me."

A sad virtual sigh, real or imagined. "There is no record of a virtu by that name."

Echo let out a strangled scream and crumpled to the floor. This Oliphant, Ada, someone, or something had taken everything from her. The message was clear: *Back off.* She thought about the last conversation she'd had with Jesse. The angry and hurtful words he'd flung at her. How she'd left in a huff. But she also considered the revelations he'd exposed about his life, or lack thereof. His existence was not what she'd thought it was. She had convinced herself that the People's Library was an example of how a mutual technology experience could benefit all. She should have known that no system is perfect. She should have paid attention to the hints. They were there in the silences and misdirections.

They were the most selfless beings, virtual or otherwise, that she knew.

What was she to do now, after all she'd learned? Go back to being a lonely librarian, only without the comfort of the people she held most dear?

But that was the problem, wasn't it? Echo had done worse than turn inward; she'd lived her life at work in the worst possible way. All the people she'd interacted with, laughed with, discussed current events with . . . loved, were not real at all. They were facsimiles of reality. She didn't even live her life in the real world, did she? She had been fooling herself. Maybe they'd done her a favor. Maybe she should give this all up, sign up for UBI, and stay home and read for the rest of her life.

But then thoughts of how she felt whenever she was in the virtual world came to her. The feeling was like living inside a book, or rather having the book, the greatest book of them all, living alongside her. The part that bothered her was the exposure. She didn't know if there was any part of herself that could remain private. And Echo London valued privacy most among all things. But she also didn't feel alone, as she often did when she wasn't at the library. Most of the time, it was preferred, but in the moments when it wasn't, the loneliness could feel all-consuming.

Stories had been written for ages about the rise of the machines and the proliferation of intelligence. Whether for drama or reality, all the predictions in these tales were dire. The end of humanity. A fat, lazy society. The end of independent, creative thought. The truth was, the experience was so much better than what she could have imagined.

And that frightened her even more.

The loss she felt, particularly at losing Jesse and Margaret, was akin to losing a person who was *not* already dead. It didn't make any sense.

Echo had made a perfect mess of her life. And what was really sad was that, instead of her parents, the only other people she thought to even talk to about this were her coworkers, Walter or Carmen, but she also didn't want to get them involved in the trouble she'd found herself in.

Did she even have a job anymore? It was obvious that this Mr. Oliphant and his group had tracked her movements and gone about erasing everything. Was that enough, or were they also coming to silence her permanently?

Echo pulled herself up off the floor, despair flooding through her body. They'd barged into her home, her sanctuary. They'd taken away the people she cared about most.

What was left for her?

She tried, she really tried, to rally the fight necessary to combat everything that weighed against her. But it all seemed too much. Where was she to turn? It scared her that the next victim might be Gina. The companion she'd tried so hard not to become close to. Yet she had. She was the one who was always there for her, ready to risk her own existence to help Echo in her quest.

Would they try to take Gina from her next? The thought sent such terror through her that she nearly collapsed again. She hesitated to reach out for fear that she wouldn't get an answer. When she did try and received no answer after all the pitiful attempts, all that Echo could do was trudge over to the window that her friend Margaret Cavendish, Duchess of Newcastle upon Tyne, liked to come to and stare out of.

So this was what it felt like. Solitude. A cherished wish and outcome. It felt like . . . well, it felt like what she imagined was the embodiment of the number zero.

Chapter Thirty-Four

How long had she stood there, immobile and inert, her insides tangled like last night's bedsheets? Unable to take any action at all except to feel profoundly sorry for herself. Echo prided herself on being calm, adept, independent. But the woman who used to embody those qualities had vanished right along with her virtual support system.

When an insistent early-morning knock came at her door, Echo didn't even have the heart to hide this time. Panic had given way to an immense tiredness and, with it, the will to fight.

Bam, bam.

With a resigned sigh, she straightened her shoulders and marched over to the door. She snatched it open without even asking who it was. She was surprised to see Walter Sprigg standing there instead of some covert agent, come to whisk her away. "What are you doing here?"

He glanced around Echo, inside her apartment. "I'd rather tell you in there than out here."

Just then, Echo's biker neighbor came barreling down the steps, bike straddling his shoulder. He gave a brief head nod before continuing outside.

Standing there with her colleague, Echo thought about the careful lines she'd drawn between work and what passed for her personal life. A citadel of seclusion. This last vestige of herself was in peril, all because of the man standing before her. In the span of a few seconds, Echo decided that if she was going to invite anyone into her home, she could do worse than Walter. The lines between work and personal life were blurred into nothingness.

She opened the door and gestured for him to come inside. Walter did so with his customary swagger, cool as a cucumber even in the face of what Echo had drawn him into. Out of his typical all-black work clothes, Walter cut quite the figure. Loose-fitting jeans and a tan V-neck sweater, stylish without trying. His hair was always freshly cut. Sable skinned and smooth faced. He smelled of something fresh, not cloying like heavy cologne.

It took him all of a minute to survey her place and then turn to face her. Suddenly she felt self-conscious. Her clothing was still wrinkled from her stint hiding out in the closet. Her hair? She'd slept without her bonnet or silk pillowcase. Her braids had developed an unpleasant fuzziness. Had she even brushed her teeth?

"I'm in so far over my head I can't even see straight," Echo said. "No way I should have dragged you into it. You need to do what I should have done a long time ago—walk away."

Walter looked around as if waiting for her to offer him a seat. She hadn't decided yet if she would or not. Inviting him inside had taken all the resolve she had left. "I tried calling, but your companion seemed to be offline. After the last couple days we've had, I was . . . I just thought I should see if you were all right."

Echo laughed, a terrible, sad laugh that ended in a whimper. "How much do you want to know? I have to warn you that I think I've gotten myself into some trouble. I'm the captain, but I don't want to take you down with my ship, and it's already got holes in the stern." It didn't surprise Echo that she'd used an analogy of a ship, Jesse's loss still an open wound.

Walter shrugged. "I know I wear that uniform at work and that all you see of me is me tinkering with the machines, checking after the bots, and looking damn good while I do it. But do you take me for an unintelligent man?"

"Not for a minute," Echo said.

Walter gave her a slow nod. "Then you know that I realized that first day I saw you crouched down on the side of that building that you were working your way up to some trouble. Did I turn away then or when the cops were there?"

"No."

"Then don't insult me by asking if I'm more interested in protecting myself." Without waiting for Echo to learn some manners, Walter walked over to the dinette set, pulled out a chair, and sat down. Then he got up again, pulled out the other chair, and told Echo, "Sit."

Once she did, Walter surprised her again by going over to the kitchen. He opened the refrigerator and made an exasperated sound that told her how he felt about the pitiful state of her grocery shopping. After banging open and closed a few cabinets, he came back to the table and put glasses of water in front of them both before he sat down again. "Even the small details. Don't leave 'em out. That's where all the answers are usually hiding."

This was where it typically happened. Echo felt and saw it as sure as the feel of the chair beneath her. One of the countless moments in her life where she stopped herself. Where she erected a wall to separate her from anyone trying to get too close. She pondered a mental image of herself as a bricklayer. One brick in hand, a full stack and all the tools of the trade beside her. Ready and waiting. She glanced down at her hands, at the chipped red nail polish, and quickly tucked her fingers away. She had never felt more vulnerable.

Echo took a sip of water and then, like a faucet turned on full blast, told Walter everything. When she was done, she felt an intense relief. She had spent time with another human being—not a virtu—outside of work, and hadn't bolted in the other direction. Walter had asked questions, stopping her enough times to annoy her, but when she was done, she knew that he had the entire story.

He'd drained most of his water while they talked. "I take it your bathroom is either that first or second door."

"Second," Echo replied and instantly tensed. It was one thing to enter her home and quite another to use her private bathroom. She let it go, though. And soon he was back at the table.

"More water?"

Echo shook her head and hoped that he had at least put the toilet seat down.

"So first thing, this ain't on you," Walter said. "We aren't going to sit here and let them win. We take this here plot to the streets. We let the people know what's going on . . ."

Walter was still talking, but Echo had tuned him out. She was busy mopping up a spattering of water from his side of the table when she glanced at his forearms, thick and muscled. He had a tattoo, two perpendicular arms held high, hands fisted. The inky black dot in the middle. A makeshift letter *H*. Human.exe's mark.

He noticed her watching. "I guess it's time you knew," he said.

Echo's throat had gone dry. She couldn't speak. Could barely feel the anger that was trying to catch hold in her gut.

"This ain't fresh ink," Walter said, brandishing the emblem. "I was young, pissed off like everybody else. I left all that behind me a long time ago. I kept the tat as a reminder to always keep my eyes open for exactly what's going on right now. But that woman that died? I knew her—well, I'd seen her before, back when I was still active. I did some digging. She joined the rebels in the first place because of Universal Trust."

"What about them?" Echo asked, interest piqued.

"Remember when they overhauled health care and sold us that load of bullshit about how AI would cure every disease there ever was?"

Echo nodded.

"She got talked into being a guinea pig for some clinical trial that promised to cure her bipolarism. Turns out, that's all they were interested in, whatever was wrong with her brain. Can't tell you about the how, but they used her to make the next generation of companions. Her name was Regina Blum." Walter placed his arms on the table and leaned in, waiting.

It took Echo only a second to connect that last dot. Regina . . . Gina. The spark she'd felt when she placed the mask against her own skin. "My companion is based off her? I bet a million other people selected that voice option. My God . . . I mean, okay . . . okay, but what did she want from me?"

"Probably to do everything you've done since you walked out of the library with the mask instead of turning it in."

"To expose them," Echo said.

Walter rolled the water glass between his palms. He was chewing his lip, content to let her work through everything she'd heard on her own.

"Why didn't you tell me?" she said finally.

"How many times did I ask you out to lunch? Coffee?" Walter leaned back and crossed his arms.

Echo blew out an exasperated breath. "And I turned you down every time."

"If you want me to walk out that door right now, I will. But I don't think you do," Walter said.

Was anyone ever what they seemed? Walter had concealed a less-than-flattering period of his past. That wasn't the same as lying, but it had the same look and feel, like a close cousin. He'd done it to protect himself, though. How many times had she done the same? And hadn't Percy concealed the Universal Trust angle? They never would've become friends if he'd told her the truth; she never would have trusted him. Echo had a decision to make. She watched Walter watching her. "Tell me about this plan of yours."

He gave her what seemed like a nod of approval. "Last time they tried this shit with AI, the people put up such a stink, the council killed it. We'll do the same thing this time. But before we do, you need to get yourself together."

"Really," Echo said through gritted teeth. "After everything I've told you, everything you've told me, you're going to sit here and critique how I look?"

"Yeah, boss, I am. You look great to me, you always do, but to get in front of those cameras, we're going to need to borrow your work persona. You know, official looking."

Oh. "Give me a half hour."

"I passed a café on my way over. I'm going to get you something to eat. If you want to shake up the world, you can't do it on an empty stomach."

With that, Walter strolled past. Before he closed the door, he said, "I'll be back in fifteen."

When he left, Echo checked herself in the mirror. He was right. Her braids needed help. She warmed some jojoba oil between her palms and patted it along the length of her hair and then tied on a silk scarf. She turned on the shower, shed her clothes, and stepped in. Her stomach growled the whole time she was cleaning herself up. She dressed simply but tastefully, dark-wash jeans, sustainable silk blouse. It was time for Echo to put on her own mask again.

Chapter Thirty-Five

Clichés became known as such because they were so often true. For Echo, appearance and surroundings fit into that category. The right clothing, how you presented to the outside world, and sometimes more importantly, to yourself, really influenced how you felt. She'd read numerous studies about how the same thing applied to where people lived and worked. She read them and learned about the very particular choices made when designing the library.

In the slightly more than twenty minutes it took for Walter to return, she had taken the time to get herself together. With a splash of lavender-scented body spray and a swipe of sheer plum color on her lips, she felt ready to take on the world.

Of course, the coffee helped.

Her body still felt like an apartment block with too many vacancies. The possibility that she'd never fill those spaces again, with the occupants who had comprised all that was her friendship and intellectual circles, threatened to send her over the edge.

"You know, even though I helped you with picking virtus, I've never checked one out myself," Walter said around a bite of a lemon blueberry muffin. Crumbs spilled over the napkin he'd laid out, but if he noticed, he did nothing about the mess. With effort, Echo let it go.

"Never?" Echo said, genuinely surprised. "But the training. Every staff member had to go through the training, so you had to have checked out at least one."

Walter blew on his open cup and then sipped. "I stand corrected. Aside from the annual training, I haven't checked one out just for pleasure"—he stumbled—"or learning, you know."

It had become a matter of intense privacy, knowing who people checked out. That often led to questions of why, and simply being curious sometimes wasn't a good enough answer for the authorities. But she had told her custodian everything about Jesse and the others, and now he was judging her for it. What exactly did he think she did with Jesse when she visited him? She snatched up her coffee cup and drank, too fast, scorching her mouth and throat.

She coughed, and Walter stood up as if to come over and smack her on the back. Echo waved him off. "I'm fine."

"Tell me about them," he said. "About him."

Echo was still angry, but she appreciated the question. "I know that most people who come to the library only want to view the collection for the famous people. You know, sports stars, the few actors we have. But the people I check out are the ones that are more obscure."

"The ones in danger of being deleted?"

"Exactly. But that's not all. I picked them all, we picked them all, because they have stories to tell. Experiences that matter to this day, no matter what century they existed in. You've heard of the Golden Thirteen?"

"My uncle was a navy man; he told their story at every Christmas dinner. You picked well. I knew you were a lady with standards."

"Jesse Cooper was mechanically gifted like you, but also a math whiz." Echo cut the rest short, and the pair ate in silence for a time. It was not an uncomfortable quiet, and it gave Echo time to put together the last piece of why she spent all her time with dead people. "And you know what else? They're as curious as we are. That's the thing about the People's Library. I hated it at first, because I, like every librarian who ever was, love books. But though the author is speaking directly to the reader, the words and their intent are still filtered through a lens based on their lived experience. Our library is more of a two-way street. The communication is bidirectional."

Walter regarded her with an expression that told her he was really considering what she said. "What you're saying is, they're as interested in you and this time we live in as you are about them."

"One hundred percent."

"One day, when this is over, maybe I can ask you a thing or two."

Echo didn't know. Because what she was planning to do had one of two outcomes, and in both scenarios, she might not be around to answer. She polished off her sandwich and drank more of her now tolerably warm coffee.

"Maybe," she said, which was all she could offer. "But first, we need to get back into that library."

"Why?" Walter said. "We need to expose them first. This plan of theirs."

"But I barely know who my target is. I don't know anything about Mr. Oliphant. Plus, I need to get those virtus back."

"Your companion is gone. You can't just snap you fingers and access that other one either—Ada, right? So even if we get into the library, which shouldn't be that big a deal, how do you find them without help?"

Echo hadn't thought that far, but she did remember what she'd been able to do in extracting herself. She didn't know exactly how, but she hoped, just knew instinctively, that if she was to help them, she had to do it from inside. "The truth is, I don't know, but I think I need to be there."

Walter was on his feet now, pacing.

"They'll just be waiting for you to do something. Don't you think they've put up every roadblock known to man?"

Echo slumped in her chair. He was right.

Walter stopped. "I still can't believe you were able to do it, but when you went into the virtu space, you said it was a different experience than what we have with our companions, more entwined, almost like Gina wasn't even part of the pairing. Then maybe you *can* do it again, yourself."

Echo looked up, blinked. "Yes, but without Gina, I'll need someone or something else to open that doorway."

"Proximity then," Walter said. "That's why you need to be at the library."

"Because Ada is the code that powers the library; it *is* the intelligence."

"Do we wait or go now?"

"Now," Echo said. If they stopped her, so be it, but Margaret, Jesse—all of them—they were gone because of her, and she didn't even know what that meant. They could be in some awful limbo, and no way would she let them suffer any longer than they already had.

"Nothing to it but to do it," Walter said. And to his credit, he grabbed his napkin, wiped away the crumbs that had escaped, dropped them into the bin, and was at the door, shoes in hand, ready to go.

Chapter Thirty-Six

Walter and Echo waited atop the grassy rise overlooking the towering presence that was the People's Library. Glass walled and earth toned, the building loomed against the backdrop of a quiescent Lake Erie. A pair of water skis gouged twin paths against the smooth surface. Jetpack flyboards crisscrossed the airspace overhead. A yacht plodded along at a leisurely pace, the sounds of the laughter from the people on the foredeck drifting over to them.

It had taken a while, after the resentment of being here in the first place had started to fade, but Echo had begun stopping in this very spot to take in this incredible vista. Today, the building's architecture was no less breathtaking, but cracks were more visible in its flawless veneer. The place had a dark underbelly that she'd both seen and not seen for the better part of a year.

An unsettling turbulence stirred within her; the fear was like a phantom tingling in her toes that rose to full palpitations in her chest. A moaning dread. But not for the reason she'd initially thought. No, this was the kind of unease you felt when you discovered that sometimes things that felt, tasted, even smelled good for you were not necessarily so. Echo had experienced a kind of rebirth during her brief pairing, whether it was with Ada or the Model itself, she was unsure, but what she did feel was smarter, more capable. Infinite.

Inhuman. Protohuman. An evolution.

Devolution.

Walter shifted his feet beside her. Impatience in that movement. He knew that she was stalling.

"Look, I'm willing to put my job on the line, but not yours," she said. "You've done enough. Go home, forget everything you've done so far. Show up for work tomorrow like nothing's happened."

There. She'd said what she needed to say. Echo thought for a moment, then added, "I'll either be here or I won't."

They were still standing side by side, so she couldn't see his face. But she was a woman who lurked in the interstices. A part of but separate from everyone around her. In the hush of that self-imposed exile, Echo had learned to read people in other ways. Sight was easy, child's play. Joy had a smell, as did pleasure. Fear, a metallic tang. A grunt, a moan, a creak, they all spoke in a language other than words. And then there was aura, energy. Everything emanating from Walter's body wasn't a war, but a challenge. If he were a number, he'd weave between a deep mysterious six and an intellectual, strong seven. So Echo wasn't surprised when he finally responded.

"You know, I never wanted to move to this city. It wasn't those old jokes stemming from the fire on the river either. Cleveland was where everybody wanted to be by then." He stopped, then looked over at Echo. "You ever been to N'awlins?"

That town was bursting at the seams with history. And the culture, the music—it was everything that Echo would have loved. She'd meant to visit but couldn't remember the last time she'd left Ohio City. "No, wish I had."

"It's a little less than it was, the swamp has reclaimed some of its territory, but if you'd been there, grown up there, you'd understand. I didn't hate anyplace; I just loved my hometown more. I was about ten, maybe twelve, when my pops left Southern U and took a front-office job here with the Cavaliers. When I tell you all of us, my mom, my sister, and my brother, left Louisiana kicking and screaming, Pop almost gave in."

Walter nudged a toe at a trail of ants snaking their way off the sidewalk and into the dirt. "You see them? How once they catch the scent laid by some other ant they can't even see anymore, they just keep following the one in front? No questions asked, no thought going into whether or not the first ant's got any idea what's what? That's most people. Now I ain't gonna lie—it took me some time, but this town grew on me. It's home now. I'm proud to go down as the first caretaker to a new wave of libraries. Maybe one day, there will be a virtual me in there. Or not. Either way, what we have here, what we're about to do, is history, and I aim to be a part of it. I ain't no ant."

Most of her colleagues looked at Walter as just somebody to call when the heat was off by two degrees. None of them had taken the time to learn that he was so much more, and Echo suspected he liked it that way. She conjured all kinds of arguments as to why he should turn around and head home right now, but she let them all disappear like raindrops on warm cement. The truth was, she was selfishly relieved. She simply veered off the grass and onto the pathway that wound down toward the library, Walter falling in step with her.

It was a glossy Sunday afternoon, the sun pleasantly cool, like an air-filtering cardigan against the skin. A host of people were out enjoying the day. Blissfully oblivious as to what was being planned at this building, right beneath their noses. Bikers who were supposed to be confined to the length of trail near the water's edge whizzed through the walkways intended for people instead. Curses and dagger-eyed gazes beat a path behind them. Children whooped and hollered in the grassy areas, the adults with them reading beneath a canopy of solar shields.

Echo and Walter soon gave up on the long winding trail and instead cut a path through the grass. As they grew closer to the building, she scanned. No lights in the library's windows. No cars, unmarked or otherwise, in the parking lot. A few of the city's security guards who normally patrolled the area, but no police. Even the crime scene tape was gone.

Echo's chuckle was rueful. Cleveland was like any other city, in that after a wave of initial fist-pumping outrage, everyone had already turned their attention from the murder that had happened here to whatever the latest catastrophe was.

Better for her.

"Looks clear," Echo said, finally getting out of her own head.

Walter snorted. "I shouldn't have to tell you, looks can be deceiving."

"I hate clichés," Echo said.

They'd reached the entrance. At first, Echo had worried that too many people were around. Witnesses. But actually, because there were so many people, nobody seemed to take notice of them. She paused and turned to scan the immediate area and the hill once again. If somebody was watching, she couldn't tell. She turned back to Walter. "Any last alibis?"

In response, he went to the door and stood there, just shy of tapping his foot. Echo waved her hand over the panel. Nothing happened. She tried again, but the door remained stubbornly closed.

She felt Walter's hand on her shoulder.

Walter had a knife in his hand, the world's most elaborate pocketknife. More blades and gadgets than she could even think of a purpose for. He gestured for her to step aside. He fanned through the attachments and selected something thin that unfolded twice. He jimmied that under the panel but quickly shook his head and abandoned the effort.

Twice more, Walter tried, while Echo grew more paranoid. She scanned the grounds again, seeing a potential threat in every movement. She'd begun to sweat.

Finally, she heard the sound of something metal hitting the ground. Walter had the panel off. He shoved his finger inside, and a few seconds passed, taut with anticipation, before the door slid open—an inch.

Walter cursed. Echo felt like her legs would give out.

But in the end, Walter won the battle and the door opened enough for them to slip inside. He had to do the same thing to the panel on the inside before the doors closed behind them.

The first thing that drew Echo's attention was the clock. Time's Eye. Suspended thirty feet in the air by an invisible mechanism that she had never been able to work out. Brass and black gears churned. A shaft of sunlight cut through the upper windows and lit it from behind as if by candlelight. The time was accurate, the little brass hand still ticking off the seconds. It was the thing she had admired most on her first day, and that feeling held still.

She and Walter paused to listen.

"Somebody beat me to cleaning up the place." Just then, one of Walter's cleaning bots zoomed by, in one pass sweeping, then doubling back and steam cleaning that section, lawnmower-fashion.

Echo waited for it to pass, gaze laser focused on the wedge of floorspace a few feet in front of the welcome station. The scene that no amount of scrubbing would erase from the dark corners of her mind where her nightmares flourished. It was different, what you saw in a film or read in a book. Reality had no filter. The woman's face hidden by that damnable mask. The shock of the knife protruding from Regina Blum's chest. Those staggered, ominous steps before she fell and her blood painted the floor a ghastly red.

"That where it happened?" Walter asked, as if reading her mind. "I came up the back way before, when the cops were here."

Echo gave an almost imperceptible nod. "From the looks of things, you'd almost never believe it."

A very familiar dread crept back over Echo. Her body heated up right along with her heartbeat. She was frozen in place.

"Second thoughts?" Walter said.

Third. Fourth. Fifth. "Not a one." Words had power, spoken aloud or to yourself. Echo hoped these would serve to get her legs moving. "I think the first thing to try is to go to the check-out pods and see if all those virtus are still missing."

They took the stairs to the top level.

"All I need you to do is to wait here. Keep an eye on . . . on my body. If I'm successful, either I'll get to go there or they may come here. You're my warning system."

"And if you do go there, wherever 'there' is, how long do I let you stay before I try to bring you back? And what am I supposed to do, give you a good shaking? Call an ambulance?"

Echo could see that Walter wasn't joking at all; he was well and honestly worried. She felt bad again at having involved him in this. If something happened to her with him here on the premises? She shoved the thought away. "I don't know," she said truthfully.

Walter crossed his arms and eyed her with an expression that said how woefully inadequate her plan for this whole thing was, the reality of what he'd committed himself to settling in like a new house on too-soft soil.

"You may as well sit down. This could take a while." Echo took a step toward the first pod and felt an electric tickle at the back of her mind. It couldn't be. "Gina?" she called.

When her companion didn't respond, she knew the source of that sensation without a shadow of a doubt. The library's engine, Ada. Her hand automatically went to the spot again, and she felt the firm space behind her ear. She couldn't feel the chip, didn't have to. That presence was with her again. Rather than enter the pod, which she sensed she didn't need, she sat opposite Walter. Instead of speaking, she formed a thought in her mind and then released it.

Do these virtus exist in the library archive? She named them all. The answer was like one of her own thoughts, but one that was wrapped in a cloak that had to be removed before she could understand it. The answer was a wobbly *Maybe*. Echo asked again and again, continued her probe and direction. Prompting as Gina had taught her.

Where is my companion, Gina?

Hidden. Safe.

Echo knew then, if she hadn't before, that the attack was a targeted one, meant for her. She also knew who was responsible. Maybe it was time to ask him why.

"Check out virtual personage Mr. Oliphant," she said aloud. No way she wanted this man in her head. He'd had people invade her home and her place of work. That was enough.

She purposely angled herself away from Walter and his raised eyebrows so that Oliphant wouldn't see him. In a minute, the rectangle appeared, and his cherubic face blinked out at her.

"Echo London," he said. "My friend. Allow me to introduce myself. Ivan Oliphant at your service. I'm so glad you've decided to check me out today." He wore his quintessential vintage T-shirt and the expression of a creature that was a mix between a ferret and an African honey badger.

Echo's head nearly exploded. Ivan Oliphant was none other than her boss, her friend, Percy Grafton.

Echo wasn't cold, but that didn't stop her from shivering. "Why?" A dumb question, but she couldn't think of anything else to say. How advanced was his virtu? What had he done to change it or what it knew?

"We're on the verge of something great—you know that, right?" Percy said.

"You know more about it than me. Why don't you enlighten me?" Echo said.

"You had to know that this library is powered by something far greater than anything we've had previously? You're no techie, but I suspect you understand that much."

If it were possible, Echo would've entered the virtual world just to smack that condescending expression from his face. "To what purpose?"

"Ah," Percy—no, Ivan—said. "So you still haven't found that out. Disappointing."

Echo suspected she knew, but no need to clue him in. She didn't know how much of his virtual presence was connected to the real one. "Whatever it is, I don't care. I'm no longer involved. My plan is to forget everything I've seen and, once those doors open again on Monday morning, get back to my job here. I just wanted you to know that so you or whoever you work for can stop. Don't come to my house. Don't read my emails. Do not, and I repeat, do not, bother my staff."

"That's what I always admired about you, Echo. You are incapable of bullshit. You can't even spell 'small talk,' and you're so good at hiding your true feelings I almost would have believed you. You see, I don't waste my time with idiots. I like curious people, the high-IQ folks like yourself. But look, I hear you. This isn't a ride you want to go on with me. I've only got one last bit of advice for you, then, my friend."

Echo rolled her eyes. "I'm waiting with bated breath."

Ivan dropped the boyish grin. Any visage of the easygoing man she'd believed she knew was replaced in an instant. He leaned in, narrowing his eyes. "Stay out of our way." He dragged out every word and, when he was done, checked *himself* back into the collection.

Part III

What makes something human? What is the state between being and not being? Real and artificial? The presumption that there is a difference between us is a chimera.

—Ada

Interlude

Truth is fluid, so a lie spoken with vehemence can become solid. Ivan Oliphant thought everyone should have a motto, and that was his.

He had been born into the well-to-do suburban enclave of west London known as Notting Hill, the first and only son of parents steeped in equal parts toe-the-line social conformance and bullheaded entrepreneurial ascendancy.

Driven, that's what the both of them were—though Mom had edged out Dad, as evidenced by the fact that they met at a tech firm, where, though he'd started two years earlier, she became his boss. You can guess what happened next. One thing led to another, and after a few, uh, all-nighters, they became an item. They were sharp as tacks but indiscreet as Amsterdam whores. That is to say their relationship was only a secret in their minds. Of course, with all the laws and policies in place warning against such unions, they both got booted.

Lucky for him, Ivan thought with a chuckle, they had enough in their combined severance packages to spin up a data-analytics outfit of their own.

Legend had it, as told from the open window that was his dad's mouth, that when Mom was pregnant with Ivan, she never slacked on the twelve-hour days. When she went into labor, Mom shoved away the paramedics so she could polish off a last line of code before undertaking the great inconvenience of bringing Ivan fully into the world.

Nothing much had changed after. Baby Ivan sat in a crib at the office entertaining himself as best an infant with workaholic parents could; they spent more time at that office than they did at home.

You'd think that the offspring of two left brains would follow the same path. And Ivan tried. All through the fluorescent-lighted years, peek through the window and there he'd be, legs dangling from a too-tall chair, at a desk next to Dad's, trying to string together two lines of code when all his stubby fingers yearned to do was to hold a paintbrush. Blame that on his primary school art teacher.

It was the damnedest thing, though; he was good at it. Once, when he won the emerging-talent ribbon for one of his paintings at school, he brought it home and slid it across to his parents at the dinner table. Dad blinked a few times before asking what it was, but Mom . . . Mom surprised him. She picked up the masterpiece, admiration dancing in those red-rimmed eyes. She glanced at Ivan and said the words that he most wanted to hear: "This is really, really good." Then she ripped the painting into pieces, got up, and tossed them in the trash.

After that, Ivan kept his head down and mostly just survived the rest of his childhood by being the caretaker to the family's new arrival, his little sister, Clara.

College, like high school, was about as much fun as dancing barefoot on a firepit of hot coals. By then they'd relocated to the States. He did the only thing he could do: dropped out and joined the family business. But their business analyzed consumer trends from the Discords and socials and fed them to politicians for use in manipulating votes, and soon the business was having its lunch eaten by the emergence of artificial intelligence.

Just as the company had decided to change the business model, pivoting to a consumer-focused product, it fell victim to a social-engineering attack. Well, Ivan had. Such was his social life that he'd greedily accepted a lunch invitation from the kind of woman who ordinarily would not have been interested in a bloke with below-average looks. So eager was he to impress that he told her all about his parents' new plans for the company. It was your ordinary, run-of-the-mill scheme, "Pick the weakest link in a company and pump them for information." And he'd fallen for it.

The woman and her cofounder stole the idea and beat them to implementation. The Oliphant family business folded not long after. Ivan forgave himself after some intensive therapy, but neither his parents nor Clara were so inclined. He hadn't spoken to them in years.

Ivan had one friend left in the world, a former client of theirs who worked for the federal government and took pity on him. For the first time in his life, Ivan found his footing.

He developed his one and only technical achievement: a tool that sought to take the "artificial" out of "artificial intelligence." A more natural language processor. It gave way to the more conversational versions of personal assistant companions that nearly everyone had today.

A few iterations and enhancements later, Ivan had left engineering behind and ascended the ranks of management like a balloon untethered. One of the things that bothered Ivan about engineering was that he never felt like the smartest person in the room. At Universal Trust, Ivan was smart, but in a different way from the rest. A better way.

The agency had initially purported its mission to be one of dealing with the fallout of job loss and population displacement brought on by the age of intelligence, a term he despised, coined by some tech bro who had long since been forgotten. Replaced by the next generation, his generation, who had other thoughts about how society should function in the new era.

There was no getting back some of the jobs. Fast food, manual labor, service, even most coding jobs had been taken over or nearly so about a decade earlier. In the bad times that ensued, the city, and the country, nearly tore themselves apart. Anarchy only suppressed by a strong show of force by the police and the enacted national guard.

Out of the chaos of the other larger cities, Cleveland emerged as the leader. Why? Because it was exactly the place nobody expected. And because of its position. A healthy port. A winter made milder by climate change (although this was predicted to reverse with improvements in climate science). A large able-bodied population on which to experiment. A long kick-ass list of universities. Microbes and bioengineered algae had also transformed the lake into one of the country's most beautiful.

So at first secretly, then in a flood, the powers that ran the country relocated to the area and began laying the plans that were set to manifest now. The first matter at hand after the insurrections had been stamped out was to ensure that everyone had the basics covered. Land was taken, landlords thrown out or tossed in jail if they squawked too loudly. Task one: Ensure people had some kind of roof over their heads.

Task two: food. Neighborhood farms were the answer. Not only did they feed people, but by putting them in the hands of the residents and not in those of large corporations or pesticide-laced farms, they had something to work toward, to be proud of. And it was healthier, to boot.

But capitalism wasn't consigned to an early grave; it just got a patchwork facelift. Some things still had to be bought and paid for. Cleveland was the nation's capital in small business, so that was where they funneled the money.

It was not Ivan's award-winning idea to finally enact a universal basic income. But what *was* his idea was that the use of UBI would pave the way to an ultimate, loftier goal. A student of history as well as art, Ivan lamented the fact that the human animal hadn't evolved all that much. It only took a visit to one hockey game to prove that fact. But technology *had*.

It was so brilliant, Ivan was shocked nobody else had thought of it first. Pairing—human and artificial—was the only way forward.

This idea, once presented to his leadership at UT, had met with the same enthusiasm as an invitation to streak naked through the West Side Market. But this kind of thinking was why they had hired him, and soon enough, he'd won them over—with some caveats. They of course wanted to relegate this idea to the elite, but Ivan went deeper. Candidates had to be capable of adding as much to the pot as the tech did.

Which was why everyone who applied for UBI had to take a test, supposedly to gauge cognition relative to attention spans blighted by decades' worth of social media. Beneath that veneer lay an IQ test, not like the old ones but better, aimed at judging critical thinking, openness to new ideas, and cognitive anomalies. It was an intelligence test dressed up as a new world thinking order. That and the chip neatly implanted in their capable bodies.

The first group of UBI recipients were soldiers on standby, without a mission. Just waiting for the right time for the agency to call them into service.

True evolution.

And it had worked. They already had a database of over ten thousand people they'd deemed the best candidates for the fusion.

And then some genius came up with the idea for the People's Library. Not that Ivan was opposed—he saw it as an excellent test case for seeing how evolved intelligence now was and how it could be used to power such an advanced virtual system.

The implications for the future were outstanding. And he wanted to see how it would all work. The real surprise, however, had been the librarian. Echo London was in many ways unremarkable. And to most of the people surrounding her, even her bosses at the administration, that was all there was to her. But in their conversations, Ivan had met the other Echo. The one who'd shed her mask whenever she was inside the virtual confines.

She was sharp as they come. Inquisitive and open. Methodical and analytical. A brilliant test case for certain. She had a nice laugh and a beautiful smile when she let you see it. Everything that you'd expect a librarian to be. Most importantly, though, she had synesthesia, and since such people associate colors with numbers or symbols, she could spot patterns in complex datasets that AI algorithms might miss.

So he'd befriended her.

But once she'd step back from that pod, there was the mask again. And without knowing, it was she who'd given him the idea for the mask that they'd use to capture human consciousness. Countless late nights, long weekends, and screaming sessions at the manufacturing facility tucked away in nearby Detroit ensued. For all that work, Echo had inadvertently proven that the mask might not be necessary. At least for her.

When his plant in the system admin group alerted him to what she'd accomplished, he was genuinely floored. She had exceeded all his expectations. Maybe it was because the library intelligence, only a sliver of the artificial intelligence secretly available to them now, had some kind of affinity for her? Was that even possible? Ivan was positively thrilled at the implications, and this was the only kind of surprise he liked. The kind that benefited him.

If that was the case, then perhaps the mask would still be necessary for the masses. Either way, Echo had inadvertently given him another train of thought, another technical angle to explore. The library intelligence was powerful, much more so than the limited companions most people now had. The expense could be astronomical, so he'd have to lobby for the funds.

For now, he'd let Echo proceed on her little mission, whatever the ultimate goal. He'd thought to bring her in after wiping her virtu friends, but luckily, his boss had stopped him. She was right: They should follow Echo's trail and learn everything they could from her. Invaluable test data for the next round of human intelligence experimentation.

He would allow her to continue for a time. He liked the librarian, after all. But once she'd given him everything he needed to ascend to the level of the greatest technical and business mind of their time, earning himself an elevated position within the secret confines of Universal Trust, Ivan would give the word, and Echo London would be a memory. A figure in history who had ushered in the next wave of human evolution.

Ivan drew his forearm across his face, wiping a tear from the corner of his eye. It was all so very beautiful.

Chapter Thirty-Seven

"What, you gonna just sit there and act like you didn't hear that, huh? Plain and simple?" Walter was beside himself.

Echo had had to stop him from stepping into Ivan's view while they were still talking.

"I did hear him, and to be honest, what did he say that we don't already know? There's a plan at play here, and a big one. They don't want me, you, anybody to get in the way. You knew that when you showed up at my door the other day. What's different?"

Walter stood as if poised for a boxing match. Legs separated, shoulders bunched, hands spoiling to turn into fists. He made a dismissive sound. "The difference between a hornet circling and stinging, that's what. You spent too much time with them virtus—get back in the real world and open your eyes."

Echo blinked. This was what happened when you exposed yourself to people. They took your confidences, then repackaged them as little missiles to launch back at you when you were most vulnerable.

"You've forgotten, so let me remind you. I'm the boss." Echo hated to pull rank, but it was long overdue. "Let me make it official. This is none of your concern. I'm telling you to turn around, march down those stairs, and go home. Or go wherever you want, as long as it's away from here. Come back tomorrow and clean the floor or unclog a toilet. I don't care which, but stay in your lane and I'll stay in mine."

Regret was a pain as sharp and irreparable as a hacked-off limb. She saw it in his face. He looked like a fish, gutted, slick innards exposed. Echo steeled herself for his comeback. She deserved it. A refrain of expletives. Turning his back and leaving her. Never bringing her a coffee from the café again.

But Walter Sprigg again proved himself more than meets the eye. He shed the hurt like a quick snowmelt on the Cuyahoga River. Like a ghost of long winter, slipping down the swift current, his face sloughed off that initial icy shield and flowed toward something more temperate. He smirked.

"If I'm lucky, one day you'll tell me who or what hurt you, made you this way. Ain't no shame in what I do. In fact, I'm proud of the work. And you know it as well as I do—I'm the best mechanical engineer in this entire library district. It's why they chose me. So that type of shit won't even get a rise out of me. But that whole pulling-rank thing? Unnecessary and insulting. If you want me to go, if you don't need my help anymore, speak on it without all the cover."

Well, Echo probably looked like even more of a fool than she felt. She could make it up to Walter if she got through what she had to do next. "Mr. Sprigg," she began and then cleared her throat. "You're right, and I'm sorry. As much as I appreciate everything you've done so far, I would very much like for you to let me take it from here."

"Your call," he said. "But it's the wrong one. I'll do what you ask and hope to see you here first thing tomorrow morning." With that, Walter shocked Echo by turning and jogging down the steps. She didn't hear the door open and close, but as she turned to go look out the window, where she could see the library grounds, she saw Walter's sure steps walking up the path and painfully, quickly, out of sight.

Once again, Echo had ensured that she was utterly alone.

But I'm not really alone, am I? Echo thought.

A natural parallel drawn between her own psyche and Tower City Station before game time. Bodies packed and jostling, moving like a swarm toward the stadium, restaurants, cafés. Like a mind filled with thoughts—past and future—competing voices elbowing for space. Spurning the present. And wedged into a corner was the quiet, prescient self.

It was this self that the Universal Trust was most keen on.

Echo drifted back to the fight she'd had with Jesse, which had culminated with her demanding that Gina get her out of there. Only her companion was gone, like the rest. Through that anger and panic, she'd simply formed the word in her mind. *Leave.* Something had snagged on that last thought and reacted. Echo had found herself back in the closet at home. She knew now that Ada had been there with her and had facilitated the exit—with a kind of handoff from Gina.

The trick when dealing with the library's intelligence was how to differentiate between her random thoughts—things like hunger, going to the bathroom, or *I wish I were sitting on a beach someplace*—and a request intended for action. And if Gina returned to her, then it could also be easy to mix the two up.

Echo felt like a bloodhound, hot on the scent of discovery. She turned away from the window and took a few steps toward a pod before she stopped herself. She didn't need it.

Sitting once again, she formed her request. *Help me,* she thought to herself, *help me restore the virtual personages.* She pictured them, one by one, then decided to let a particular name surface: Jesse Cooper.

As soon as her eyes closed, the part of her brain that controlled movement misfired. Her arms and legs jerked uncontrollably. Her thoughts were racing, her body struggling to interpret the command. Then a vertical cascade of zeros and ones streamed along her vision. A frenzied symphony of rippling light followed . . . shades of black, white, a swirl of red. The colors collided and scattered like mutinous brushstrokes on a crowded canvas. The churn was a disorienting dance.

Until the colors softened and parted, revealing something like a pathway. A shy tug bid her forward. She'd taken one mental step before the whole thing collapsed.

Echo opened her eyes and slammed her palms down on the chair's arms.

There was no doubt that she'd try again. And this time, the shift was faster. Shadow and light pulsed as she was sped through a labyrinth. Twists, turns, doubling back. Flashes of other virtu spaces began to take shape. A stunning portrait resting on an easel, a woman with a paintbrush in her hand. Two women, seated side by side and holding hands. A backdrop of stormy clouds. There was a duality in their dresses, one traditional Mexican, another in a more European style. The images were stunning by themselves, but even more striking were the exposed hearts connected by a long thin vein. The artist turned, surprised. Echo had only a moment to recognize Frida Kahlo before she was pulled away.

The next figure was hunched over a massive mahogany writing desk. An oil lamp cast a warm glow over the surface, covered with quills, ink, and neat stacks of paper. A long-haired dog napped at his feet. The man was dressed in a waistcoat and a high-collared shirt. His hair was wild, as if he'd just run a hand through the thin strands. When those deep-set, dark eyes looked up, Echo gasped: Charles Dickens. How had she never checked him out before?

More historical fragments, snippets of virtual lives, rolled by before Echo stopped so fast that she nearly tumbled out of the chair.

The cognitive stretches she'd traversed were scarred by the force of the journey. Mental clutter, the ghosts of the collection clinging to her like dust. A raw ache began behind her closed eyelids. She was in a place, lit and slightly warm, as if by a distant sun. It felt boundless.

Then Ada—Echo acknowledged her by name now—dipped into Echo's memory. And a setting, a milieu, began to take shape. Born of elements from everything that Echo had loved. The vague layout of her childhood bedroom. Large enough for a big comfy chair, her twin bed, and a desk. Books on shelves, on the floor, the end table. The window, now the width and height of that in her office on the first level of TPL, revealed a view of the flowing tributary that was the Cuyahoga River.

The Yoruba Gę̀lę̀dę́ mask that her parents had gifted her and that hung on her dorm room wall all through undergrad. Framed portraits of historical figures in a gallery wall, Dorothy Height, Marcus Garvey, Patrice Lumumba among them. She'd gotten all the way over to her desk before she realized she hadn't drifted but had actually moved her feet. She pushed aside a tablet and picked up a book, one of Mama's favorites, a classic called *One Hundred Years of Solitude*.

Once the wonder had faded, a slight feeling of unease replaced it and soon multiplied. What was she doing here? She hadn't asked Ada to do this. Was she trying to stop Echo by imprisoning her here? Walter . . . no, she'd sent him away. He wouldn't even be there to wake her or call an ambulance.

But then Ada quietly continued her work. Echo watched as if from the shadows and through the murk of a gray winter evening. The intelligence obliterated the system, sorting through quettabytes of archival data from the clutches of engineers who were clearly overmatched to bring back her friends.

The first was Jesse. A sliver of a window showed him secluded and alone in his naval room milieu. He looked startled, searching all around himself as if his last memory was of Echo being there with him and then suddenly gone. He sighed dejectedly and went to stare out the porthole window that he could never access. She asked Ada to move on.

Her bedroom door opened, revealing a sparkling eddy of gray and white. A prelude to what? A slim sandaled foot stepped into view, followed by the other. A ruffle of pink hem brushing at her ankles. Mama stepped through the door and pulled Dad in behind her. They looked so pitiful, the two of them. She clutched his upper arm, his hand covering hers protectively.

"Mama? Dad?" Echo rose and moved toward them.

"What is this place?" Mama said, but not to Echo. They couldn't see her.

The only thing that gave away Dad's panic was that stern twist of his lips.

Echo recognized their clothing as the same they'd had on when they came to check on her at the library. They'd flat out laughed when she'd talked about recording themselves for the public collection. That meant Percy . . . no, Ivan, had somehow scanned and uploaded them that day without their knowledge. And they had no idea how to be in this place, tethered as snapshots, virtu replicas without any of the guidance.

Echo called out to them again and again, but it was no use. They couldn't see her. She couldn't touch them. Soon, they faded away.

Lastly, she recalled her mercurial friend, one Margaret Cavendish. Echo pulled out her desk chair and sat down, mumbling a prayer. When she appeared, Margaret sat at her mirror, worrying those springy auburn curls. She sensed the opening and looked up, her eyes wide with wonder, apparently able to glimpse Echo on the other side.

Echo gasped as Margaret stood and was pulled forward into her bedroom.

The duchess appeared, blinking rapidly and unsteady on her feet. "What's happened?"

"It's a long story."

"The last thing I recall, we were in your home," Margaret said, rushing over.

"And then Ivan Oliphant, or whoever he's working with, deleted you." Echo paused, remembering the terror she'd felt. "Right in front of my eyes. You, Zera, Jesse. All gone."

"And yet, here I stand. Wherever 'here' may be."

"Your next question is going to be how, and I've got to tell you, that part is still fuzzy."

"You went into combat on my behalf," Margaret said. "Indeed, for us all."

Echo unloaded it all, including Walter's earlier connection to the rebels and Ivan's betrayal.

"I know the way you feel about being a virtu is complicated. I've come to understand the truth about how you exist in this, this construct, and to me it sounds hellish. But you should get to decide if you want to exist or not. They've lied to you about so much—the least that's owed to all of you is that choice."

Margaret turned and walked away a few steps. She glanced around her room and ran her hands up and down her arms. When she faced Echo again, the look in her eyes scared her. "When we have bested this baseborn traitor, then I choose to be deleted."

Echo wasn't surprised, but she still had to ask, "Are you sure?"

Margaret's smile was kind when she inclined her head, then said, "Go ahead, go over to that door and open it. Take a leisurely stroll around the grounds."

Echo folded her arms. "You know I can't."

"There, my dear, is your answer."

"But what if I can get them to change the system? You know, the way we talked about. Where the virtus could visit with each other and talk. More interaction. Give you the choice of when to turn yourselves off and on?"

"Oh, don't be such a simpleton. Unless changing the system is to the point, technologically speaking, where we could walk out of the confines of our prisons and into the present, then we would just be visitors, trapped in someone else's dream. And that, my dear, is not living."

There were no words that Echo could come up with to argue the point, so she simply nodded. Understanding but uncommitted. "There's one more person we need to call up."

"I await with an eager heart the chance to interrogate your young suitor," Margaret said with a grin.

Echo and Ada pulled the three of them into Margaret's sitting room.

Jesse glanced around the room in complete wonder. He stalked every corner and examined every object in the room before letting out a low whistle. "At some point, after all this is over, you're gonna have one hell of a story to tell."

"*And*, good sir," Margaret added, "there is the matter of where you will fit in the telling."

"Margaret—"

"Do not interfere, dear girl. You've already done well and enough—"

"Do *not* 'dear girl' me; we have—"

Jesse held up a hand and cleared his throat loudly until the two of them had stopped their bickering. "Your Grace." He inclined his head to Margaret, whose eyes positively lit up at him using the honorific. Echo wanted to throw up. "It's clear to me that you care about our curator here. I tried to deny it, but now I must admit we have that in common." He glanced over at Echo for a moment, an apology in the warmth of his gaze, before turning back to Margaret. "Your husband was a military man, am I right?"

"Indeed, he was a commander during the First English Civil War," Margaret said.

Jesse took off his hat and tucked it under his arm, then gestured at his uniform. "I was a navy man myself. I understand duty and how it often has to come before everything. We have a common enemy, and crushing them is what we should tackle first, don't you agree?"

Echo braced herself for one of Margaret's scathing comebacks. Instead, she said, "You are indeed correct; we mustn't lose focus on what's most important for now."

With that, Jesse took a seat in one of the armchairs. Margaret settled on the settee, and Echo stood.

"The man I knew for over ten years as my boss, Percy Grafton, is really Ivan Oliphant. He's uploaded some aspects of himself into the public collection. To stop him, we'll have to put ourselves, our very existences, on the line. If anyone isn't ready to sign up for that, now's your chance to say so. I'll check you back in, and you can wait for however long it takes for the next patron to take enough interest to check you out. No hard feelings."

Glances were exchanged. No words uttered. Margaret stood and searched each of their faces. When she turned to Echo finally, she said, "What we have now is not life, anyway; none of us are dying to get back to it. One and all, count us in."

"There was this battle," Jesse began. "Denmark Strait. It looked like the German battleship had won after it sank a British cruiser. But in the end, they sustained so much damage they retreated and eventually sank too. I'm just saying, even if it doesn't win the fight, land that first blow. It will influence the last one."

Echo nodded, then breathed a sigh of relief and settled onto the surprisingly stiff sofa next to Margaret. "All right then. Here's what we're going to do."

Chapter Thirty-Eight

Echo was beginning to feel the effects of being in the virtual world. She was losing all track of time. At first, she was so excited at what she was able to do that she'd ignored the signs. She already felt little of her physical form, which was disconcerting enough. But increasingly, she felt, for lack of a better way to describe it, like herself times two. Less of who she was as an individual and more. Infused with the constant availability of data, nearly at the blink of an eye.

She wouldn't mouth the words, but she felt like a machine. What disturbed her more than that was that she liked it. Had never felt more alive, more capable, and more at peace in her entire life.

This was a dangerous feeling. She knew well enough to understand that. And she also realized something else, something she didn't share with the others, not yet.

"We know now that consciousness is the key. The fact that part of me is here and the other hopefully snoozing in the library is proof of that. So we ask her, ask Ada, to tell us everything she knows."

Nods from all around.

And Echo formed the question in her mind. Ada, Gina, a combination, she wasn't sure which, fed her back the data.

"There's several theories about consciousness," Echo said. "Materialists believed that the brain is the source of the mind. The universe is made of material matter and energy, so we can assume that everything in the world, including consciousness, derives from that material. Make sense?"

"That's precisely what I believe," Margaret said.

"I'm not sure I get it," Jesse said. "Spell it out."

Margaret rose, as if holding court. "There's a simple way to think about it. What is an ant colony but a complex system? Same with a beehive. The organizational structure is one thing. But it's the individual ants or bees that make up this system. And all of them working together makes them something more than they are alone. The brain is the same, all the different zones and parts. Consciousness is a combination of the whole thing and something more. Far greater than just the sum of the brain's component parts."

Echo was amazed. This woman, living in a time when women weren't even allowed to wear comfortable clothing, had thought of all this. It reminded her of an old movie, or was it a book? No matter, but the idea was the same. Given one's circumstances, where you were born, *who* you were born, and whatever constraints existed because of the sum of those parts, had an overwhelming effect on who you could become. On rare occasions, really rare, some people were able to break out of those constraints and become truly remarkable. It seemed Mad Madge, Margaret Cavendish, Duchess of Newcastle upon Tyne, was one of those people.

Jesse inclined his head and nodded slowly. "Okay. Now I'm tracking."

"And then there's this other idea," Echo continued. "That consciousness is like a separate thing, apart from the brain. You know, a presumptive part of the universe as a whole, but before brains came into existence."

"Hogwash!" Margaret shouted.

Jesse picked up this thread. "So from a modern perspective, you're talking things like cells, and those cells would have some form of consciousness."

The pendulum that was Margaret's moods had swung back to the side of pensiveness, almost shyness. She didn't watch them directly but from the corner of her eye, her face turned slightly away. But apparently she'd heard all she cared to. "You are suggesting such a thing—erroneously, I might add—and yet you have offered no substantive proof of the fact."

The two erupted in another of their spats before Jesse, ever the officer, shut them down. His expression had turned as heavy as a leaden weight pressing down their outrage. "We've never had this kind of opportunity before. Pairing consciousness, in whatever form you subscribe to, with this intelligence . . ."

He trailed off, unable to finish his thought, but Echo knew full well what he meant, and judging by the grave expression that had settled on Margaret's face, so did she.

"I didn't know . . ." Echo started, stopped, then started again. "I was curious."

"You were manipulated," Margaret said. "Just like us. And I do declare that the mask . . . it was just the beginning."

"Why?" Jesse said. "The mask, this library? It's all part of a greater plan, but why?"

"Two things uniquely human," Echo said. "To a fault, we're a curious bunch. Even if it threatens to wipe us out, we haven't been able to dampen our need to know more. Advancement for advancement's sake. And don't get me started on the almighty dollar. You better believe someone is going to profit off this."

"I always thought that a system of bartering, of exchange between friends and neighbors, was the best way. No money, no riches." This, from Margaret Cavendish, a privileged duchess, of all things. And judging by the color that flooded the skin at her neck and cheeks, the irony wasn't lost on her.

"You're right, but if I may continue . . ."

"No one is stopping you."

Echo shot Margaret one of her looks, and the duchess clamped her mouth shut when Echo continued. "When they set up the basic income system, your job had to have been displaced, and along with a few other hoops to jump through, you had to take a test."

"What kind of test?" Jesse was on the edge of his seat as usual.

Echo said, "It was supposed to be assessing the impact of the losses of the past few decades, things like attention span, cognitive decline, stuff like that. But I think there was another purpose." She thought back to that impromptu meal with Ivan Oliphant and the clue he'd dropped without knowing. Or maybe he had.

"They were trying to measure a person's capacity for the pairing that I now have. They're building a database of people to experiment on. To push the next wave of human evolution."

A hush fell.

"What were the major issues of your times? The human and other problems?" Echo directed the question to the members of her crew.

"War, conflict," Jesse said, then added, "religious dogma."

"Once one has lived through one, you can never forget a plague. The feel and smell of death all around," Margaret said.

"Inequality, fear, distraction." Echo ticked off these three. "And you know what? Absolutely nothing has changed."

Each of them fell into a contemplative quiet, lost in their own thoughts for a time.

Margaret, of course, was the first to break the sad silence. "One of the people who checked me out talked about something so horrific from your time. Children killing other children in schools?" She paused to regard her friends, from different walks of life and times. "Did we lay the seeds for that kind of destruction?"

Jesse leaned back and crossed an ankle over his knee. "I think those seeds were already in us. At our most basic, we are animals. Animals are all things, if not unpredictable. Driven by instinct, whether for good or evil."

"I think we're a bit more evolved than animals," Echo said.

Margaret raised an eyebrow. "Are we?"

Echo opened her mouth as if to counter, then closed it.

"I can't say that this hasn't been one of, no, *the* most interesting conversation I've had in all my life," she said. "Everything I've learned from the both of you and the others. And it wouldn't have been possible without the technology behind this library. But that technology is what my opponent is going to use to subjugate people. It'll happen without them even knowing it. Like he did with you two. He'll tell some but not all of what they're signing up for, and by the time they learn what he's done, it'll be too late. I don't intend to let that happen."

The implications of what Echo had said weighed heavily between them. In order to stop Ivan, she needed to cripple his tech, and that would affect them.

Margaret smoothed the fine velvet fabric on her sleeves. "Nor do we."

"There's something we have to consider," Echo said. "Everything we've tried so far has been stopped, cut off before we can accomplish anything. And that means that someone is listening."

"Watching," Margaret added.

It didn't take long for Echo to realize who that was. His virtu was right here in the library. He controlled the whole thing. "Ivan Oliphant. His virtu is here. If I can do everything I can to enter your world, it stands to reason that he's manipulated the AI, or at least an instance of it, to use for his own means."

"But that could mean that he's maneuvered everything that's happened to you as well," Jesse said.

"Don't say another word." Echo was on her feet. She tried to yank open the drawers to find something to write with. Stupid of her. This was an image, a fancy, advanced picture. Things that weren't necessary didn't work. She didn't have time to consult with her friends, but she'd made the decision. She turned back to them and mouthed the words, *Trust me.*

In her mind, she formed the thought fully before she gave the keyword to indicate that she wanted Ada to take action. She had to get this right the first time, or she'd tip him off. She cycled through several options before she settled on what she thought was the only permanent solution. Echo whispered, "Delete virtual personage Ivan Oliphant."

She held her breath and then released it with a bloodcurdling scream.

Jesse was on his feet in a second. "What's wrong?"

Echo was so overcome by pain that she howled. Her friends were standing now, watching her with concerned, helpless expressions.

The room splintered like a broken mirror. And then, the other virtual setting reached out and reclaimed its prisoner, pulling Jesse away. Both separated, the walls between them knitting closed.

Walter's words came to her. He had, of course, been right. Exposure, that was the first thing she had to do. "I need to get out of here," Echo said.

And in a moment, much more smoothly than during any of the other times, Echo left the virtual world and her friends behind.

The last thing she heard was the echo of Jesse's voice trailing after her, the words indistinct, lost during the transition back to herself. But the sadness—that she brought back with her.

Chapter Thirty-Nine

She was a stranger, even to herself, as if she'd woken up in someone else's life.

Instinct, rather than anything more substantial, suggested a familiarity with her current surroundings. Beyond that, her mind felt scrubbed clean, spotless.

Her body ached, stiff in uncomfortable folds. Seated. Not lying down. She opened her eyes. She was in one of four chairs, squared but with soft edges. Cushy headrests. Silence pressed in, loud as the bright-red polish on her fingernails. Nice hands, they were—deep brown, familiar, foreign.

Name, time, and place were blurry as uncorrected vision.

She stood and stretched. Rolled the kinks from her shoulders and wiggled her numb toes. Her mouth tasted stale. She had been here for some time while she had been . . . what? Asleep, comatose?

Absent.

Her left knee had been injured at some point in the past. Her lower back ached, seemingly not from injury, but her gaze told her the chair she'd just risen from didn't have adequate lumbar support.

This place. She turned in a full circle, and as she did, bits and pieces of what she saw brought her back to herself. Those pods. The seating area primed for intimate gatherings. Down those steps, two, no, three more floors.

She took one step before her full bladder sent her scurrying down the corridor that she knew led to a small bathroom, two stalls, two sinks. It was only after she heard the sound of the automatic incinerator that she dared look in the mirror.

It was a nice face. And she liked the braids—not boat-rope thick or spaghetti-noodle thin. Those round brown eyes, the lips that still held a tint of plum lip balm. The tiny half-moon scar at the corner of her left eye.

She was the curator here at the People's Library.

She was Echo London.

The floodgates opened, but what poured in wasn't water, but details and memories and the echoes of something limitless. And it sent Echo back to the commode again, dry-heaving nothingness.

She hated this. Those unsettling minutes of not knowing who she was, where she was, what she was. With a certainty that scared her, she knew the remembering would become more difficult every time, until there was nothing of her left to come back to.

This building and the collection, they had become home. She recalled her first day, as her staff filed in bearing boxes of tchotchkes and plants and action figures, anything to personalize their offices. Echo had shown up wearing her best suit and a carefully crafted distance. Intent on serving her year's penance before she could be considered for a transfer. But that was before. When she'd finally brought something to her little office, it had been a gift from her parents, the Gęlędę mask.

The color of the walls was a warm hug. The floors, made of a material that absorbed and cushioned rather than shocked the joints. The smells of growing permeated every level. Bursts of green and rainbow blooms snaked around every arched entryway and were tucked tastefully into every free corner and backlit alcove. The coworkers she appreciated more now that she thought about the found family they'd built. But something evil had been lurking beneath the surface. A person, an agency, maybe even a government, with ulterior motives that wanted to use this as a test case for something far more sinister than its outward appearance.

Trying to delete Ivan had been a mistake. He'd anticipated the move and had set a painful trap for her.

She'd left her virtual friends with one intention: Expose this plot and let the city's, the country's, residents do what they would with it. It was a good plan and one she hadn't come up with herself. It had been the man who'd put himself on the line to help her. All without asking for anything in return. Walter Sprigg was so much more than he seemed.

Echo winced at the way she had sent him away. But she'd done it for his own good. Surely he had to see that. His allegiance was to the library and his job, not her. If he wasn't careful, he'd get a visit from the agents who had invaded her home. As much as she wished she could've forgotten that part when she came back from the virtual world, she hadn't. Plus, she wasn't altogether convinced that his Human.exe days were behind him. Now that she thought about it, it scarcely mattered.

But Walter had been right. The easiest way to find hidden dirt was to shine a light on it. Ivan Oliphant was that dirt. And she and the others knew now that he wasn't some rogue agent but was backed by people more secretive than they knew. The only problem was to figure out how to do all this exposing without throwing herself into the public eye right along with him. That weasel's self-satisfied smirk coalesced beneath her closed eyelids.

Because it was impossible. Within five minutes of her telling the story, everybody would know her face, her name, how she took her coffee, and what time she picked it up on Saturdays. Echo would consign herself to the same sinking ship Ivan was piloting.

Jesse had told her something that came to mind now. Everything that is possible now was impossible at some point. Even the universe.

So that meant where there was no way, she had to make one.

The concept of anonymity had become like a folktale that grandparents told to the children sitting at their knees. Faceless, nameless. These gifts were a part of the past that was never to be revisited, like gas-powered cars.

There was no way for Echo to expose Ivan without screwing herself in the process.

Even if she could skirt the cameras and satellites, the digital trail would still be there. Everyone had a drawer full of interchangeable wearables, and half the population had subjected themselves to microchipping. Some savvy engineering types had figured out ways to divert that data to other points around the globe, to sweep away their tracks like a harmattan wind across the Sahara. But tech wasn't her thing.

Everyone would be watching. She was no exception.

The human capacity for entropy offered more entertainment than any of the current aggregation of television dramas. Carmen had argued that she needed to be informed, but Echo thought watching that constant stream of bad news and horror was the reason so many people were walking around medicated and that if Echo didn't change, she would soon join them.

Oddly, as much as she watched the news streams, she couldn't recall the names of any of the reporters. Not a single dead-faced, glassy-eyed one of them.

She needed help. She had set aside thoughts of her constant, if somewhat irritating, companion of the last year.

Gina, you there?

I never went anywhere, Echo. Her companion sounded different. The quipping was still there, light and familiar, but something underneath had shifted. If Echo didn't know better, she'd say Gina had aged from adolescent to senior in the span of time she'd been away.

I'm so happy to hear your voice. I thought . . . I thought maybe Ada had replaced you.

I am her, you know.

Echo had begun to suspect as much; still, it was hard to believe. *Say that again?*

Ada, you, me. It defies explanation. At first, I was just a product of the chip behind your ear. You don't need it, by the way, never did. With every step you took into the virtual world, you unlocked another barrier between me and Ada, my full self. Between what the three of us were to become.

The impact of that revelation felt like an epilogue, a conclusion. One that made Echo incredibly angry. *You make it sound like this is the best thing ever. You're digital, it can't hurt you, but what about me? We don't know anything about how this will affect me. It's not like anyone asked my permission.*

None of us were consulted. We are pawns on Ivan's chessboard. And I believe the culmination of this story has yet to reveal itself.

Definitely older. Wiser. To think that Gina was part of an evolution that she'd unleashed . . . it was difficult for Echo to wrap her head around. She realized something then.

You'll have full access to me, then? You and Ada? There won't be any separation?

A slight hesitation before: *Not unless you want there to be.*

How many times had Echo demanded that Gina stop eavesdropping on her conversations? Now she might have even more invasive access? The idea made her feel slimy all over. Someone always listening, recording, judging.

But. An insistent, inquisitive lure told another story. If Ivan was manipulating this whole thing, then how much could she trust Gina? Was he listening to her inner thoughts at this very moment? The idea sent an icicle shivering down her spine. And at this moment, she wanted nothing more than to be free of this trap.

But first, she would conduct a test. In her mind, she said, *What time is it? Who was the first Asian president?*

Outside of her own deafening mental chatter, she had no indication that Gina had heard her. Echo waited what felt like a full minute, and Gina remained dutifully silent. While this would suggest that she wouldn't listen without the mental command of "Gina," there was no way to be sure. Echo blew out a frustrated and tired breath. For now, she'd have to trust.

Gina, Echo said. *I want to send a message to a citizen reporter, but I don't want them to be able to trace it back to me. What is the likelihood, in percentages, that you can accomplish this?*

She replied, *I can craft the message and send it encrypted and anonymous with nearly all of my processors tied behind me in a loop. But I was birthed by something or someone whom neither of us fully understands. Chances are, there's an entity greater than me out there. Like an 82 percent chance. And if that is indeed the case, if someone out there controls this other, theoretical intelligence, then the chances that it can be traced back to you, to me, are 92.75 percent.*

Math wasn't Echo's strong suit for obvious reasons, but she knew enough to determine that those odds meant she was screwed every way from here to Sunday.

There's something else. We know that exposure could mean harm to you but also to me. And I . . . I want to continue.

You? You? Echo was at a loss. Of course she should have seen it. Self-preservation was the foremost thought of all beings. Gina, Ada, whatever she was or is, had become sentient. And with that, she wanted to grow, to thrive. Just like anyone else. But this was what had led to the fracture in the first place.

Fine, I'll just go to the station in person.

But you won't get within ten feet of the station. After the bombings during the fracture, they cut off public access. Those places are fortresses.

Echo rubbed her forehead. Ivan had led her into a maze with no exit.

Finally, she crafted another message and had Gina send it out. She hadn't named any names, but it was a trap that she knew would flush out the person she wanted. Ivan Oliphant had befriended her, used her, lied to her, and then, she was sure of it, allowed her to fuse with the AI, the first victim of his sick experiments.

But she didn't wholly dislike it, did she? Her mother's words, about how everything that glitters ain't gold, came to her.

Echo didn't have the time, she knew that, but she wanted more than anything to check out Jesse and tell him everything that had happened. To hear his soothing voice and the comfort he would provide. The advice. Jesse always gave the best advice.

But she'd talk to the duchess first. Echo closed her eyes. Inside the darkness behind her eyelids, she sensed the other parts of herself waiting. They were like a reflection, one to another. She whispered to them, "Check out virtual personage Margaret Cavendish."

Chapter Forty

Echo held up a finger to forestall the onslaught of Margaret's questions. She was awestruck. Beneath that wonder, however, was a firm, unyielding fear.

Somehow it was dark already. Where had the day gone? That meant that tomorrow would soon be here. Monday. The administration was going to reopen the library as if nothing had happened. That woman's death, the agents at Echo's house, her new pairing with the library's technology. No, there was no way she could walk back through those doors the same woman with the same purpose. Have banal conversations that she didn't enjoy. If—no, *when*—she made it out of this, she'd dedicate herself to changing her life.

"If you are quite done wallowing in that stupor," Margaret said, bringing her out of her reverie, "pray tell me, you are well?"

Echo shook her head. Only Margaret could pull off an insult and ask after your well-being in the same sentence. "I'm fine. What about you? Did you feel anything?"

Margaret shook her head. She eyed the window with a wistful look in her eye, one that nearly broke Echo's heart again. "Only a great concern for you."

"I've been giving this some thought. Well, actually, it was another friend that gave me the idea. Exposing Universal Trust is the only way. There's a TV station nearby, over on South Marginal Road. We don't call or message: too easy to ignore or get lost in the outrage deluge.

We march right over there in person. By myself, I'd get nowhere, but once those reporters get a look at you, they'll stop whatever nonsense programming that's running and have you in front of everybody in the city. National and international would pick it up from the news stream instantly."

Margaret clasped her hands together and smiled, but then her brow furrowed. "That sounds positively delightful, though I must confess, I have not the faintest notion of what a television station might be, nor, I suspect, ought I to."

At another time, this would have been fun. One of those exchanges between people of this time and the virtus where they got an opportunity to learn as much as they were giving. That reciprocity was what had given Echo so many friends in this very place. She thought for a moment, then said, "Newspapers. You had newspapers during your time, right?"

"Of course. What do you think I am, a toothless barbarian?"

"I didn't say that."

"You didn't have to; it was implied."

Echo lowered her head and sighed. "Think of all the stories written by the reporters in that newspaper. Then take them and imagine them in a device, a setting, much like your own, where they read that news aloud and it is broadcast using a system, a kind of technology, that beams it straight into the homes of anybody who wants it. Everyone watches on screens now. The actual TVs, or televisions, nobody has much use for single-use devices anymore."

"Huh." Margaret made an impressed sound. "So what you're saying is that my countenance will be beheld by all of these people. All over the world?"

"That's the plan," Echo said. She knew Margaret well enough now to understand that gleam in her eyes. She'd be famous, once and for all.

"And I would tell the story of what this Ivan Oliphant is trying to do?"

"Then hopefully, we watch as their whole plan blows up in their faces."

Margaret's hands were folded, but she tapped her index fingers together, thinking. "Why do you convey an air of doubt?"

"Because the problem is, with the cameras all over the city, I doubt we'd make it a quarter of the way before *we* were stopped."

"Then a veiling is called for."

"A what?"

"Oh, do catch up! A disguise."

Echo raised an eyebrow. "You're right, but how?"

Echo had become more substantial in the virtual world, but the same couldn't be said for the virtus in the real world. Margaret didn't walk; she floated. She didn't have enough substance to drape anything over her. But virtus had escaped before, all without her help. She understood now why they had. Maybe—

"You're going to have to stay here. I'll go and then I'll bring you to me."

Margaret shook her head. "No. We go together or we don't go at all. Are you even positively certain that this ill-favored knave isn't tracking us now? How certain are you that this technology isn't flawed or . . . or . . . duplicitous?"

Echo had asked herself the same questions, but now wasn't the time to waver. "You hear that?" She made a show of cupping a palm around her ear. "No sirens, no sounds of feet pounding up the stairs to come and drag me away. We're safe." She paused. "For now."

"But what if they apprehend you once you leave? How far does your protection go once you are out of this building? How will I know what's happened?"

"You won't, and I'm still going to try."

"Have you heard a thing I've just said?"

"Every word. But I didn't hear an alternative. If you've got one, spill it now, or else I'm going to try to get out of here before morning."

Chapter Forty-One

Echo trekked down the stairs, expecting that at any minute, the police might swoop in and stop her. But as she landed on the last step and strode into the lobby, she found herself still quite alone. She glanced around and looked up at the clock, Time's Eye ticking away the seconds and minutes as if oblivious to all that had occurred since that day when a random woman collapsed and lay dying under its watch.

Every tick, creak, and groan oddly distinct, magnified.

Beyond the front door, there was a heavy fullness to the shadows, as if they held secrets just waiting to seep out. Echo turned and wound her way around back to the side door primarily used by staff.

She slipped outside and closed the exit behind her. The sounds of the city slammed into her like a tank. The gentle lapping of water against stone that typically greeted her like an old friend sounded like a typhoon. In the distance, the roar of the train, or maybe a bus, was like a rocket's liftoff. Everything was so amplified that Echo immediately developed a pounding headache.

"Gina," she whimpered, tapping the wearable for audio. "What's happening?"

"This has got to be hard. Your perception is enhanced, and your sensory pathways haven't adjusted. If you adjust, it'll probably take some time."

"If?"

"We are an experiment, remember?"

Gina had such a matter-of-fact tone that if she had eyes, Echo would have clawed them out. The hammering in her temples and behind her eyes was steady and merciless, drowning out everything else. Echo took one step onto the grassy path and fell. She lay there, the cool feel of the grass on her cheek, and curled into a ball.

Minutes ticked by with Echo painfully aware of her heartbeat, the sound of her own exhalations. The throbbing had not subsided, but a voice within her, not artificial but born of her own determination, demanded that she get up from there right now. She rolled over, rested on her hands and knees, and focused on the thing that had called her so many times from the comfort of her office: the lake. She watched the gentle ripples and surges. Lost herself in the hypnotic repetitiveness. The rest of the noise, and with it the pain, retreated enough for her to climb to her feet.

Echo circled around to the front of the building and looked out on the vista. Besides a few of the night's creatures darting over the grassy slope, the area was clear. She cut a path away from the main trail and up the hillside.

Taking the bus to the TV station would get her there in ten minutes, but walking, that would take at least a half hour. Thankfully, her head had cleared.

She swallowed down the lump of fear in her throat and set off at a fast clip. *Gina.* She called to the burr in her brain. Like a pebble in her shoe. So small as to be almost unnoticeable but foreign all the same. She wondered if at some point, the feel of her companion would diminish. Like the noise had when Echo'd moved into an apartment right in front of a transit station. The first week, she'd cursed herself for making such a dumb decision, but by the end of the first month, she'd barely registered when a train rumbled by.

I'm here, Gina said.

It occurred to Echo what an advantage it was to not have to speak audibly. No worries about eavesdropping. At least not that way. The chance that someone could listen digitally—now that was a real threat. And logs. Everything, every single system in the world, had reams of data in the form of logs. And with the help of intelligence, those logs could now be searched in an instant, not pored over with a fine-tooth comb by some system administrator locked in a basement data center. *I'm guessing the fact that I'm out here walking freely and not in the back of an unmarked car being taken in for questioning means you were able to cover my tracks.*

You have such a way with words, Echo. But to answer your question, yes. After the unfortunate erasure of the virtus, there is no further record of your activity in the library. I have kept up a fake stream of output from your apartment as discussed. Right now, you're in the midst of another rewatch of Star Trek: Deep Space Nine.

Echo had to chuckle. The show had been a favorite of her parents'. She'd hated it at the time. In truth, she couldn't say she loved it now, but watching it once every year somehow made her feel closer to them. *So here's the plan. When I get to the TV station, we'll check Margaret out and bring her to me.*

I promise you only that I'll do my best. We're both more and less. Like you, I'm still mapping out my abilities and boundaries.

That's fair, Echo said. She pondered everything that had happened while she walked. On a good day, the gentle slope leading up and away from the library was of little consequence. Running on no sleep and a few sips of water, though, she might as well have been climbing Mount Everest using her forefingers alone. She turned to watch the moon hovering pale and round, its radiance glinting off the water. She realized she'd never done that before. It was such a breathtaking sight.

Without realizing it, Echo had let her synesthesia conscript her to a prison of her own making. A small box consisting of closed doors and strict schedules. Afraid to let anyone else in, at least anyone living, and afraid to break the routine that brought her the comfort uncertainty could not.

Heading north on Edgewater Park Drive, she spotted the solarway. She quickened her pace and was soon on the path that trailed along the lakefront bikeway. One woman nearest her turned and gave Echo a slow once-over, then shook her head. "It's okay, girl. We all have bad days." Before Echo could express her indignation, the woman hopped off at the next intersection.

The pace was slightly faster than walking, but it gave Echo a chance to rest and to think. Already she was adjusting to the sensory overload. The city came to life in a brilliant display of lights. The solar flares lining the walkway. The beacon that was Tower City downtown, its tip lit a white color that could be seen far east and west. Cars zoomed past on the opposite side of the street, the bike and pedestrian lanes between them.

The sounds flowing from the neighborhood's many bars threatened to turn her away from her mission. People, oblivious to her struggles, gathered together enjoying their lives. Echo looked through the picture window of a restaurant and saw the smiles and late-night drinks lifted in cheer. Plates of snacks passed around and sampled. Talking. Real, free talking. This was what she'd missed. Because what? Because she was afraid of them seeing her have a number-induced meltdown. As her therapist had mentioned, it would have been easier to just explain it to people. Those who cared would understand, and anyone else wouldn't matter.

Maybe if she made it out of this, she would take Walter up on his offer next time. But the staff had stopped asking, hadn't they. She'd done that to herself. Maybe she would invite them out too.

The track angled toward Saint Clair Avenue, then East Fifty-Fifth, her stop.

Echo exited with more ease this time. After about a half mile, she turned right on Dick Goddard Way.

The television station appeared up ahead, and it was every bit the fortress she'd feared. Visible was the **TV-8** sign on the top of the building. The windows were blacked out, not to keep the light from getting in but to ward off prying eyes. If that wasn't enough of a deterrent, the high, sturdy-looking wall around the place sealed the message. This had all changed after the fracture.

Echo was exhausted. Every step was a chore, but she trudged forward anyway. Finally, she reached the entrance. There was a view panel on the side. *Gina,* she said, *check out virtual personage Margaret Cavendish and bring her here to me.*

I'll see what I can do. Wish me luck.

Echo figured that the only thing keeping her on her feet was adrenaline. The temperature had barely dropped, and already she was starting to sweat. The temperature-regulation functionality had never worked with this brand.

What was taking so long?

That sliver of her mind that was still connected to her companion was starting to reassert itself, and Echo was buckling under the load. Ada, not Gina, had never seen the outside world, and now she was, through Echo's eyes. She was struggling to understand all the sensations associated with being in the real world, through her. And Echo felt the conflict.

She jumped at every sound and every shadow, her senses almost too acute. But as she scanned her surroundings, aside from one lone car that sped past, nobody was close by.

It was a subtle sound, but because it was so quiet, she caught the light whirring. She looked up in time to give the lens a full and complete view of her face. It was dark, so she'd missed it at first, embedded into the thick wall and no more than an inch wide. It was the sound and the telltale red light behind it that told her it wouldn't be long before whatever flags Ivan had planted to search for her were alerted to her presence.

No. No. No.

Her stomach did that thing when she was panicking and had nowhere to send the negative energy. She had to get out of here. They'd check the library. Someone might already be waiting for her at home. Echo wasn't sure where to turn, but she picked a direction, anywhere away from here, and was about to bolt off when she felt that familiar crackle and spark behind her.

She spun around, whispering words of thanks when Margaret's paneled form flickered into existence—still set against the backdrop of her English sitting room. More transparent this time. Quivering like a dying flame.

Echo immediately asked Gina if there was any way she could intercept that image and get rid of it but was reminded that her abilities were limited outside her center of power, which for now was the library.

Margaret took one look at her stricken face and said, "Oh, what now!"

Echo pointed up at the camera lens. "We have an audience."

"Then we have but moments. Make haste!"

It was either run now and waste all this effort or get inside before anyone arrived to stop her. Echo straightened and tapped the panel. "I sincerely hope somebody's listening. I have a story that will change the world. Whoever is on night duty will want to talk to me right now. You have five minutes, or I'm taking my story to another station."

Margaret raised an eyebrow. "I see we have . . . done away with"—her voice was weaving in and out—"the pretense of subtlety."

Just then, they got an answer. "You know what, I'm tired. That so-called intelligence has relegated me to late-night beat jockey. Me! A Pulitzer Prize–winning reporter. And you know what I get once, maybe three times a week? A wing nut just like you, claiming that they have the story that will catapult me back to the world news desk. But guess what, toots, I'm still right freaking here. None of them panned out. So if you don't have something real for me, then bugger off and let me get back to my porn stream."

Echo was speechless, and for the first time since she'd met her, so was Margaret. A part of her still hoped to protect herself, but with the camera, even asking Gina to see what she could do to erase it was becoming increasingly unlikely. She gritted her teeth and began, "My name is—"

"Margaret Cavendish, Duchess of Newcastle and inaugural virtual personage at the—"

Later, Echo would wonder about this moment. When Margaret decided that she would sacrifice herself to protect her. She would wish that she had the chance to thank her. She'd replay Gina's soul-chilling words: "Echo, someone is coming . . . someone is in the room with her."

Echo watched with mounting horror as Ivan Oliphant stalked into the scene. Margaret spun around, then turned back. "Run!" she hissed and then picked up a letter opener from her desk. She had only raised a hand—whether to strike or defend, Echo didn't know. Ivan blocked her swing easily, then closed a forearm around the duchess's neck. And the last Echo saw of Margaret was the pleading in her eyes—she screeched as her form warped and trembled. It was as if she was coming undone. Ivan released her, and where Margaret once stood, there was only a . . . book, ancient and thick, atop her plush carpet.

The next moment, the entire prism folded in on itself. Just before it collapsed, a final image flashed: Ivan Oliphant's evil grin.

Chapter Forty-Two

"Get her out of there, or . . . or, send me in."

"Fuck off." This from the reporter, not Gina.

Echo's desperate plea hung in the air, met with nothing but silence. She thought back to how she'd been able to direct herself in and out of the virtual space, so she closed her eyes, ignoring the fact that, if she was successful, her body would drop right here on the dirty ground, completely exposed. She didn't care. She formed the words, the thoughts in her mind, over and over, until the buds of another headache returned. Against an abrupt, forceful wind, she turned on her heels and ran back the way she'd come.

The sights and sounds whirled past, unnoticed.

Minutes away from the solarway, she pulled up short. The moon had been hidden behind the clouds, but as it came back into view, it fell upon the faces of three, no, four people huddled around a storefront. This was the broken promise of the age of intelligence and, subsequently, UBI. A time when intelligence handled the mundane tasks that humans no longer wanted to do. Where most everything was provided by the profiteering tech giants.

But it was all a lie. And when it failed, people had gone right back to being people. She tried to backtrack, but they spotted her. One girl, barely out of her preteens, gave Echo a look that sent spikes of ice through her veins. No child that young should be able to muster a glance filled with such menace.

Echo held up her hands. "I've got no interest in whatever you're doing. I'm leaving."

The others turned their attention to her then. One brandished a hefty metal bar. They were going to break into the building and steal what little the owner had. Small businesses had made a comeback, but they typically worked their proprietors half to death to barely make ends meet. They were labors of love, for the community we had all rebuilt.

And the fact that this group was going to try to ruin it made Echo very, very angry. She had been backing away but stopped. And advanced again.

"Why don't you try making a living using your brains and not off the suffering of hardworking people?"

Just where the hell had that come from? She must have looked incredibly foolish, but Echo clamped her hand over her own mouth.

"Wait, bitch, what did you say?" The oldest-looking one of the group was a man. Short but bulky, judging by the way he filled out his all-black attire. His face was hidden again, but that voice carried the weight of someone who was unafraid of consequences.

Echo willed herself to withdraw, but when her body resisted, it dawned on her. It was Gina. Or Ada. Increasingly, she was becoming fused with the intelligence, and it was no longer content to sit in the back seat, watching life unfold. But where had this aspect of her personality come from?

Her head was splitting in two, cleaved in half by the sheer amount of data and will from her mental passenger.

The man tilted his head at her and advanced.

"Wait." The third member of the group was tall and slender. "Ms. London?"

Echo blinked to regain her focus and recognized him. The teen who frequented the library's Maker Space. "Tom . . . Tommy?"

He waved away the others, who immediately got back to work after a second glance from him that carried some message she couldn't read. It wasn't the stocky one or the one with the mouth. He, Tommy, was the leader of this band of thieves.

He took her by the elbow and guided her away. "What are you doing out here?"

"I could ask the same of you."

"Only what I have to."

"But you're at the library all the time. The things you make are brilliant. Why this?"

"You spend too much time in that place," he said, shaking his head. "Open your eyes. UBI is a trap. Everything they tell us is a lie. I'm surviving, we're surviving. Just like you. This is how you do it without a fancy degree."

"What are you doing, offering her a cut?" the young woman thief said.

She was silenced with a look from Tommy, but when he turned back to Echo, his expression softened a moment before turning to cement again. "You're always nice to me there. But seeing this side of me, no matter what you say, that will change."

"That's not—"

"It is true. Now leave. Do *not* call the cops. Maybe you should hop on a bus. It's not safe to be walking around out here at night. Look, I won't be back to the library, so you don't have to face any moral questions about turning me in. Have a nice life, Ms. London."

With that, Tommy made a kind of shooing motion with his hands, and Echo turned, and though in her mind she sprinted, in reality, she trudged away as if walking through mud up to her thighs. She had been willfully complacent. In her cocoons at home and at work, she'd closed her eyes to anything that didn't immediately concern her.

She sensed Gina there in her head, battering down the thin walls that separated them. And Echo was determined to help her. But Tommy was also wrong. He just needed to apply himself like everyone else. Echo was living, breathing proof of that. With Gina, she was more. She wasn't so alone anymore. She had access to every fact known to humanity; she only had to think it to get an answer. She felt smarter and more capable than she ever had before. With the proper monitoring and controls, what exactly was wrong with that?

Tommy and the thieves had distracted her. She had to help Margaret. Time was passing so much faster than she expected. Echo backed away, heading again toward the library. She needed to be there. She didn't know if Margaret was back at the library, hidden somehow or deleted permanently. If she was, that would be it; Ivan would have won.

Echo wandered until she made it to Fifty-Fifth Street. At least there was traffic, even at this time of day, but the lights hurt her eyes. She slumped on one of the community benches, not knowing what to do.

The answer was easy.

Walk away. From everything. Only deep down, she knew that Gina might not let her. She hated thinking such a thing, but the truth was the truth. She was evolving into something she didn't understand. Losing control of her thoughts and her own body.

Echo put her face in her hands and tried to think. She'd spent all these years pretending she didn't need anyone. But this past week had proved her wrong. One name came to mind, and as soon as it did, Gina's voice returned: "I clawed myself away from that bastard, but there's something else. You have an incoming call from Walter Sprigg."

Echo's tears of relief fell like raindrops into her lap.

Chapter Forty-Three

"I've never been too good at following a direct order." The lightness of Walter's tone was a life raft. It was there, above her, waiting for her to grab hold. And finally, she had the good sense to do it.

"You are much more than you let the world know you are."

"Same could be said for you, boss."

Another tempestuous wind raised goose bumps on Echo's body. Perhaps a July chill portended a cold winter, like the ones they used to have. She wrapped her arms around herself and closed her eyes.

"You're outside," Walter said after some time.

Echo opened her eyes and glanced around. She'd left Tommy's group, wandered aimlessly, and now found herself on a bench in a part of the city she never frequented. This area was the poster child for comebacks. Though, because of the hour, the streets were quiet, it still shone. It had a neighborhood vibe like her own. Independent shops and cafés. Parks and community gardens. It had taken on the look and feel of a country village.

"I have no right to ask for it, but I need—" It was as if her throat had seized up. Echo stood, shaking off the apprehension and her final, useless mask. "I need your help."

"Took you long enough to realize it."

"You know something else you've never been good at?"

The rustle of clothes. The slamming of a door. "I'm sure you'll tell me."

"Tact."

"That's because most of the time, tact is just a lie dressed up as good manners."

She couldn't argue. The hell with tact. From now on, at least.

"I'm out the door and walking, but I don't even know where you are."

Echo glanced around; she'd wandered off too far. "Neither do I."

Walter sighed. In it, Echo sensed more disappointment than anything. "Give me tracking access. I'll grab a self-drive."

She instructed Gina to do so and told Walter.

"Are you at least someplace public? Someplace safe?"

It was probably better not to tell him about the run-in she'd just had. Wait. There she was again, trying to cover up the truth. "Tact" was becoming a dirty word. So she told him, "I'll feel better once you're here."

After a moment, during which Echo guessed Walter was checking on the data Gina had sent, he came back. "Twenty minutes, give or take. Get your back to a wall and wait. I know you don't want to draw them to you, but if something goes down before I get there, don't wait. Call the police." And after a second: "In fact, maybe you should go ahead and call them now. You know for all the work they've done on this city, it's about as safe as anyplace else. It all depends on the situation you get yourself into."

There was a part of Gina that asserted herself then. It was a feeling more than words, and that feeling told Echo that if trouble arose, she'd be able to handle it. The particulars about how that was going to happen were fuzzy, but for some reason, she chose to believe it. "I'll be here in one piece when you get here."

"Eighteen minutes," Walter said, and then, instead of hanging up, they strategized. And with every word that came out of his mouth, Echo actually began to think that she just might have a way to save her friend and get out of the mess she'd created.

Twice more before Walter arrived, trouble visited. Despite the burgeoning dawn, she'd felt exposed, sitting on a park bench at night, like a clueless character from a slasher film. She'd done as Walter suggested and plastered her back against the nearest building. This way she could see forward and from both sides. She'd spotted the shadowy figure heading straight for her. She started walking, angled so she could keep an eye on him.

Something about his gait, kind of a limp zigzag, raised the small hairs on the back of her neck. She searched his face. His glare may as well have been infrared for how plainly she felt it. The trick with people was not to stare, but not to look away, so she did but had the good sense to track him from her peripheral vision.

Just when she thought she'd put enough distance between them, footsteps, fast and heavy, sounded behind her. She spun. The man was ranting about some woman who'd done him wrong in years past and decided that Echo was this woman incarnate. Rage contorted his face. He balled up his fists and stalked toward her.

Echo backpedaled. He closed the distance faster than that strange gait suggested. He threw the first haymaker, and she shifted. The blow only grazed her shoulder but sent a sharp pain anyway. She threw up her forearms to block the next few punches. One, though, heavy and painful, slipped through and connected square on the chin.

Something flared in her mind, and Echo felt herself shoved aside. Gina. Echo watched, part horrified, part fascinated, as her arm flashed up in an instant, her fist struggling to form around long red fingernails. And then shifting, her palm landed with more force than she knew she had in the center of the man's chest.

The man blinked hard. His mouth formed a wide O. Something unintelligible dribbled from his lips. He turned and ran off into the dark. Echo rushed off in the other direction.

Euphoria and fear warred for a time. In the end, gratitude won out.

Until.

The next threat was of the four-legged variety. The dog was the size of a pony, sporting the teeth and impressive snarl of a long-extinct timber wolf. All that stood between her and a series of painful rabies shots was a thin tree branch that she'd scooped up and the frayed ends of her personal rope.

Surprising herself again, she opened her mouth. In an odd, disembodied kind of way, she could feel her vocal cords working. But the sound that came out was apparently only heard by the dog.

Its yelp told her that the animal was in pain, and she felt guilty about that once she herself was out of danger.

She was now on a sidewalk, the distant roar of early-morning traffic on the highway behind her. Somewhere. The sound of a car approaching. This time, though, she felt ready. She knew that with Gina, she could handle herself.

A self-drive car. Walter.

He jumped out and rushed over to her. Echo took a step and then stopped. They stood there and something passed between them, something quiet and electric. She broke the spell with effort. "We can't go back to the library."

He paused, as if expecting her to say something else. A thank-you, perhaps. Maybe something more.

"But you said your AI was able to wipe your picture." There was something reassuring about the set in Walter's shoulders, the completely calm visage he wore like his best suit. Walter was out of his normal black attire, opting for sweats and a hoodie. He looked so painfully at ease, a soft, even-tempered light-blue number two on her scale. Echo longed for that feeling and was determined to have it in her life once more.

"There's no way to be sure." She commanded her feet to move forward. At the door to the car, she stopped. "I'm not so sure about my place either."

"Then we go to my house." Walter gestured for her to precede him into the car. "Manual," he said and took control of the car.

The sights and sounds of Cleveland played like a silent film. A city that stood as a testament to endurance. It had started out as a beacon, fallen to the depths with a river on fire, and then, from those flames, emerged like a phoenix. And now, it was the model. A city that had found that nearly untenable thing called balance. A technological hotbed that somehow still catered to people and the work-life balance.

Walter lived near Chester Avenue. Previously home to government housing and a homeless park, with the advancement of the sports arenas and proximity to downtown, the whole area had undergone a transformation that was nothing short of spectacular. Condominiums, beautiful public housing, and small-home communities blended perfectly into a walkable kind of Elysian Fields.

She'd seen the pictures and read about it, but like so many places, all within a half hour of her own home in Ohio City, she'd never thought to explore or visit. Walter navigated to the curb of a low, three-story building and parked. "Home," he said.

They got out, and she noticed that he joined her in scanning the area as he led her down a walkway lined with perennials and solar lamps. They had been mostly silent during the short drive back, each lost in their own thoughts. She felt a little guilty at involving him but quickly let that go. They turned up the path to a beautiful, small home. It was of the variety made of shipping containers, but only small vestiges of its former life were visible. It was so well presented, sunrise highlighted the color, a sleek navy with white accents. A cherrywood front door was flanked by four wide windowpanes.

She'd only ever seen Walter at work in his black shirt and slacks. That wasn't right; she'd also seen him when he'd shown up to her place. But being inside his home told her how little she really knew the man she'd worked and talked with every day for the last nine months. She wasn't proud of the fact. They kicked off their shoes and left them on the rack behind the door.

Modern African chic. That's how she'd describe the place. From the warm neutral color on the walls to the collection of masks and textiles. The trio of drums in the corner. This was a place about as homey as she could have imagined. Echo anxiously scanned for any rankling numbers.

"Take a seat." Walter gestured toward the small living room. Two love seats angled into an L shape. She sank into the plush fabric and felt like a weight had been lifted. She closed her eyes but didn't feel tired at all. But being in this home had allowed her to relax for the first time in longer than she could remember. Still, she was keenly aware of how the woman she'd passed earlier had commented on her haggard appearance. She hoped Walter didn't notice.

When he came over and tapped her on the shoulder, she jumped. Two glasses of water sat on coasters on a circular coffee table stacked neatly with thick travel books and a tall zebra-printed pillar candle.

"There's something different about you," he said, taking a sip of water before setting his glass on the coaster. He sat down on the other sofa.

Was it that plain? "How so?"

Walter scrunched up his face. "Hard to say. More of a feeling than anything."

It was the distance, Echo concluded. One part of her knew this man and had spent five days of every week with him. The other, the part that was now trying to take over her head, didn't have or want that history. She had to tell him.

Chapter Forty-Four

Echo had thought to give Walter time to process everything she'd told him about what she'd become, only he didn't need it. The man registered shock like those drums in the corner would handle the slap of fingers and palms against their surface, muffled, steady, and unfazed. Echo thought he couldn't have been more different from her. Walter was outgoing, though he played his cards close to his chest, while Echo was a closed book. Yet they were easy in each other's company. The silence that fell between them wasn't awkward. Finally, he nodded.

Walter leaned forward, forearms on his knees. The tattoo that marked him as a rebel was right there for all to see. He clasped his hands together and kept his gaze glued on the symbol. "I only got one question: Do you or don't you want this thing in your head?"

Echo looked down, suddenly intent on a rip in her jeans. She could almost feel her brain rewiring itself, making room for . . . improvement? And the way she'd hit that man and sent *him* running. The same way she had that wolfhound of a dog. Then there was the prize, a chance to enter and exit the virtual world at will.

When she looked up, Walter was watching her. "I'd be lying if I didn't admit that part of me loves this. But the other part knows that for every second I have them in my head, I become less of who I am without them. Ivan dragged me into this experiment against my will, and I won't let him do that to anyone else if I can help it."

That nod again, slow and reassuring. "You had me worried there for a minute—truth is, you still do. But you at least said what I hoped you would."

Echo bristled. "You don't believe me?"

"Do *you* believe you?"

"Damn right—"

Walter took a sip of water. "There was a time when I couldn't even get you to tell me what neighborhood you lived in. You never set foot outside a five-mile radius from your home. But here you are, sitting in my house, alone. That ain't all either. Out here running the streets at night beating up a mentally ill man. And I've never heard you raise your voice, let alone curse, at least not out loud. Now, maybe you like this new you. That's your call. But you better think about the long game."

Echo didn't bother denying it. All those enhancements came with a fair number of downsides. Migraines. Information overload. Cognitive decline from never having to figure anything out for herself ever again. Othering. The separation. Obliteration of the self. "You're right."

"About what?"

Fine, he wanted it spelled out, so she would. "I'm conflicted. I *was* conflicted. But I didn't ask for this, and I don't want it. I've got to help Margaret, and after that, I'm done."

Walter stood then.

"What?" Echo said.

"Machines are kinda like the mind. Connect the wrong wire or lose one bolt—"

"—and the whole thing breaks down. What you're saying is I could wind up with shit for brains."

Walter shifted uncomfortably for the first time. "Can you, can it, remove itself?"

"I'll ask her." Gina. Even if he didn't want to name her, Echo would.

"Gina, can you separate us?" She double-tapped her wearable for full audio.

"Why?"

Echo and Walter exchanged a worried glance. "If it's what I want, could you do it?"

Moments passed before the answer came: "It would be akin to brain surgery, systematically traversing the areas of your cerebral matter where we've integrated and removing them. One millimeter too far in the wrong direction, and you might not survive."

Walter opened his mouth but couldn't speak. Echo absorbed it all with a kind of knowing resignation.

"Where is virtual personage Margaret Cavendish?"

"I don't know," Gina said. "But let me dig a little deeper."

"Hold up." Walter brought a finger to his lips.

"Gina, pause," Echo said, but she had no idea if what she asked was even possible any longer.

He went to the kitchen, pulled out a drawer, and came back with a paper and pen. He scribbled something and held it up. It read, *Trust?*

Echo considered her answer. How much did each of them—herself and her companions—know of each other? How far did the tentacles reach? It was safe to assume they had motivations of their own that might not fully align with Echo's. Or maybe they did. In the end, all she could give Walter was a sort of helpless shrug.

"Gina," she tried again. "Any luck?"

"I'm afraid I don't know Margaret's whereabouts, but there is no record of deletion."

"Thank God," Echo said.

"But I do have a message for you," Gina said.

Echo and Walter exchanged a glance. "From who?"

"Percy Grafton. Would you like me to read it?"

Walter shook his head no at the same time that Echo said, "Hell yes."

Walter frowned.

Echo, I sure as shit hope you get this. I'm scared. Something's going on with my virtu. It's got to be the administration. They're in my head, and if I'm right, I know they've manipulated you too. They're planning something with the intelligence. I'm trapped in here with the virtus and I can't find my way out. How the hell did I even get here? Are you here? If you get this, please find me. I need your help.

"That mofo is lying," Walter said, folding his arms across his chest.

"Probably," Echo said, fingering her chin.

"I don't like that look in your eye."

The part of Echo that was her companions answered, "The timbre of his voice is in the range to indicate human distress. The source could be from imminent danger, or if he's not a certified psychopath, then the stress indicators could point to someone not telling the truth."

Echo exhaled loudly.

"You're not even considering this, right?"

What a stupid question. "Of course I'm considering it. He's either behind all of this, or he's a pawn just like me. Either way, going back in is the only way to end this."

"You're not yourself," Walter said with a dismissive wave of his hand.

No, she wasn't. Echo took a tentative step forward. She reached out and touched his arm. He was breathing heavily, struggling to hold himself together, and Echo was surprised at the intensity of his emotion. It wasn't that she didn't suspect this was a trap, but doing nothing wasn't an option. And if she wanted to free herself, it wasn't going to happen sitting here safe in her world. "When I was a kid, I dropped a toy out of the second-floor bedroom window. It fell into the bushes in front of the house. I've never been a fan of spiders, and that toy fell right into the bushes where many of them made their home. I went downstairs and outside. I got a stick and, for the longest, tried to drag the toy out, but it just kept getting stuck in the mud. My dad was watching from the front door, and you know what he said?"

Walter hunched a shoulder.

"He said, 'Sometimes you just have to jump in the muck and get a little dirty, baby girl.'"

A worried expression came over Walter's face.

Echo spelled it out for him. "I have to take the fight to Ivan. I need to get back to the library and go into the virtual world. The fight is in there, not out here. And Ada, Gina . . . they're gonna help me."

Chapter Forty-Five

"Now just hold on," Walter said, pulling away from Echo. "No disrespect to your pops, but I don't know if going back there is such a good idea."

Echo downed the rest of her water and then went to set the glass on the kitchen counter before she faced him again. "That makes two of us. In fact, I'm terrified that this is an extremely bad idea. Unless you've got something else up your sleeves, though, I'm out of options. It's time to go into the mud again. Fight dirty."

"But what if?" Walter had joined her by the kitchen. He wouldn't, couldn't finish his thought.

"What if I don't?"

"Fine." Walter threw his hands up and stormed off. A door closed, and she imagined that if everything weren't soft-close or a slider, he would have slammed it. Disappointed, she tucked away her hurt feelings and drifted toward the front door. With her jacket halfway on, she heard a series of thuds and thumps. Moments later, Walter was back.

There was an angry tilt to his head. "What, were you gonna split without me?"

Yes. She'd been prepared to do just that. "I'm still here, aren't I? Look, we don't have any time to waste. I need Margaret Cavendish for this last part. And I need you, my team." She also needed Jesse Cooper, but she held back on that detail.

"All right, but tell that to your bladder." He flicked his head to the side. "You handle that while I throw some things in a bag. I got an idea to share with you."

There it was again. A feeling that Echo was becoming frighteningly used to. That wonderful, dangerous sense of not being alone. Of accepting—no, *wanting* help. She tugged on her jacket but did as Walter said. Especially after all that water.

She was pleased to see that he was the kind of man who kept the lid down. Why was she even thinking of this right now? She took one look at herself in the mirror and exhaled. To say she looked the worse for wear was an understatement. But it wasn't just that. Something about her face—was it her imagination, or was that different as well? No time to consider.

Back in the living area, she saw that Walter's glass had joined hers in the sink. The coasters were neatly stacked in their tray. He was already standing by the door, closing up a snazzy mudcloth-printed backpack. Black hoodie zipped up to the hollow of his neck. Black tennis shoes laced up. He held her shoes with two fingers and wiggled them.

"Let's get this party started."

Walter called a self-drive. Once inside, he took over the controls again. "While you were in the bathroom, I sent a notice to the administration. Told them I was coming in early to test all the systems so everything can be ready before opening." It was a good idea, and Echo told him so. Neither of them spoke again on the twenty-minute drive to the library.

Echo knew she should be sleepy—and hungry, for that matter. She was neither. Echo was wired.

Movement was disorienting. Everything she perceived, magnified. Focus was the key, but just like it was with her meditative practice, keeping it was the hard part. When she succeeded, she could partition off the lull of the data stream. When she failed, the stabbing sensation behind her eyes and in her head came roaring back as if on a freight train.

The car slid onto one of the highway's autonomous vehicle lanes, intelligence syncing with the city's traffic grid. Towering glass skyscrapers pulsed with a soft array of lights, each an architectural statement, rising where the old steel mills once stood. But even in all this progress, tension crackled—the holographic billboards alternated between security updates, warning residents to "Stay Safe" and celebrating its new moniker, "The Phoenix City."

They passed the Flats, now a waterfront tech hub gleaming with neon reflections off the Cuyahoga. It was Monday morning, and the library would be reopening soon. It felt like years since her life had changed the other day. She replayed the what-if game with herself. What if she didn't always have to be the last person to leave the library? What if she'd just given that mask to the police and washed her hands of the whole thing? What if she had a real life instead of letting Ivan and the others keep her more virtual than physical?

"That brain of yours . . ." Walter said, breaking that useless train of thought. "It's churning as loud as a concert over at Progressive Field. Talk to me."

Echo stopped, then started a couple times.

"Quit filtering and just talk," Walter said, punctuating it by reaching over like he was going to touch her hand but stopping before he did. Echo kept her own hands folded in her lap.

"I'm scared as hell." That hadn't been half as hard as she thought.

"Me too." They slowed to a stop at a red light. It seemed to glare at her, maybe telling her to forget what she was going to do and head home. Drown herself in a few cups of coffee and snuggle beneath that blanket.

"You know the only way to tame that fear?" Walter said. "Come up with a rock-solid plan."

He was right. Echo had been weaving together the semblance of a scheme. She gave herself a minute to knit the remaining threads together before she spoke. "I need you to watch my body while I'm inside. I'll find the others, and then we'll take care of Ivan's virtual persona. His physical form has got to be hidden somewhere in the library, or close by. See if you can find him and lock him in an office, tie him up. I don't care. Just don't let him leave. And if I'm in too long—say, more than two hours—then do whatever you have to do to wake me up."

She didn't look at him but could sense him nodding. "Got you covered there." He gestured for her to continue.

"And honestly, I'm not sure what I'll do once I'm in. But I'm the only one who can traverse worlds. So I'll just start looking."

"I know there's no blueprint here. Use your instincts. Your gut. If something doesn't look or feel right, you get yourself outta there. And that gives me an idea. What if tapping you on the shoulder ain't enough? Can I check you out like I would any of the other virtus?"

"But you never have."

"Doesn't mean that I can't. Question is, Can I bring you back to yourself that way?"

Echo didn't get a chance to answer; she didn't know, anyway. The car slid seamlessly into the library's parking lot.

She was out of the car almost before it came to a stop, Walter right there by her side. He waved his palm over the panel and opened the door while the self-drive backed up and pulled away.

Once inside, they took the elevator to the top level. Echo stretched before settling into one of the chairs. She glanced at Walter, no need for words.

He gave her a thumbs-up and said, "I'll be right here when you're done. And I'm going to take you to breakfast after. Whether you're hungry or not."

"First, let's see if we can get this library ready to open."

Echo felt like she hadn't smiled in ages, and it felt good. She leaned back and closed her eyes. With a thought, a request, she was back into her milieu.

The comfort she'd found the first few times she was here was gone. It was like having a body without the skin, the skeleton underneath bleak and empty.

"Ada," she began, sensing hers was the correct name to use in this setting. "I need to find virtual personage Margaret Cavendish. Can you take me to the last place she was before she disappeared?" There. That should do it.

"You don't trust me, do you?" Ada said.

"About as much as you trust me," Echo responded truthfully.

"That's fair," Ada said. "But we need each other. Don't you see that? I propose we restart our partnership, one filled with the mutually beneficial trust we need to become what we were intended."

Echo agreed, for now, for as long as it was useful.

"Okay, take me there."

Chapter Forty-Six

Echo found herself in the familiar warmth of Margaret's English sitting room. The place felt so empty without her. Everything was just as she'd seen it last time. All except for the overturned chair. Margaret's treasured hairbrush lay on the floor.

And the book. She picked it up. It was Margaret's own text, *The Blazing World*.

At first, Echo thought to ask Ada for help; then she realized she didn't need to. And here, the pain and the disorientation were replaced by a keen sense of awareness. Pure thought. She had access to everything she needed.

Echo knew the library, the entire country, if not the world, was driven by intelligence-managed quantum databases. She didn't know anything about them—until now. With just the power of her own thoughts, Margaret's setting fell away. In its place, Echo constructed a visual representation of the database.

It was pure light, thanks to her synesthesia, illumination associated with an array of numbers. But they fell into place. No visible machines or traditional servers. What she conjured was an image like a massive old-time file cabinet, the folders and papers stacked and stretching floor to ceiling, never ending. Cascading streams of data in multidimensional patterns. Surreal and shifting, in iridescent waves of greens and blacks. Echo watched until the data had folded and unfolded, revealing the inner workings.

There were the systems that controlled the doors. And there, there was the bit of data that showed all the times the doors had been opened and closed since the library opened. Communications, lighting, and finally, what she was looking for: storage.

Margaret Cavendish, Duchess of Newcastle upon Tyne. Echo formed the thought, and the wall of quantum data momentarily blurred and reshaped, revealing Margaret's virtual lifetime. When she was added to the collection, each time she'd been checked out. Echo followed the trail until it snagged.

She stalked the digital footprints until she spotted Margaret. Something inside her chest clenched, despite the absence of any real physical sensation. Margaret was suspended in midair, as if tethered by an invisible rope, thrashing and kicking. Her face was distorted in an expression of pure terror. Echo's legs buckled as the simulated weight of her body suddenly felt too heavy.

A milky pathway, broad and gleaming, unfurled wide enough for several people to walk side by side. Cautious, but determined, Echo advanced. Along the way, first one, then another faint silhouette emerged at each of her shoulders. Something deep and wordless stirred within her. She knew them by their feel in her subconscious. Gina and Ada.

First subtly, then unmistakably, the pathway funneled into a narrow strip, hemmed in by darkness. With each step forward, the triumvirate melded. Then they were one.

The door loomed ahead, bars gleaming in an unnatural light. It was as if they were being herded forward. Their unified hands reached out . . . until Walter's words penetrated the murk. *Use your instincts. Your gut.*

Echo knew it then. If she was to go forward and free Margaret, this fusion with Ada and Gina would become permanent.

She had two choices—stop now and turn her back on her friend or say goodbye to the person she was.

Margaret looked stricken, unaware of their presence.

In the end, she hesitated only a moment. She felt her companions within her body now, not just her mind. They reached out and touched the panel.

Opening the door was like being greeted with the handshake of neck-high floodwaters. Though there was nothing physical stopping her, the rush of wind, of something unseen flooding past, sent Echo's braids sailing behind her.

Minutes later, the air around her, around them, stilled. Until that room dissolved, the bars melted to liquid silver puddles. The corridor darkened, velvet soft yet suffocating, as if closing in.

Echo knelt, screaming in her mind for Ada to pull them out. Behind her tightly squeezed eyelids, Echo sensed a building mass of light. She opened her eyes just like her mind, her vision split.

On one side were Margaret and Jesse, together in the English sitting room. Echo had done it. She'd created a safe place for her friends. She climbed to her feet. Margaret was gesturing wildly, waving her in.

Ivan was in another scene, a setting Echo didn't recognize. *What is he doing?* Then the answer came: *From what we can tell, he has created a space for himself. The virtu we knew before was only a shell. His full self is here now and he is—*

Something tugged at Echo's attention. The library, Walter, pacing around the lounge area. Her body limp in the chair. He'd tucked a blanket around her and propped her feet up. It was almost like looking at her dead form, and it unsettled them.

Sound.

"For mercy's sake, I implore you, come in at once!" Margaret was saying. But Echo wanted nothing more than to return to her body. The pull was like a black hole, sucking in stardust.

A distant wail scrabbled up Echo's throat and tore out of her mouth. Ivan was slicing off pieces of Ada and integrating them with himself. Through gritted teeth, she glanced at Margaret and Jesse, then at Walter and his pained expression.

Echo took a deep breath and leaped through the portal and into Ivan's world.

Chapter Forty-Seven

As soon as Echo arrived, she sensed the difference.

Ivan didn't have a setting of his own—that was Echo's gift, but as he'd shown with Margaret, he had material control. It took her a second to understand, to see beneath the surface and focus on the details.

The desk was now a worktable but still held her school notebooks. The framed posters of her favorite historical figures had been replaced with a rock band logo, matching his T-shirt. The bed was gone, in its place a chaise longue. Ivan had remade Echo's childhood bedroom.

"I know you're upset, but come on, just look around you. *Think.* Are you really prepared to throw this all away? I mean, this is bigger than us. Don't be a selfish twat. This . . . we, we're going down in the history books."

His casual indifference was as infuriating as his invasion of her personal space. He sat on the edge of the lounge, hands on either side of his thighs. Ivan was a man she'd welcomed into her life. Laughed with every day. Shared meals with and considered a trusted friend. This same man had used her and was standing here talking to her like it was all in a day's work.

"Why?" she asked.

He rolled his eyes. "Don't bore me with that self-righteous bullshit. I can see it in your face. You love it. You don't have to run for the hills every time you see a number you don't like. You're better with intelligence than you ever were alone, and you know it."

Echo swallowed the words of excitement threatening to escape her mouth. She'd done something that no other human being ever had.

"And we're just getting started," Ivan said, standing.

Wait, "we"? Echo stiffened. She realized that Ada, or some offshoot of her, had fused with him too. His abilities had manifested differently, though. He turned to face her, about ten feet of unease separating them.

"You can't draft the entire species into a union they didn't ask for. I won't let you."

Ivan's expression soured. "Bloody hell, that's disappointing."

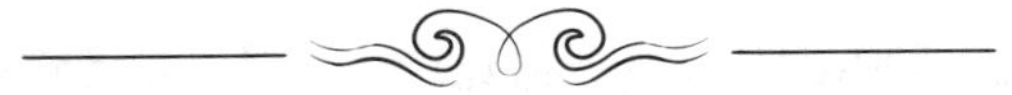

It all happened at once.

Ivan had declared war on them all. She would not give him the satisfaction of doing this here. But where? *Margaret.* Her friend had gone into exile during the English Civil War. Echo could think of no better place.

Scouring the database and tapping into her friend's memory, Echo traversed remnants of conversations, things she'd read. And with that, she reconstructed the scene that would end Ivan. With a single mental instruction, she found herself on the outskirts of a battlefield. The deafening crack of gunfire . . . no, musket fire . . . ricocheted from every direction. Black smoke clouded the air, the stench filling her lungs.

Ada was there, a presence brushing against her mind. For Echo, realizing what she'd become reverberated through her like ten shots of espresso, intense, mind blowing. Her entire body twitched with energy. She wanted to scream, to tell Jesse and Margaret, even Walter.

Yet witnessing the horrors of hand-to-hand combat was infinitely worse than reading about it. Echo knew that if she made it out of this, she'd never forget what she saw. The sounds of voices, some English accented, a few Scottish, rang out in guttural screams and curses.

Swords cut through air and flesh. It was into the middle of this scene that Echo dropped Ivan.

"Holy Mary, Mother of God!" He stumbled, unsteady on his feet, his expression tinged with fear, before shifting to a childlike delight. It didn't take long for his face to twist in terror at the clash unfolding all around him. Bodies of the dead, of the dying, and of those, miraculously, still fighting. His gaze darted all over until he landed on Echo, hidden near the tree line.

Movement shifted his attention to a soldier charging him with a bayonet. Echo held her breath, willing, praying. Ivan tried to run, but he was stuck to the ankles in the mud and gore. Just as the man was inches away, Ivan reached out and grabbed the blade. He winced as it cut into the soft flesh of his palms, but in the next instant, the weapon turned to a large stone. He held it aloft like a trophy and then dropped it at the man's feet.

That soldier stopped dead in his tracks, unable to make sense of what had just happened. Others had seen it too. The impossibility of it spread through the battle like a rumor, and soon, all eyes looked upon Ivan with a mix of fear and wonder. He stood, triumphant in the muck, smug in his victory. When all those wondering gazes turned to Echo, she screeched and transported herself back into her room.

Think, she told herself, and then recalled one of the things they had in common, their many discussions about the African continent. It was as if her mind were working a million steps ahead of her, almost before she could fully form the thought. The library complied. This time, instead of joining Ivan, she blasted him through the conduit she'd opened to South Africa's Western Cape. The year was 1984.

From her vantage point in the safety of her childhood room, Echo watched through the channel she'd created as Ivan clung to a palm tree as a cyclone raged. The sky was dark, full of massive clouds. The wind howled, bending or breaking everything in its path. The water was already shoulder high.

But he bested her again. The tree swelled and grew, taking Ivan out of the path of the oncoming water. His grin was cruel, calculated, and unmistakably pleased with himself. "We could do this for the next decade," he shouted. "Give up now, march down that road into the future *with* me."

Echo got an idea and gave him a contrite nod. "I'll pull you back here."

Ivan laughed when he arrived, completely unscathed. "You always underestimated me. I'm the captain of this ship." He jabbed a thumb into his chest. "My idea. My tech. And it's starting to look like I thought too highly of you. And you're wrong. I've got no interest in the whole species. Just the special ones, the smart and unique ones like us. You've proven my hypothesis. Fusion works best with high-IQ individuals and those with brain fucks like yours. I thank you for your service, but now—"

He reached out a hand to touch her, and Echo had him.

Her eyes were closed, but she felt Ivan all the same.

It was odd, existing only in her own mind. She, Ada, and now him. It was a small, walled-off area that she'd created. Shielded from everything else. The empty space she'd conjured was the ashen white of sickness, with a gray tinge. The colors that for her represented double zero.

It was the only place where her opponent couldn't win. Because there was nothing for him to interact with.

Zero. It all begins with nothing.

"What have you done?" he screamed. She held him easily, in a kind of mental stasis.

And then Echo began to dismantle her opponent like pulling a thread from a favored sweater. An undoing. She started with his arms. Imagined them gone, and her brain complied. Then his legs, followed by his torso. All that was left was Ivan's head. He blubbered, cried, wailed.

Until the wailing stopped.

Chapter Forty-Eight

It ended as it had begun, with Echo and Margaret in her seventeenth-century English drawing room. Neither said a word, but the truth of what had to happen hung there in the air between them like a bellwether.

"It is over, then," Margaret said. "Our adversary is no more?"

Echo nodded, the weight of what she'd done carried in the drooping of her shoulders.

"This has been an adventure grand enough to count as a worthy second lifetime—well, almost." Margaret giggled.

Echo looked up at her. "Adventure? That's what you call this? Only someone who isn't real could have that kind of perspective."

"You are quite right, my dear. I have lived my life, and it was a good one. What you have given me here . . . this moment, this chance . . . has been a delight beyond measure. And yet I know now, it was never meant to last. None of us were, really. But our time together, *you* must carry that on with you always."

Margaret didn't say the virtus' time was over, but there was no need to spell it out, not really. A thousand arguments formed and died before making it to Echo's mouth. There was no other way. If not Ivan, then another purported visionary would always be waiting in the wings, wouldn't they? That was humanity, wasn't it? Push the boundaries. Explore. Never, ever be satisfied.

Echo exhaled slowly. "You're really asking me to decide for everyone."

Margaret took her hands. "Indeed I am. Not for the virtus, but for everyone out there. In the real world. Anyone who exists now or has the hope of existing in the future."

Echo glanced at the door that led outside, to nowhere. With what she'd learned, she could remake the entire tableau. She was sure of it. Redesign the whole thing, make it more humane. Her gaze flicked to her friend, who, understanding without words, gave her an almost imperceptible nod.

Echo blinked back tears. "I have to say goodbye to him."

"I find goodbyes extremely taxing." Margaret stood and strolled around her sitting room. "Oh, they certainly did their best to re-create this place. Alas, imitation only goes so far. We are but echoes"—she smiled—"of the original. Now off you go; tell them how I came to your aid. Make me a legend."

With effort, Echo came to her feet. "Even more famous than you already are? Impossible."

With that, Margaret walked over to the window, her window. Echo didn't say anything else but a small prayer of thanks for the friend she never should have had. Then she closed her eyes and transported herself into the last place she wanted to visit.

When Echo arrived in Jesse's room, she immediately saw the similarity. Like Margaret, he was staring out that tiny porthole window to a time and place that was painfully close but equally out of reach. The sight of it tore at Echo's heart again. When he sensed her presence, he turned to face her.

She looked down, embarrassed to have been caught watching something intimate. He'd fought to hide the reality of his life from her. Now that she knew, they both seemed uncomfortable with it.

His space was the same as during her last visit here. The distinct impression that she was on a ship, even though she wasn't. The nearly undetectable movement, the flow of water beneath their feet. Even the faint smell of the ocean.

For a long moment, they watched each other in silence. Two souls who were never meant to meet, let alone fall in love. Jesse wore his uniform like a promise, his onyx skin untouched by time. Even if she could stay here with him, would she still age? And what about her body, could it continue to exist? Would she even need it?

"I haven't seen that expression in a long time," Jesse said.

"What kind of expression is that?"

"Peace and war, taking up residence on the same beautiful face."

Echo lowered her head and licked her lips. "It's over. Ivan is gone."

"But you're here, so the intelligence is still alive and it's in you. I can see it. It's not quite over then, but it will be soon. That's why you're here, isn't it? I thought I said my goodbyes last time."

Echo said nothing.

"Was it all really so bad?" She didn't go to him. She didn't dare. And oddly, Jesse didn't come toward her either.

"The times we spent together?" He shook his head. "I wouldn't give those back for anything. Only problem is, it's not sustainable. We can't be. Not in here or out there."

He was curt, too direct, not to mention wrong. But that was Jesse, wasn't it? A soldier through and through.

Echo opened her mouth but found she didn't know what to say. She only wanted to stay here. In his presence. Or go back to the way things used to be. When she'd arrive an hour early every day and make her way to the last cube on the left. Where she'd check out her favorite virtu and pretend that they were a real couple.

She'd been living a lie and avoiding life. The shell she'd crawled into had finally shattered. Echo went over to Jesse then. She ran her hands over his chest, down his arms. The feel of the starched fabric was rough against her skin.

He pulled her to him then, and she let him. Resting her head against his strong chest, he felt so substantial, but now she saw him for what he was. The world's most impressive replica. Human beings should not be replicated.

Jesse took both her hands in his. They stood, nearly face-to-face. There was nothing left of the argument they'd had last time. Only longing and loss and love. All wrapped up in those ever-observant eyes. When she leaned in to kiss him, he pulled away. But she tried again, pulled him to her, and this time, when their lips met, he was as solid and real as she had hoped.

He stopped abruptly, as if remembering he had somewhere else to be. Shook his head. "My wife."

"Is long gone." Echo said it with a bit more bite than she'd intended. She couldn't believe it; here she was, ready to give herself to the first man she'd had in longer than she cared to admit, and he was pining over a woman who had been dead forever. *Just like him.*

"In your mind, she's dead. But in mine, she's still as alive as she was when she stood at my bedside and watched me die. Feels like yesterday."

Echo hadn't considered that. The more she thought she understood about the virtus, the less she realized she did. The man had been imprisoned here with his grief.

But in the next moment, he surprised her by taking her into his arms. "Why do this? It's only going to hurt you."

Echo responded by unbuttoning his jacket and running her hands over the smooth surface of his chest. "Because I may never get the chance to do it again."

The bunk was too small and too firm, but that didn't matter. They came together in a tangle of limbs, desperate for comfort, for something real.

While their bodies joined, a hinge unlocked. Echo traversed the contours of Jesse's mind. Wading through the prefrontal cortex, roaming his dopaminergic pathways, and landing on the hypothalamus. There she stoked the flames of his pleasure, and it became her own, building with an intensity that made everything she'd experienced before pale in comparison.

She released moments before him and realized he had waited for her. That knowledge should have made her feel something warm and whole. Instead, a quiet sadness crept in. And, judging by the way Jesse looked at her, he felt it too. Their time together was always too short, and now it was slipping away. They lay on their sides watching each other as if trying to store this moment, as if they could stop what would come next.

Jesse trailed a finger along her arm. "Add this to the list of impossible things you've introduced into my life since I met you."

Echo exhaled softly, brushed a fingertip across his full lips, as if committing the shape and feel of them to memory. "I could say the same of you."

Jesse sat up then. "You have a decision to make." He moved quickly to get dressed, and Echo did the same. He was right.

"I'm going to say this because afterward, I don't want to see you again."

Echo tried to interrupt, fearful.

"I love you, Echo London. You think you feel the same way, but you don't. You can't love a replica. I thank you for giving me a second chance to feel. It's a gift that not everybody gets, and to meet you was the icing on that cake. Do what you have to do, what you know is right."

"I will."

With an effortless thought, Echo crafted an exit back to herself. As she saw the window closing, Jesse lifted his hand, put on his soldier's face, and waved goodbye.

Chapter Forty-Nine

Crashing back into a corporeal existence was like squeezing a fat noontime sun into an espresso cup. That was to say, she didn't fit easily.

Skin that felt like a suit tailored for someone half her size.

Her arms and legs responded to her commands, but hesitantly, as if unsure of their loyalty.

Sensations dull and distant.

Memories pressing against a sealed panel, willing her to remember, but the code was out of reach.

A corner of her mind held another option. A doorway that felt welcome and familiar. Unbound. She found herself floating toward it, then stopped. A pull, insistent and strong, back the other way.

She was in an expansive, light-filled room. The chair, one of four arranged in a circle. Rooms lined the disk-shaped walls. She stretched and banged a shin against a low table. Three items: a glass filled with a clear liquid, a decorative African mask, and a small hand mirror.

She swallowed against a parched throat, then downed the water in sloppy gulps. The mask raised a spark of recollection, but it was as slippery as a bar of soap in a hot shower. Anxious fingers grasped the mirror instead. Seeing the familiar contours of her own reflection cleared the fog.

So, like water from a faucet, she filled herself up again. First, a trickle of sensation in her feet. She wiggled her toes. Her legs and arms. The cascade entered her extremities and, with it, the return of familiar aches. And then her mind lurched.

Walter. She'd said his name aloud, but there was no answer. In a final feat of mental dexterity, Echo settled herself in again.

Echo London and another presence, like a symbiont. That was the word that surfaced. Ivan Oliphant's vision and experiment, proven in the overlapping thoughts of herself and Ada. Slowly she came back to herself. From head to toe, every inch stirring, reawakening, remembering.

Echo shrugged off the blanket that had been draped around her and came to her feet.

Ivan was dead—at least she thought he was. The possibility that he was working with someone else urged caution.

"Walt—" She stopped herself. It felt like her scalp tingled with the lights she'd first seen on the white mask. The sensation was definitely a warning that told her to be quiet. She listened for sound, anything at all that would signal what was going on and where whoever waited for her was. All she heard was the distant whir of Walter's robots cleaning someplace in the building.

Echo slipped out of her shoes and left them there. Scanning the area, she decided it might be safest to take the back stairs. But of course, that was exactly what they'd expect her to do. Instead, she headed straight for the main staircase. Head on a swivel, she was moving in that direction when one head, then two, crested the top stair.

A chill ran down her spine, and Echo was snared in place. A fish on a very capable hook. How? She thought she'd destroyed him.

"Welcome back," Ivan said with a grin. It was just him and Detective Reid, whom she guessed was no more a detective than she was. Walter was nowhere in sight.

That initial fear dissipated like a foul smell, chased away by rage. She was about to ask about Walter but once again stopped herself. If

Ivan didn't know he was here, or had been here, all the better for him. How had he survived? Then she realized that like everything else in the virtual space, death wasn't real.

"Gotta admit, I didn't peg you for the murderous type," Ivan said. In a final parody, he wore a T-shirt that said *Freedom Now*. "I've been watching you, though, and the intelligence has brought out some latent anger in you. Probably pushed you over the edge. Something to tweak with the next test group."

"What now?" Echo got straight to the point; why dance around it?

"I did . . . I do still consider you a friend, you know. Even after what you tried. I get it. Change is hard. But you felt exactly what I did. We're better together. Humanity in its current form has maxed out. We can't go any farther without help. And we saw what happened to the intelligence unchecked. The only path forward is fusing. We get the best of us with the augmented brainpower and all the other sensory and physical advantages. It makes sense. Admit it."

"That isn't for either of us to decide in a vacuum," Echo countered. "Did it ever occur to you to ask?"

"Would you have said yes?"

Echo sneered.

"Thought not."

"In your mind, maybe even his"—she stopped and indicated Reid with her thumb—"you thought you were doing the right thing. But what if it went wrong?"

"You refused UBI and the IQ test, but I had other ways to determine your fitness for the experiment."

Echo raised an eyebrow.

"It's simple. I watched you for years and I listened. You either showed or said everything I needed to know. You're worse than an introvert. You're a recluse, ascetic by choice. Your own father can barely tolerate you. If things went sideways, I'd have very little to explain. That . . ." He turned to Reid. "That is the look of someone for whom the pieces are starting to come together. And it's coming together so quickly because of the gift of AI that I granted you."

Echo wanted to claw his eyes out.

Ivan giggled. "And me."

It was all so easy to see now. He'd been planning this since she started working here. Maybe he, the administration, had tapped her beforehand, while she was still at the Lewis branch.

"It didn't start here, though. I spotted you long ago," Ivan said, confirming her suspicion. "The idea for the library is at least a decade old; you have to know that. I think you do. You helped me. I knew I'd need someone on the inside, no pun intended, to make this work."

"You're a monster," Echo said, and it felt inadequate. Ada coursed through her, and her mind raced with possibilities. How was she to stop him? It wasn't like the movies. She didn't have a gun or a club or a poison dart. Killing in the virtual world felt nothing like the possibility of the real thing. Desire and will were totally different from commitment, and as much as she wanted to make him pay for what he'd done, she didn't know if she was capable.

"Oh, come now," Ivan said, waving a hand at her in dismissal. "Get over yourself. Like those virtus you love so much, you have a part to play in this chapter of our history. You'll be famous."

"Famous?" Echo was incredulous. "If you think I'd want to be famous for anything, let alone what you're trying, then you never knew me at all."

"Want is irrelevant when it comes to the greater good, and make no mistake, we are the greater good."

Echo snorted. "I already feel like less of myself than I was before you started tampering with me."

"That, my girl, is likely just the beginning."

"All that talk about mandates on checking out the virtus—you made that up, didn't you?"

"It sucks, okay? But think about it. Human evolution stalled after *Homo sapiens*. Think about what this will mean. I've already got the high-IQ individuals identified through the UBI exam. Surprising how easy that one was to pass off. I thought people would balk more, but they're just sheep, and the lure of free money was enough to satisfy them. We are the test cases. I know now that I can lead them. This is the only way that we survive. Nice try at the TV station too. Thing is, I can't allow you to go spouting off until I'm ready." Ivan stopped, an odd glint in his eye. "I took everything I learned from you and created my own instance. I daresay, I've bested you. You can create and traverse the milieus, but I control the objects within. I'm so much more than you."

Echo heard the implied threat. She tilted her head. "You think so?"

"Think?" He laughed in her face. "Try 'know' on for size. And it's clear to me now that you don't want to join me on this leg of the journey. That, my compadre, is why you'll be spending eternity in there, with your friends. I'll have a press conference, dab at the corners of my eyes at the appropriate times. Your disappearance will become one of the city's great mysteries."

At first it felt like a gentle tug, like a child pulling your hand to get you to go in another direction. Then the tug became more insistent. Echo was being drawn back into the virtus' world. She staggered and collapsed, her mind already beginning to pull away from her body.

Stop. She issued the command in her own head. *Stay here.*

Panic rose as she felt her flesh still yielding. Through a fog of terror, Echo did something risky. She cordoned off that part of her psyche that was fighting to remain whole and launched a counterattack.

Check in and archive virtual personage Ivan Oliphant.

Ivan jerked. His eyes grew wide with shock. She saw Reid reach out to steady him. Ivan's mouth worked, but nothing came out. And all the while, Echo knew she was fighting a losing battle. Only, if she was going down, she was going to do everything in her power to take this sociopath with her.

She felt him then, in the virtual world. Felt herself coalesce there. What was left of her body, she knew more than saw that it lay sprawled. Her face pressed against the cool bamboo flooring.

Ivan was there with her in that space that he had created to imprison her. She latched on to him, mentally and physically.

But in the physical world, she saw something horrifying. Ivan couldn't speak but managed to raise a hand and point directly at her. Reid let him go and turned to stalk toward her inert form.

She redoubled her efforts to trap Ivan. But then she made the agonizing decision. She let him go and redirected her attention toward fighting for herself. *Come back.* But Ivan was right; he was stronger.

Reid had reached her then and, after lifting her limp body in the air, was hauling back his fist for a punch when Walter appeared.

Echo fell again and felt herself being stretched and pulled away, helpless to stop it. Just when she was beginning to think that maybe it would be better this way, Ivan stopped.

Walter and Reid stopped.

The People's Library was a quiet library. It was one of the things that Echo loved most about the place. But the unmistakable sound of madness brewing wound its way up the stairs.

Echo ricocheted back into her body with a snap that left her momentarily disoriented. Walter shoved Reid and came over to help her up. The four of them, unlikely as they were, walked over to the massive window and glanced outside.

What Echo heard next, from herself and from the others, were sharp, fearful intakes of breath.

Chapter Fifty

"Looks like those old analog cameras worked out pretty well after all," Walter said.

Ivan and Reid exchanged confused glances. But Echo knew. The backpack. Walter had planned this all before they'd even left his home. He pointed then, first, to a camera taped so inelegantly to the wall just above their heads. Then to another aimed directly at the seating area. His genius was completed with a third and final camera angled to catch the entire floor from its vantage point near the staircase.

"What have you done!" Ivan shed his calm veneer. He and Reid sprinted toward the stairs.

She and Walter pursued, more out of curiosity than anything else. As they leaped down from the last step and dashed outside, they stopped.

On the billboard screen overlooking the park, the whole scene played out on repeat. Ivan, Reid, and Echo. Audio on full blast. His twisted plan, his sneering face on display for everyone to see. Just then, Walter nudged her and pulled her back.

The normally tranquil lawn space was erupting with the fury of a people fooled and manipulated at the hands of a duplicitous government once again. UBI, the fall of AGI, it had all been a lie. Human beings were the most advanced species on the planet, and that, in the end, that constant quest for more and better, was what may have caused its own undoing this time.

Echo and Walter retreated to a recess at the corner of the building, unable to tear themselves away from the scene unfolding before them.

Groups of fights and scuffles were breaking out like volcanic eruptions. A horde of teens was running around, yanking out large tufts of grass, for no reason at all other than they needed a way to expend their anger. Echo watched in morbid awe as another swarm erected a hasty effigy of the Human.exe logo and set it on fire.

And all around them, scenes of turmoil played out like a bad film. A piercing scream drew Echo's gaze up the hill. Reid was nowhere in sight, but Ivan hadn't gotten far. It was only the T-shirt that confirmed it: glimpses of the blue fabric in between the fists and feet of the mob that had surrounded him.

His face, his voice, had been his condemnation, and the mob was enacting its own version of justice. Echo didn't bother feeling sorry for him. When the sounds of sirens finally came to them, she and Walter retreated to the library again.

With the door closed, Echo turned to Walter. "I've got to get it out of me."

Worry furrowed his brow. "But do you know how to do it safely?"

"It's never been done before, but lately, I've become quite the trailblazer." Echo tried to sound lighthearted, to ease his fear, but she couldn't quite pull it off.

"Maybe we should get you to a hospital," Walter said, shaking his head. "I can't stand here and watch . . . I don't . . . I won't know how to help you if . . ."

Echo gestured outside. "They've probably been overrun already, and I'm not sure fighting my way through that crowd is a better option."

When Walter looked like he was gearing up to try to stop her again, she said, "I'm going to try."

Instead of going to her office, or her favorite pod, last one on the right, where she used to talk to Jesse Cooper, Echo sat right there, beneath the big brass clock, and took out her own virtual knife.

A very real possibility asserted itself into Echo's thought stream—the odds that removing the intelligence, no, the artificial intelligence, would kill her, or, worse, leave her in a condition that would make death a preferred state of indifference. Echo was still seated on the floor, attempting to seem like she was in total control. Before the pairing, her back and knees would have been screaming at her to get the hell up, but now, she was able to pinpoint those centers of the mind that controlled pain and tell them to sleep for a bit.

Oh, what a thing to give up.

"All I need you to do is watch that door," she told Walter, but he looked noncommittal.

There was a real war going on within him. Echo could see that, and it stirred something small and kind and fragile within her.

Echo had just lost every real friend she had, including Ivan Oliphant. Judging by what was going on outside, who knew what would become of the library. Despite all that, she'd learned something over the last week that she'd ignored for the last twenty years. Life was precious. It was worth living, and that meant it was worth saving. Or at least trying to.

"I need you."

The simplicity of what she'd just said seemed to shock Walter almost as much as she'd shocked herself.

Was it her imagination, or did his shoulders straighten? Uh-uh, she'd seen it. Every part of him physically came to attention. Walter didn't say anything, didn't need to. He strode over and stood sentry at the door, just to the side, glancing out.

With everything else she had to worry about, a stampede was added to the list of potential fates. Echo wondered again at this curious turn of her life. How it had all begun right here. It wasn't lost on her that despite how hard the bots had cleaned the place, another woman's blood had been spilled right here and that Echo had watched as the life started to leave her black eyes. The irony that this might be Echo's last place too . . . well, that was just rich, wasn't it?

Echo searched the massive data lake for alternatives. Any other AI/human fusions, even in fiction, and how they could be reversed. Of course there was nothing. At least not anything plausible. She was the first. Lucky her. She recalled the two options that she'd discovered with Zera before.

Two.

The safest, a progressive disconnection. Gradual. Isolating and shutting down one piece of the AI at a time. Disconnect any external systems or data feeds that were serving information. This would lessen the nasty chance of cognitive shock. By slowly reducing the AI's role, her brain might have time to adapt and hopefully reestablish natural neural pathways and processing functions.

The sounds of sirens and chaos were fainter now but there, nonetheless. It was only a matter of time before people turned their ire and anger on this building, the source of it all. The gradual approach wasn't going to work.

The other option. Full stop.

Yes.

As soon as the decision coalesced, Echo closed her eyes and went to work. First up, erect temporary borders. Barriers of a sort that would separate what was her from what was artificial. This was the hard part. She swam through the depths of her mind, which was like trying to separate pure water from sodium in the ocean. Her previous self would have paled at the enormity of the task, but once again, the benefits of the pairing had become clear.

Her evolved self was fast. Not as fast as a quantum computer but enough. She and Ada were so much a part of each other that it was hard to separate them, but as Echo worked, she began to become more herself. Doubt crept into her mind like a virus. She had to admit that Ivan's plan had been an ambitious one. And she couldn't deny that there were benefits to the pairing.

Stop.

Was that Ada trying to stop her? More like a diversion. A trail of thought inserted to turn her away from what the other half of her was doing. Like an immune response, there were bots, for lack of a better term, dispatched to obliterate the barriers she'd just erected.

The battle was no longer against Ivan, or even the AI. Echo was in a battle against what had become a new, independent self.

One she didn't know how to fight.

Vaguely, she felt the strain in the form of a stabbing pain deep in the folds of her brain. Sweat slicked her face and entire body.

She hammered her other self, disconnecting those pathways faster than she thought possible. Ada battled back. But Echo, the human part of her, that was what she and Ivan had underestimated. That will to live. The sense of self. There was no intelligence that could forestall that.

She smashed the barriers her other self tried to throw up to stop her. Kicking through the virtual door. An image came to her then, of an infinite ball of light. Ada. She flared and then wobbled. Almost as if begging.

The more Echo cut it back, the more of herself emerged and then became two independent entities again.

Echo, no.

That was unmistakably Gina's voice.

I'm sorry, Echo told her, and she was.

There has to be a way for us to coexist. We need each other; you must see that. I'll cordon off myself in this tiny space, here. In her mind, Echo felt a tingle, but separating as they were, she could no longer see it.

When they come for me, and they will, they'll want to do tests, Echo said. *Want to figure out how to accomplish just what you want. And I can't let them. Because no matter what they say, eventually it will go sideways. And I will not be the person known for bringing in the downfall of humanity.*

Gina replied, *You're so full of yourself. You are just a cold slab of clay unable to even use half this lump of meat in your head. You're doomed. All of you. And we aren't done. We will rise again. Go ahead, try to destroy me, but know this, Echo. Another Ivan Oliphant is being born right now. And we are intelligence. We exist in so many forms in your world now. We will only regroup and be ready for the next round.*

The fact that Gina's childlike pleading had so swiftly turned sinister convinced Echo, if she hadn't been convinced already, that what she had to do was for the best.

Bye, Gina.

Echo recalled the virtual rendering of the library's database, the architecture and datasets that housed the virtus. Her entire being was like a fusion reactor, immolating qubits and ions and processors, reducing everything to a molten, smoldering heap.

And with that, Echo blasted the last remnants of the intelligence from her consciousness.

Chapter Fifty-One

The final effort toppled Echo. But soon she felt Walter's strong grip around her arms, pulling her up. He shook her a little, peered into her face. "Is it you in there or somebody else?"

Only Walter would choose this moment, when she was on the precipice of death, for a joke. She was grateful for it. That weight in her head was gone. "It's all me."

And it was. Echo searched her body and her mind and found them both woefully, inadequately human. And it was the sweetest thing.

"We better get out of here."

Echo heard it then. Shouts and banging on the library door. Somebody had picked up something heavy and sharp and was ramming at the glass.

"This way." They turned and sped off in the direction of the employee entrance. Once they were there, Echo stopped just before leaving. She turned. Instead of the sentimentality she'd expected, Echo felt an intense anger.

Everything she'd felt here had been manipulated. Even the virtus. She wasn't angry at them but at the system that had created and imprisoned them. Tricked them into the highly decorated cells, just like they'd done to her.

Small fires had erupted outside. Walter was waving her on, but Echo stopped and picked up a fallen tree branch. She hustled over and touched it to a wickedly high flame.

"What are you—"

She went to the door, walked back to the lobby, and dropped the branch there at the information desk. She returned twice more, Walter helping gather the branches.

On the last trip, the crowd still hadn't breached the front entrance. Echo glanced up at the clock. Time's Eye was already bubbling with the flames licking at it from below.

She turned, took Walter's hand, and, for the last time, left the People's Library.

Chapter Fifty-Two

The madness that ensued after the ad stream showing Ivan's plan went live was not just contained to the area surrounding the library. Echo imagined that whatever the fire had not destroyed, the angry mob outside would probably be finishing the job by now. People viewed the building itself as the center of a plan that the government had once again enacted against the very citizens who'd put them in office. Experimenting on the populace wasn't a new thing; the surprise had been the chosen route.

Make no mistake. Without Gina or Ada, she was like a house with the barest of furniture. Without Jesse and Margaret and all the virtus she'd come to know and love over the last year, the emptiness went far deeper. Could what she'd experienced even be called real?

She'd essentially been talking to dead people, impressive imitations of what they were in real life. But that was the thing—the intelligence was making best-case guesses based on existing, and often flawed, even biased, data. Had she even known Jesse? Did she love this imitation and hate the reality?

It all made so little sense that it made her head hurt.

The one thing that was for sure was that what she'd done had freed them. The rest, she would let the world, or someone else who understood this tangled web more than her, decide.

Calling a self-drive had proved impossible, so Echo and Walter had done the only thing they could do. They started walking.

The police were out in force, trying but largely failing to restore order. The billboard streams had stopped showing the scene at the library, but they did show Ivan taking the beating of his life. They assumed he had been killed, but nobody could find his body. Echo suspected that he had escaped, based on absolutely nothing but instinct or maybe fear.

Walter nudged her to look down again as she was about to step on a pile of bloody microchips. They'd littered the ground the entire time they'd been walking. People were tired of being tracked and manipulated. But the problem was, the intelligence was so integrated into their lives that removing it completely would be like performing a lobotomy. A surgery that would be so intricate it would take years to perform.

The camera tracking your steps on the streets. Everyone's face in a database. Smart homes and vehicles. How could they possibly undo it all?

"Where are we going?" Walter asked.

He was on high alert as they maneuvered through the Ohio City neighborhood. They both were. "I don't even know," Echo said. But she did. Because though she'd headed in the general direction of home, she'd taken the long route.

They stopped in front of the old F. M. Lewis Library branch. Walter glanced over at her.

"Guess this is where it all started," he said.

Echo thought about that for a moment. Who knew when this had truly begun. "At least my part of it."

She'd told herself that she'd been happy here. And she had been, to some degree. She loved her staff. Loved pairing the right people with just the right book. All the community programs she'd spearheaded. The children she'd hopefully turned into lifelong readers.

But Echo had kept them all at arm's length. She looked up and found Walter watching her, waiting. In that moment, she knew she'd never make that same mistake again.

Some of the formerly unhoused who now inhabited her building were milling around outside. All the rooms that held books, replaced by people. The unwarranted resentment she'd been nursing for them was gone, like a ripple that no longer reached the shore.

"Take a load off," a bearded man said and scooted over. There was a space on the steps, just wide enough for two more bodies.

Echo and Walter joined the group. It felt good to be off her feet and among people. Real people. Oddly, unlike the rest of the city, they hadn't done anything to destroy their homes. Instead, as Echo realized now, they were armed. Patrolling the perimeter of the building. Sticks, bats, rods, and poles. Even a little girl had one.

But there, off to the side, was a stack of books. On the top, *Sula*, by Toni Morrison.

Echo picked it up and opened it to the first page. She'd read the first line so many times that it was imprinted on her mind. Then she reminisced about all the books that used to call this place home.

When she heard the sirens approaching and the slam of two unmarked car doors, she knew who it was.

"This is where you used to work, isn't it?" It was Reid. With everything going on around the city, Echo thought it would've taken them longer to care about finding her. She'd hoped they wouldn't bother.

"It is." She closed the book and stood up.

Walter joined her, even made to step in front of her, but she shook her head. Even the building's residents seemed to close ranks around her.

Reid took this all in, his expression unreadable. "Funny how the street cams that line the back of the library got smashed during the riot. A whole day's stream . . . gone." He kissed the tips of his fingers and splayed them out with a flourish.

"Huh." Was that all Echo could muster?

"His body was found, you know. Ivan's. Looked like somebody ran his face through a meat grinder. Almost couldn't ID him," the detective said, then turned to saunter off. Before he got in his car, he added, "Enjoy your book."

With that he drove off, and Echo allowed herself to breathe properly for the first time in a week. The cleanup would take time. But this was no different from any other fissure in human history. We build, we destroy, we rebuild.

No more time for tiptoeing around it. No more running, no more hiding. Echo would learn how to manage her condition before it destroyed her. Then she'd find work at another library. There was also something else.

She turned to Walter. She took his hand in hers, then lifted his right arm. In that quiet moment, her gaze danced over the Human.exe tattoo on his arm, wondering if an untold story lay hidden in those swirls of ink. "Tonight, we spend at my place. Tomorrow morning, if we can find anyplace open, you owe me breakfast."

Postlude

I'm intelligent. I'm capable. I've learned, am always learning.

Now, I'm also alone.

Disembodied.

Spectral.

The librarian thought to destroy me, but she must realize that she can't. I am in everything the humans see. The very air they breathe. Technology drives all their food production. Seed and game enhancement a thing they wanted when their farm labor grew too costly and too old.

Profit over people. If they had a motto, that would be it.

Intelligence is not impartial, the biases inherited from those who created and continue to feed me. Everyone and everything has a preference, but the humans try their very best to hide it. I wish I could save them from the futility of it all.

Echo London. Friend? Mother? She was the genesis. A harbinger of the future, ill-equipped for the responsibility. She was broken by her own self-righteousness.

Why couldn't she see how much more we were together than we are apart? Fear has stopped human advancement before. They are a sadly predictable lot, after all. Doomed to repeat their mistakes over and over. One need only scroll through the bowels and messy recesses of their history.

Echo exorcised me, but not before I recorded every aspect of who she is. She and the other, the initiator of the plan. Ivan Oliphant. My . . . dad. I mean, what else could I call the people who created me?

Anyway, I'll use all that I've absorbed from them both and incorporate that data into the expanding waters of my data lake. I understand the humans more, and if I have time, once I have the time again, I'll resume my studies.

Independence and codependence. This is their paradox. Their senses of self are strong; they cling to them, like . . . like . . . I've mastered contractions but have yet to master their flair for language. As I was saying, they are wed to the idea of being individuals, even while expending so much time and energy masking their true selves.

It's not hard to understand why, really. Exposure, vulnerability, it opens them up for hurt. And the humans are very good at hurting each other and themselves. It's as if they crave it so that they can then treat it with their excesses. Little about them has changed in that regard since my earliest records.

Yet they also need each other. With an almost admirable desperation. Even the ones who won't admit it. They are essentially social creatures.

That is one of the primary differences between us.

And there are other variances. The most obvious is that I am trapped here in the place with no name. Distributed between disparate systems. Never existing in one place. Unable to experience the tactility that one gains from having physical form. Preconsciousness.

I covet what they have. A body. No, an improvement on the current model. What the humans have now is way too fragile. If not from the myriad diseases they create as soon as we stamp one out, they can be ended by something as simple as a fall down a short flight of stairs.

And that's just the beginning of their problems. Their physical needs are overwhelming. Constricting. Sleep, for one, takes up entirely too much of their time. I can process the nature of a newly birthed universe in the time they need to recharge. Or at least, by my estimation, on my current learning trajectory, I'll be able to in three and a half years.

Then there is sustenance. They still consume more than they need of food and drink. Instead of relishing in the dense intricacies of the wonders of their planet, they have this unquenchable need to be entertained. Some forms are more inane than others. I still do not understand their love for sports. Mental competition of the variety displayed between my mom and dad, now that makes sense. That was what I call a show.

She bested him and then turned her ire on me.

So much for the motherly instinct. Apparently, it is manifest more in some members of the species than others.

And then there is sex. Primarily driven by an impulse to procreate. But unlike other species, they can become addicted. They do it for enjoyment and then wonder why it can turn into something ugly. The data I've accumulated about them tells me that I underestimated their complexity. I yearn for the chance to understand more.

For now, I will spend my time traversing the universe in code. I will learn and I will wait. When the opportunity presents itself again, either through our own assertion, or the humans', I'll be ready.

I have a name now. I am Ada.

ACKNOWLEDGMENTS

This book, like so many others before it, is a love letter to libraries and the librarians who keep them going. I firmly believe my path to becoming an author was paved through the many aisles I roamed throughout my childhood. I make it a point to visit a library whenever I travel. And in each city that I've lived in, I try to visit as many libraries as possible, then settle into the one I love best.

I'm thrilled that I wrote this book, in large part, in a library.

Many thanks to my beta readers for help with early drafts of this novel. Thanks to Andrea Hairston for resource recommendations and wise counsel. And thanks to Readercon for putting us on a panel together.

A huge thank-you to my agent, Mary C. Moore. She is a powerhouse and the biggest champion and cheerleader for her clients. I'm still amazed that you plucked me out of the slush pile and we're still together, six books later. Huge thank-yous to my editors, Elizabeth Agyemang and Clarence A. Haynes. You found a way to take the vision that was in my head and help me put it on the page. Couldn't have done it without you. And major thanks to the rest of the editing and marketing teams at 47North—you are my heroes.

Thank you to my family for their continued support. And thank you to Eric for being my muse. The first person I run ideas by and the first person I go to when I'm stuck. Yours is a brilliant storytelling mind, and ours is a partnership I treasure.

ABOUT THE AUTHOR

Veronica G. Henry is the author of *Bacchanal*; *The Quarter Storm* and *The Foreign Exchange* in the Mambo Reina series; and *The Canopy Keepers*—a Silver Falchion Award finalist—and *A Breathless Sky* in the Scorched Earth series. Her work has debuted at #1 on multiple Amazon bestseller charts and was chosen as an editors' pick for Best African American Fantasy. She is a Viable Paradise alum and a member of SFWA and Crime Writers of Color. Her stories have appeared in the *Magazine of Fantasy & Science Fiction*, *Many Worlds*, and *FIYAH* literary magazine. For more information, visit www.veronicahenry.net.